SNAKE OIL

Look for these exciting Western series from bestselling authors William W. Johnstone and J.A. Johnstone

The Mountain Man

Luke Jensen: Bounty Hunter

Brannigan's Land

The Jensen Brand

Preacher and MacCallister

Fort Misery

The Fighting O'Neils

Perley Gates

MacCoole and Boone

Guns of the Vigilantes

Shotgun Johnny

The Chuckwagon Trail

The Jackals

The Slash and Pecos Westerns

The Texas Moonshiners

Stoneface Finnegan Westerns

Ben Savage: Saloon Ranger

The Buck Trammel Westerns

The Death and Texas Westerns

The Hunter Buchanon Westerns

Will Tanner: U.S. Deputy Marshal

SNAKE OIL

A Texas Moonshiners Western

WILLIAM W. JOHNSTONE

AND J.A. JOHNSTONE

PINNACLE BOOKS
KENSINGTON PUBLISHING CORP.
www.kensingtonbooks.com

PINNACLE BOOKS are published by

Kensington Publishing Corp.
119 West 40th Street
New York, NY 10018

PUBLISHER'S NOTE: Following the death of William W. Johnstone, the Johnstone family is working with a carefully selected writer to organize and complete Mr. Johnstone's outlines and many unfinished manuscripts to create additional novels in all of his series like The Last Gunfighter, Mountain Man, and Eagles, among others. This novel was inspired by Mr. Johnstone's superb storytelling.

First Printing: March 2023
ISBN-13: 978-0-7860-4886-1
10 9 8 7 6 5 4 3 2 1

Printed in the United States of America

Chapter 1

Pike Shannon rested his hand on the side of his smooth leather holster. His lightning-fast draw filled his fist with the Colt. A callused trigger finger tightened, but not enough to send a bullet blasting from the barrel.

He relaxed his hand just a mite and savored the slickness of the familiar worn walnut grips. He had worked to polish off as many of the sweat stains as possible from the wood, but the oldest ones remained. That didn't matter. How the gun felt in his grip mattered.

And the memories. Those mattered more.

The memories of being a hired gun handler returned to taunt him. The long rides and fierce battles. Friends standing with him and lovers leaving. But the worn, trusty pistol carried a reminder of so much more.

He imagined the stinging bite in his nostrils from the gun smoke that filled the air. Then he heaved a deep sigh and slowly returned the revolver to its resting place. It had been a spell since he'd fired it, even in practice. For the last few months, there hadn't been any call for him to do any of the things he'd done over the years, some legal, some not.

The Shannon family had even stopped moonshining . . . again. Pike had to admit that the long, lonely nights and sudden death of his former life weren't things he missed. But running the family still—the sharp tang of corn mash and the slow, steady drip of potent moonshine into a crockery jug—left a yearning not easily replaced.

He smiled ruefully. Not only had the family forsaken a tradition going back to their days in the Arkansas hill country before moving to Texas, but Warbonnet County had gone dry.

The temperance movement had convinced enough voters to close the saloons and make corn squeezings illegal. He licked his lips. It had been a while since he had even tasted liquor. He missed it more than a little and the way it drove away all the small aches and pains from long days in the saddle.

He looked around. The two-story family ranch house that stood behind him was sturdy and secure, and their spread was prosperous. The Shannon clan hardly needed revenue off moonshining.

He still missed it, despite their continued success without it.

As he turned to climb the steps onto the front porch, someone frantically called his name. Pike swung around again. Jimmy McCall, a youngster from Warbonnet, waved and yelled to get his attention as he trotted toward the house.

"Mr. Shannon, Mr. Shannon," the boy gasped out after he skidded to a halt beside Pike. "They . . . they—"

"Settle down," Pike advised. "What brings you out here from town?"

"Mr. Shannon, sir, thieves! Horse thieves. They're comin' after your best breedin' stock!"

"Take a deep breath and tell me the whole story." Pike looped his thumbs in his gun belt. Jimmy wasn't one to tell tales, or even exaggerate much. Those fine traits got drowned at times by his inability to control his excitement.

"I was outside Miss Truesdale's shop—" The boy looked up at Pike to see if he was in trouble for mentioning the young lady's café. It was common knowledge Pike and Sophie Truesdale had a prickly relationship. As much as Pike liked her, and he thought she liked him as much in return, they never agreed on much more than she made about the best pie in town. She was a leading light in the temperance movement, and this came between them more often than not.

"Go on."

"Well, Mr. Shannon, sir, I heard these two cowboys boastin' on how they intended to come out here and steal all the horses you have in the south pasture. Those are your best bloodlines, aren't they?"

Pike nodded. Jimmy's detail added credibility to his claim.

"There was two of them coming out of Miss Truesdale's café, but two more joined them in the street. They was all laughin' and jokin' and talking about how they could sell those horses in the wink of an eye."

"I'll send somebody down to the pasture this evening to stand guard. Thanks for the warning."

"No, sir, that'll be too late. They was comin' on out right *now*! In broad daylight!"

"Did you run all the way from town?"

"Yes, sir, I did that. They was still talkin' when I lit out, but on horseback they'll be rustlin' your horses by now."

Pike considered the distances. Any horse thieves would skirt the Shannon spread to keep from being noticed. They'd ride along the road that swung a long way south and curled back toward the pastures where the thoroughbreds were pastured. If he rode straightaway, he'd likely catch the thieves in the act since he'd cut across the ranch instead of circling it.

"You go on up to the house. See if Nessa can scare you up some lemonade. She and my ma spent the morning squeezing a bag of lemons."

Pike sent the boy up the steps for a double reason. Jimmy had to be parched if he ran the entire way from Warbonnet. Hospitality required Pike's sister, Vanessa, to remain here and take care of their company. That was a good thing, because she was like iron to a magnet when trouble came a-calling. If she came with him, Pike would be more inclined to worry about her, although she was capable of looking after herself. She was almost as good a shot with a six-gun as he was, and from the rifle reports during the long, hot Texas afternoons, she practiced enough to be a better shot with her Winchester.

"Whoa, son, where you goin' in such an all-fired hurry?"

Pike glanced over his shoulder. Jimmy had run headlong into Fiddler. The grizzled old man carried his fiddle, coming onto the porch to practice. Pike had heard better players, but not around Warbonnet County. Fiddler ran his hand across his balding head and smoothed the few strands of graying hair. With an arthritic twist, he moved aside just enough to let the boy run past him into the house. He put his fiddle down on the porch railing and joined Pike.

"There's something in the air," he said. "What's going on, Pike? That boy's always as calm as a new spring day. The way he's all riled up means he knows something and is bursting to tell it."

"Rustlers," Pike said. "It's probably nothing, but I'll check."

"You want me to fetch Torrance? He's up in the house, reading one of those books of his."

"No need to bother him," Pike said. "Jimmy might be letting his imagination run away with him."

"Are we talking about the same Jimmy McCall? That boy's as steady and rooted as that old post oak yonder." Fiddler pointed to a huge tree that had spent the last fifty years protecting the road to the Shannon house's front door. He peered hard as if reassuring himself that the tree hadn't moved.

"That's why I'm heading out to see for myself. It might be something innocent."

"Or it might actually be rustlers," Fiddler said, growing more excited. "Let me grab my shotgun. I'm coming with you!"

Pike started to object, then realized Fiddler wanted to get away from the house. He and Pike's ma got along real good—too good for Pike to spend much time thinking about it—but Mary Shannon was a demanding woman. Pike knew that better than anyone. It had been part of the reason he had taken to the trail years earlier, that and the constant fighting with his pa, Elijah. There hadn't been much holding him to the family homestead.

Returning hadn't been too pleasant, either, when he heard that his pa had died under peculiar circumstances.

He had gotten to the bottom of that and brought the men responsible for murdering Elijah to justice. Hot lead justice. By his own hand.

"Saddle up, partner," Pike said.

Fiddler let out a whoop and slapped him on the back. They went to the barn and readied their horses.

Pike's dun was as anxious to head for the distant pasture as Fiddler. Being penned up too long did that to a restless spirit. They trotted out a few minutes later, and Pike began to regret letting the old-timer ride along.

"Yes, sir, it's been mighty quiet around here of late,"

Fiddler said. He bounced in the saddle, showing his eagerness for something to take place.

Pike had to agree. The ranch routine kept him occupied, but that was the problem. It was routine. Nothing new ever happened.

"Are you expecting a gunfight, Pike?"

"Don't get worked up," he advised. "When lead flies, men can die."

"But it's so *quiet*. The tranquility driving me right out of my head."

"Are you getting itchy feet? Thinking about pulling up stakes?"

"Oh, no, nothing like that. Your mother, well, she and I are still on good terms. She's a better woman than an old galoot like me deserves. And I haven't had so much as a taste of liquor in months. I never figured to be free of that demon riding on my back."

"I can testify to your sobriety. It must be a challenge."

"I'm up to it. But, Pike, it's so danged *quiet*! It's almost enough to drive me to drink. Almost."

"Be careful what you ask for," Pike said. He drew back on the reins and stared across a rolling pasture to a small herd of horses a quarter mile away. Several riders were moving around over there . . . riders who shouldn't have been anywhere near those horses.

"I count four of the varmints," Fiddler said, squinting his rheumy eyes. "They're attempting to cut out the best of the mares. See how they're moving all about?"

"Jimmy wasn't passing on worthless gossip, after all." Pike pulled his carbine from the saddle sheath. "You stay here. I'll circle around to the other side and we'll get them in a crossfire."

"You be careful about shooting any of those horses.

They're valuable." Fiddler snorted and shook his head. "What am I saying? You never miss."

"I usually hit what I'm aiming at," Pike agreed. He wasn't too rusty but wished he had joined his sister during her afternoon target practice, just to keep his hand in.

Pike urged his horse down into a ravine to sneak up on the rustlers without being seen. Fiddler was sensible. If things got hot, Fiddler wasn't going to do anything crazy. Even after spending the ride out here bemoaning how dull life had become, he was levelheaded. Pike knew he could depend on the old-timer not to panic.

The ravine wound around and went away from where Pike intended to confront the four men. He snapped the reins and began the climb up a steep slope. He came within a few yards of the crest, when a head appeared in front of him. With the sun halfway up the sky and on the other side of the hill, the rider's face was hidden in shadow. Pike saw right away that he had been found out by the way the man jerked at his reins and galloped off.

"Come on, let's mix it up," he urged his horse. The dun struggled to the top of the hill.

The bullet coming his way caught the crown of his hat and jerked it off his head. The chin string kept it from flying away, but for a moment the sun blinded him.

Pike swung his rifle around, hunting for a target. Who was the hunter and who was the hunted became apparent rapidly. Unable to see, Pike held his fire.

The air around him filled with the sizzle of half a dozen rounds. The fight was on!

Chapter 2

Pike Shannon jerked around, bent low and galloped along the ridge, not caring where he went as long as it was away from the worst of the fire. He heard horses neighing and the thunder of hooves as they stampeded. Twisting around until his joints popped, Pike leaned far left and shot across his body.

The bullets went wide, but they got the rustlers' attention. He turned the mare around until he had the outlaws directly ahead of him again. With methodical movements, he fired one shot after another. One rustler jerked and clutched at his right arm. Another's horse spooked and bolted in front of the other two. Confusion reigned.

"I got 'em, Pike. I got 'em all!" Fiddler's triumphant cry echoed across the pasture an instant before the boom of his shotgun added to the chaos.

Pike applied his heels to his horse's flanks and rocketed forward. Such a frontal attack was the last thing the rustlers expected. This caused even more disarray. With the rifle pulled in tight to his shoulder, he got another horse thief in his sights.

His bullet hit the rustler smack in the middle of the chest. The man threw up his hands and toppled backward.

The outlaw's horse reared and threw its rider. The man's boot tangled in the stirrup.

Fiddler hollered and sent the horse galloping off, dragging its flailing rider.

"Stay back," Pike ordered. His friend was too caught up in the heat of battle—or his hearing was playing hob again.

Fiddler fired the shotgun's second barrel as he galloped into the fray. Pike saw what the other man didn't. One rustler had dismounted and had taken shelter behind a rock. With his rifle balanced on top of the boulder, he had an easy shot at Fiddler.

Pike let out a rebel yell and changed direction, letting the only still-mounted owlhoot get away. His intentions centered on the man behind the rock. As he tried to draw the outlaw's attention, his horse stumbled and threw him. Pike went sailing head over heels and landed hard on the ground. He gasped to get the wind back into his lungs as he rolled over.

Thrashing about to find his rifle, he gave up when he couldn't find it quickly. Fiddler's life depended on how fast he distracted the sniper. Pike rolled onto his side and drew his pistol. He thumbed back the hammer and let it fall when the weapon had barely cleared his holster.

He wasn't sure who was more surprised, him or the rustler. His slug ricocheted off the rock inches from the man's face. The outlaw winced as rock fragments tore upward into his cheek. Such a lucky shot astounded Pike. It would be something to brag about around campfires for a dozen years, only he never tooted his own horn like that. Too many cowpokes considered a tale like that to be a prevarication spun for the purpose of entertainment and nothing more. Pike considered it not to be bragging if it was true.

"You nailed him, Pike, you did!" Fiddler drew rein a couple yards from where Pike still sprawled.

"Down!" Pike came to his knees and fanned off the rest of the rounds in his Colt. Not one of the bullets came close to his target.

The only good thing about emptying his revolver like that was driving the outlaw around the rock and ruining his aim.

"Get down, you old fool!"

"What? Who are you calling a fool?" Fiddler's outrage made him swing around to protest. The angry reaction saved him a bullet in the gut. It whipped past, barely missing him.

Pike twirled his Colt around and slapped it back in the holster. He dashed for his rifle lying a dozen yards away. With a sure grab, he picked it up, rolled over, and came to rest flat on his belly. The rifle bucked once. That was all it took. His slug knocked the outlaw back.

Over a long and bloody decade as a restless gun, Pike had developed a gut feeling for when a shot hit its target and when one didn't. The rustler was hidden by the big rock, but Pike felt confident there wouldn't be any more fight from that one.

"There are two of those varmints left." Fiddler turned back and forth, hunting for them.

"One's carrying my bullet in his shoulder. The other might be wounded, too, but I'm not counting on it." Pike took advantage of the lull in the fight to reload his Colt.

"I see sunlight reflecting off something silver." Fiddler thrust his now-empty shotgun in the direction of a towering sweetgum tree.

"By the pond," Pike said. "I see it, too."

The men exchanged looks. Pike smiled crookedly. "It's a lure. Somebody's trying to outsmart us."

"Not happening. Not today, not any day. Not when they're facing the likes of Pike Shannon!" Fiddler broke open the shotgun and thumbed fresh shells into the chambers, then snapped the weapon closed. "Or me, neither." He peered at the sweetgum tree. "You think they're hiding by the stock pond waiting for us to sneak up on them?"

"We'd have to go right by the bank of the pond," Pike said. "If I was laying a trap, that's how I'd do it."

"Let's go. Only it'll be those scoundrels who are in for a surprise!"

If he and Fiddler rode directly for the towering tree, the outlaws could shoot at them from either side of the pond. Pike mapped out the territory in his head. He'd come here to water the stock more times than he could remember. He silently pointed to a gully to the west of the tree. Fiddler began hiking for the cover it provided.

Pike went to the eastern side of the tree where the pond stretched out a watery finger. Eyes peeled, he advanced slowly. If he and Fiddler had advanced straight on, gunmen on either side would have had them in a crossfire. This way he and Fiddler had spread out even more and bracketed the two men, the pincers of a deadly tong closing on the outlaws.

At least that was Pike's plan. He edged nearer, hunting for the bushwhackers. As well as he knew the area, he failed to find any rustlers hiding in any of the places where he would set up a trap.

Pike circled the sweetgum tree. The soft ground at the base hadn't been disturbed except by squirrels. He motioned to Fiddler to join him. To keep Fiddler silent, he pressed his index finger against his lips.

That didn't work. "Where did those varmints get off to?" Fiddler looked around. "They didn't turn to smoke and up and blow away."

"Two of them aren't going to steal any more horses," Pike said. One had been dragged away by his horse. There wasn't much chance for him surviving such a deadly ride. The other he had plugged and lay dead by the big rock.

"That leaves two," Fiddler said. "You'd think they upped and . . ." His voice trailed off.

Pike got the same idea at the same instant. Both of them turned, weapons lowered and aimed toward the stock pond. Pike's sharper eyes caught sight of the ripples before Fiddler could focus. His rifle came to his shoulder, and he squeezed off a round. The bullet hit the water and sank beneath the surface.

Even though he expected it, Pike recoiled as a man erupted from underwater. The rustler began firing wildly at Pike. The second shot misfired from the gun getting wet.

It was the last thing the man did. First one slug and then another drove into his chest. The outlaw threw up his arms, his revolver flying into the air before splashing noisily in the middle of the pond.

"You got him dead center, Pike." Fiddler began his own careful study. Another ripple, closer to the bank, caused him to blast a load of buckshot into the water.

The remaining rustler broke the surface, gasping for breath. He thrust his hands in the air and shouted, "I surrender. Stop shootin'!"

Pike pushed Fiddler's shotgun down to keep him from triggering the gut-shredder's other barrel and gunning the man down.

"He's calling it quits," Pike said sternly.

Fiddler's blood was still up. "He's a horse thief! If I don't shoot him that means we'll have to hang him! It's tradition."

The few seconds Pike looked away from their prisoner was all it took for the man to jerk away, dive underwater, and disappear. The muddy water prevented Pike from seeing which direction the man swam.

"He can't stay under for long," Fiddler said. "One way or another, he's a goner when he comes up for air."

Stepping to the muddy bank, Fiddler peered over the shotgun's twin barrels and watched the water like an eagle waiting to swoop down on a trout.

"He must have drowned," Pike said when the outlaw never surfaced.

Walking along the bank slowly, he hunted for any trace of the remaining horse thief. Not a ripple showed. Nary a drop of blood betrayed where a dead body leaked out its last.

"Perhaps he's part fish," Fiddler complained. "I'm not budging until he comes up!"

"I can't explain where he went," Pike said. A man's will to live when faced with certain death lent ingenuity and strength far beyond normal. "Stay put. I'll be back."

A complete circuit of the pond convinced Pike the rustler was still underwater. No boot prints in the muddy bank betrayed an escape. Not content, Pike perched on a rock and waited. After ten minutes, he gave up.

"He'll either wash up eventually or sneak away," he told Fiddler.

"What's he doing? Sucking air through a reed? There's a thick patch of them over yonder, pussy willows and all."

"The horses were a mite spooked. Otherwise, they're all in the right pasture." Pike watched the reeds swaying about. A stick of dynamite tossed into the pond would flush out the rustler. It'd also kill all the fish they had in there. One catfish in particular had eluded Pike for too many years. Killing it to catch one man wasn't worth the effort. "We might as well leave him here. If by some miracle he's still alive, I'm betting he'll steer clear of Shannon range from now on."

"No, sir. I'll sit myself down right here, under the tree in the shade. If he's gulping air through a hollow reed, he'll get tired sooner or later. Then I'll have him."

Pike shook his head. "I can't leave you here, Fiddler, as long as there's a chance that fella is still alive."

"What?" Fiddler fixed Pike with an offended glare. "Do you think I'm incapable of dealing with one horse thief who's probably in fairly bad shape by now?"

"I didn't say that."

"Perhaps you believe I'm not enough of a man to handle trouble on my own. You should ask your mother how much of a man I—"

"Nope, nope," Pike said quickly, holding up his hands in surrender. "That's enough of that. I'll go on and deal with what I need to. But you be mighty careful, Fiddler. If anything happens to you, Ma would never let me hear the end of it."

And she would never forgive me, either, Pike thought.

But when Fiddler got stubborn like this, he was almost impossible to budge. Besides, he was a grown man and had a right to make up his own mind what he was going to do. Pike didn't have the right to boss him around.

"I'll take the bodies into town. The sheriff might have wanted posters on them."

"If he doesn't, Sheriff Burnett may not be happy with us killing them."

Pike shrugged it off. He shared some of Fiddler's restiveness. Arguing with his old friend Andy Burnett, who was now the sheriff of Warbonnet County, might rub away some of the everyday monotony. Unlike his brother, Torrance, he found excitement outside a library of dusty old books.

"Don't you stay too long. You'll miss supper."

"Tell your mother I may be out here all night." Fiddler sounded defiant.

Pike had to laugh. "You can tell her yourself. I don't want her getting angry with me over something that you've done."

Fiddler groused a bit, settled down with his back against the tree. Pike wanted to warn him about getting the sticky sap all over his shirt, then kept quiet. It wasn't his place telling another man how to live his life, even in such a small thing.

He waded out a few yards, caught the floating body by a leg, and pulled the rustler to the bank. With a heave, he lifted the owlhoot over his shoulders and headed back to where the other corpse was already starting to stink in the Texas sun.

By midafternoon, he was on the road into Warbonnet with the three bodies. Since he hadn't heard any gunfire from the direction of the stock pond, Fiddler had either fallen asleep and let the man skulk off or he still stood guard, waiting.

Pike sighed. He and Fiddler likely shared that desire for action. Both had a hankering for something stimulating.

Chapter 3

Fiddler clutched his shotgun so hard his hands began to cramp. He mumbled to himself and leaned the gun against the tree trunk to rub his hand across his denim trousers. Again and again he scanned from one side of the pond to the other, hunting for any trace of the rustler who had submerged.

"Drowned by now," Fiddler said aloud. "Nobody can hold his breath that long unless he's part amphibian. And sucking air through a reed is exhausting."

He leaned back and remembered his own youthful escapades a half century and more earlier. Spying on his brother sparking Lily Goodman came to mind. He smiled broadly. He had used a reed to swim underwater until he was less than ten feet from where they had stretched out on a patch of grass. The memory caused him a momentary pang. His brother had died only a couple years later, a victim of one of the fevers that swept across the frontier from time to time.

And what about the lovely Lily? He had no idea what had become of her, but she had lit a fire in him just as she had in his brother . . . a fire he'd never had the chance to extinguish.

Fiddler jerked upright when he heard a loud splash. He grabbed for his shotgun and pulled it to his shoulder, swinging the sights back and forth across the pond. He saw waves marching dutifully along the still surface, but what had caused them wasn't obvious.

"Could have been a fish jumping at a flying insect," he allowed. Fiddler climbed to his feet and squinted. Sunlight reflecting off the surface was blinding. "Or it might be that thieving rapscallion finally sneaking away."

He considered finding Pike to back him up, then realized he was on his way to Warbonnet with the other rustlers' bodies. If he rode hard, he could overtake Pike in an hour. Even if they turned around and returned immediately, the horse thief would be long gone.

But he had no need for Pike Shannon. The man was an expert gun handler, true, but Fiddler knew a thing or two about squeezing a trigger. In his day, he'd tangled with a lot of dangerous desperadoes.

"Or one or two," he amended. "Well, almost one." His life to this point hadn't been anywhere near as exciting as Pike's.

He marched off, circling the pond. Fiddler kept the shotgun aimed across the water. If he spotted the fleeing rustler, he'd be ready to dispense justice. No more boring days. Mary Shannon kept the nights lively, but Fiddler chafed at not having much to do otherwise.

Until now.

By the time he reached the far side of the pond, he was sure someone had slithered from the water, wiggling along on his belly like the low-down snake that he was. The wide swath pressed into the mud showed that the thief had gone close to ten yards before climbing to his feet. Fiddler paced alongside the tracks.

His legs were short, and matching the distance between prints showed the fleeing man was either taller than Fiddler by a foot or more or had sprinted off the first chance he got. The tracks led into a thicket. Following through the brambles wasn't anything Fiddler wanted to do, but once he caught the outlaw, he'd have quite a story to tell.

"Might even make Pike take notice." The notion of impressing Pike Shannon sent Fiddler hurrying ahead. His shorter stride failed to match the running rustler's, but he covered more ground faster than he had in years. Cursing the thorns cutting at his legs did nothing to get him through the sticky patch faster, but he came out on the other side with only minor scratches.

He looked around. Somewhere in the thistles, he had lost the trail. The only hope of catching the varmint was to get to high ground and spot him hightailing it off Shannon property. From his vantage, he saw movement downhill in a stand of oak and elm trees.

"Hell's bells," he said. He knew this section of the ranch like he did the back of his hand.

Working his way down a hillside brought him to a road overgrown with weeds. Muffled sounds came from deeper in the woods. He opened the shotgun to make sure it was loaded, then closed it and marched ahead. The left rut in the road showed clearly how someone had come this way only minutes earlier. The crushed weeds still leaked sap. Some weren't even black yet with swarming gnats licking up the juice.

Minutes. He was only minutes behind.

Fiddler froze when he heard more than one voice. Two? More? They argued, but try as he might, his old ears weren't able to make out the words. The debate stopped suddenly. He edged away from the road and used a tree to shield his presence. Retreating was the smart thing to do when a man was outnumbered and quite possibly out-gunned.

But Fiddler felt an exhilaration he hadn't experienced in months. His life had never been filled with excitement, especially when he had been imbibing too much liquor. Mostly then he had been locked up in the town jail more than he walked free. But after Pike had bailed him out from then-Sheriff Doak Ramsey's jail, he had walked the straight and narrow.

Along the way he had been tempted but had always done the right thing. That made him feel good. But that was months ago. Now, going after the rustler—rustlers!—gave him the satisfaction with his life that had been missing.

". . . here somewhere. It's gotta be. He said so!"

"You're full of beans. Nobody's come this way in forever."

The two argued some more, now shouting at each other. Fiddler took the chance to advance. Their loud voices hid any sound he made crushing dried leaves and snapping branches as he burst out into a clearing.

"Hands up!" Fiddler cried.

It was a toss-up who was most surprised. Fiddler hardly expected to have his shotgun trained on two youngsters. And they reacted poorly at having the gun pointed at them.

"Don't shoot, mister! We didn't mean nuthin'!" The boy closest threw his hands into the air. The other one fell to his knees and put his hands together as if praying not to be shot.

"They told us wrong. We shouldn't have ever come out

here!" The other boy was younger than the ten-year-old by a month or two. He looked up with frightened eyes.

"Yeah, Quince's right. It was all Freddie's doing, lyin' to us about it bein' out here."

"Hush, both of you," Fiddler ordered. He squinted at the pair. "You're Quincey Toms. And you're, let me think, I've seen you around town, you're Zeke Benton."

"Benson, sir, his name's Ezekiel Benson." Quince blanched whiter than a muslin sheet when he realized he had indicted his friend in some terrible crime.

"Put your hands down," Fiddler said. "And stand up like a man. It's humiliating looking down at you shaking like a leaf. Stand on your feet, lad." He glared at the two boys. "What are you doing out here trespassing on Shannon land?"

The two babbled, and he got nothing out of it. Fiddler held up his hand to stem the flow of gibberish, which was likely to be a lie, anyway.

"Wait. Before you tell me what you're doing here, have you seen a fellow all dirty, covered in mud? He'd be running like his life depended on it, which, in fact, it does."

The boys looked at each other. From their expressions and the way they shook their heads, he believed them. Such confusion wasn't easy for a ten-year-old to fake.

"We thought we was out here all by ourselves, sir. We'd never have come here if we thought anybody else was here. Not you or some dirty fellow running around in the woods."

"That's right," chimed in Quince. "We'd never prowl around here by ourselves if we thought anybody'd be here to catch us."

Fiddler looked pointedly at tin cups dangling from the boys' rope belts. They wouldn't look him in the eye when it became obvious he saw the cups.

"Now what reason would you both have for those?" He pointed to the cups.

"If we found it, we were gonna take a sip. Only a sip, sir," Quince blurted out. Zeke elbowed him to be quiet.

"It? You scallywags thought there was a still out here in these woods?" Fiddler held back a chuckle. Not so long ago the Shannon family ran a good-sized still not a hundred yards from this very spot. Since Pike had decided to abide by the law, he had not only given up the family business but hadn't had so much as a drop of liquor himself.

Fiddler cursed the temperance crusaders, not that he intended to take a nip ever again. But just a sniff? There wasn't any harm in that. But the still dripping out a steady stream of moonshine was about the prettiest scent Fiddler could imagine. Even better than the way Mary's hair smelled after she washed it.

"We heard rumors," Quince said uneasily. "We didn't mean no harm."

"Freddie told you, did he?" Fiddler had no idea who Freddie was, but the name had come up.

"He did, sir, but everyone in town knows the Shannons are back in the moonshine business."

"Do they now? Come along." Fiddler escorted the two down the overgrown road to where the still had once been the pride of Warbonnet County. He let them poke around until their disappointed looks told him they were convinced.

"Freddie's gonna get it for this," Zeke said in a low voice, thinking only his friend heard.

"He's not the only one who's going to land in a heap of trouble," Fiddler said sternly. "Come along. I'll see to it that your folks hear about your expedition."

"Please, no!" Both boys began yammering for leniency. Fiddler was having none of it. If they'd seen the horse thief, he would have been inclined to let them go. But his day was ruined. He saw no reason not to take some of his annoyance out on these two for distracting him from a more important hunt.

They left the woods, following the old road a ways. Fiddler stopped suddenly and cocked his head to one side.

"You boys hear that?"

"A rider's comin' this way," Zeke said. He exchanged a quick look with his friend. What he planned was as plain as the nose on his face.

"Take cover. Don't go running off or more than a whipping might be in store for you. That's likely a murdering horse thief coming to be sure no one can identify him to the sheriff."

Both boys dived for cover in a shallow ditch along the road. Fiddler found a spot on the far side and crouched behind the stump of a lightning-struck tree. He rested his shotgun on the jagged, burned top and waited.

Sure enough, a rider came in his direction, staying hidden in shadows. Fiddler squinted a mite, drew a bead, and got ready to take his shot.

One was all he'd need to put an end to the no-account rustler.

CHAPTER 4

"You returning to your gunfighting ways, Pike?" Sam Crow pushed his hat back and stared at the bodies draped over the horses trailing Pike. They had run into each other on the road into Warbonnet.

"Nothing of the sort," Pike told his friend. "These gents happen to be horse thieves caught in the act. Are you going into town?"

"I'm in sore need of grain for my horses," Sam said. "Rats got into my storage bin and had themselves a feast."

"Since you don't have anything loaded in the wagon going to town, why don't you see that these horse thieves get a proper reception at the sheriff's office?"

"Is there a reward on their heads?"

Pike said, "If there is, go on and claim it for your trouble. If there's any question what happened, I'll come in to tell the tale. They're strangers, though, and anyone speaking up for them's likely to be a horse thief, too." He shook his head. "There won't be any questions asked."

"I heard tell of a gang of rustlers moving into Warbonnet County from the west. You reckon these gents fit the bill?"

Pike nodded. He hadn't heard anything like that, but it had been a couple of weeks since he'd been to town. Tending his own herd and making sure fences were mended took up all his time.

"I'll see what I can squeeze out of Andy. He's so tight with county money the buffalo on every nickel bellows in pain."

"Much obliged, Sam. I left Fiddler on guard duty waiting to see if a fourth horse thief showed his face. I'd better get back."

"That's something to worry on, Pike." Sam Crow laughed. "Fiddler might just throw in with a rustler if it sounded exciting enough. The last time I talked with him he was feeling a touch of restlessness."

With his friend's help, Pike loaded the bodies into the back of the wagon. He pointed at the two horses.

"Those are yours, even if there's a reward.

Sam Crow thanked Pike, then got his corpse-laden wagon rolling toward Warbonnet. Pike waited for him to round a bend in the road before getting his bearings and cutting across country to return to the Shannon spread. The farther he had gone, the more worried he'd been about Fiddler being left alone to outwait the fourth rustler. Chances were good the horse thief was dead, but such scoundrels too often showed a spark of imagination.

What Sam had said about Fiddler feeling restless fit too well with his conversation with the old-timer, too. He might have to come up with something more challenging around the ranch to keep Fiddler occupied. If he let him ride off, his ma would blame him for sure. She'd think he had driven Fiddler away for some reason, and no amount of convincing would be enough.

Pike reached the pond in a decent amount of time. The sun was midway down the sky heading for the western horizon. Fiddler's mount was tethered where he'd left it.

Worried what might have happened to his friend, Pike caught the reins to Fiddler's horse and began tracking.

The deep muddy depression where the horse thief had slithered from the pond had hardened. Pike found the man's tracks and picked up the pace, topping a ridge to look down toward the woods where he, his grandpappy Dougal, and brother Torrance had operated a still not that long back.

Pike licked his lips. A drop or two of the prime quality 'shine they'd cooked would go down good and smooth about now. He reached the road and decided that Fiddler had followed his quarry into the cool depths. To stay out of the hot sun, Pike left the road and skirted the tall, shady trees.

Something warned him to pull back on the reins and stop. He took a deep whiff of the air. He missed the pungent scent of moonshine being distilled, but he hadn't expected to smell anything of the sort. He cocked his head to one side and listened.

His hand drifted to the holster on his right hip, but he didn't draw. Something felt wrong. He hoped that Fiddler hadn't tangled with the escaping horse thief—and lost.

Walking his dun forward slowly, he came to a halt again a few yards deeper into the forest. Two small heads bobbed up and down in the drainage ditch alongside the road. He heard them whispering urgently. Unable to make out the words put him on guard. It seemed unlikely two youngsters had laid a trap for him. That didn't mean they weren't in cahoots with the rustler and working as scouts.

He waited long enough to see how the boys kept popping up and looking across the road. He stepped down and swatted his horse's rump. The dun protested but dutifully walked forward. Pike moved like a ghost, dodging from shadow to shadow until he reached the far side of the road.

He grinned as he came up behind a tree where a man waited, clutching a shotgun.

"If you're fixing to shoot me, you should have climbed up in that tree for a better shot," he said.

"Pike!" Fiddler jumped a foot. When he came down, he whirled around, eyes bulging with surprise in their sockets. "That you? What are you doing back here from town so quick?"

Pike explained briefly about running into Sam Crow on the way to Warbonnet, then asked, "How'd you come to be with those two desperadoes?"

By now, both boys had heard what Pike and Fiddler were saying. They crawled out of the ditch and shuffled around uncomfortably, edging away, obviously thinking about running.

"You boys stay where you are," Fiddler warned them. "Pike here is about the best roper in all of Texas."

"Y-you wouldn't rope and hogtie us, would you?" one of the boys asked.

"They thought the Shannons were moonshining again," Fiddler explained. "I'll see them into town and find out what their folks have to say about trespassing."

"You head on back to the house, Fiddler. I'll escort them. I know that one's pa." Pike fixed Quince with a hard look. "After I explain what his boy's been up to, there won't be any more trouble."

"Please, Mr. Shannon, we can get home on our own." The boys exchanged panicked looks.

"You wandered into a situation where three men ended up dead." Pike touched his holstered gun. "Another'll be pushing up daisies if I find him."

"We don't abide by horse thieves," Fiddler added. He looked at Pike, then sagged a little. "You get those imps back to town. I'll let Mary and the rest know you won't likely be back for supper."

Pike slapped Fiddler on the back, then pointed to the boys.

"You climb onto that horse of yours. If we ride fast, we can reach Warbonnet before sundown."

It looked like Pike was destined to go to town today after all.

The boys grumbled but obeyed. Pike took Fiddler to where his horse nipped at a patch of blue grama. The horse was as reluctant to leave as its rider.

Astride his dun, Pike called, "Let's make tracks, you two."

They rode in silence all the way to town. The closer they got, the more nervous the boys became. Pike dismounted in front of the courthouse where Sheriff Andy Burnett's office was located and motioned for the two youngsters to do the same.

"You're turnin' us over to the law? Please, Mr. Shannon, don't do that." Quince was close to tears.

Zeke was made of sterner stuff. "It might be better sittin' in a cell than lettin' our pas know what we done."

"Who's this Freddie who told you we were making moonshine?" Pike asked as he wrapped the dun's reins around a hitch rack.

"It's not right squealin' on him. It's not right him passin' along gossip, but I won't turn him in for runnin' off at the mouth." Quince stood a little straighter as he made that declaration.

"Learn who to listen to," Pike said, approving of the boy's loyalty. "You should know my family obeys the letter of the law. We might not like Warbonnet County being dry, but we're following what the majority have voted to do. That includes not running a still."

"Yes, sir," the boys said in unison.

"Get on home. Tell your parents what you want, but don't lie."

"You mean we can just not . . . fess up?"

"Some might say not confessing is a lie. I don't see it that way. No harm's been done, and you seem to have figured out who to listen to—and who not to."

"Thanks, Mr. Shannon! Thanks!"

He watched them run off, their tired old horse struggling to keep up with the youngsters. In his heart he knew that, at that age, he'd have done the same as those two. The lure of tasting just a sip of moonshine was overpowering, and it was probably their first chance to try the potent brew. If they learned not to trust everyone who had a story, their experience turned into real knowledge.

Delivering the boys safely to town was only part of the reason he came. Letting Sam Crow bring in the horse rustlers' bodies had seemed prudent, what with the fourth one escaping the way he had. Where he'd ended up was something to ask around about, but neither he nor Fiddler had caught sight of the outlaw's face. With his partners ready to be planted in the potter's field, more than likely no one knew his identity.

Pike considered asking around. Without a saloon in town, finding someone who had seen a fourth man was a matter of going from store to store. The chances of learning anything important were slim.

Pike smiled as he turned toward the next best place to find out gossip in Warbonnet. Sophie Truesdale's pie was the best in town, and on any given day the best he'd ever eaten. The coffee was better than decent, as well.

He stepped in and looked around. Two customers were finishing. He touched the brim of his hat in acknowledgment, then settled down at a long, narrow bar. Pike couldn't hold back a big smile when the lovely blonde came from the back room, wiping flour from her hands.

There had been a time when Pike had believed that he and Sophie might be able to build something together, despite the differences in their attitude when it came to liquor. But that time had come and gone, and in recent weeks Sophie had been spending a lot of time with a young fella named Curtis Holloway, who had been part of a dust-up a while back that had involved not only the Shannons but Sophie, as well. Pike wished Sophie and Curtis only the best, if it was meant to be between them.

But that didn't keep him from still feeling a little pang inside when he looked at her.

"Hello, Pike," Sophie said. "What brings you to town?"

He expected a more cordial greeting. She neither smiled nor let her words carry more than a neutral welcome as if he were just any old customer.

"What else but a slice of your fine pie? Rumor has it you have peach as well as apple and cherry."

"Rumor's true. Peach and a cup of coffee?" She turned to fetch his pie and drink.

She slid the plate in front of him without looking up.

He caught her wrist and held it lightly. She pulled away. He let her go without any struggle.

"Not all rumors are true," he said.

"Do tell." Her lips drew back in a thin line.

"I caught a couple boys poking around my place, thinking I was moonshining again. Have you heard that gossip?"

"Well, are you?" Her Texas sky blue eyes flashed angrily as she glared at him.

"That's against the law. I'm a law-abiding horse breeder."

"That's not the way I heard it."

"Whoever told you that's a liar," he said, his voice harsher than he intended. "I'm giving you my word that there's not a still on Shannon land."

"Or anywhere else? You're not running a still away from your spread?"

He forked a piece of the peach pie into his mouth. Part of him said this was good, maybe better than the apple pie he preferred. But it turned to dust on his tongue because of Sophie's attitude.

"No," was all he said after gobbling down the last of the pie. He drained the coffee in a single gulp.

Sophie started to speak, but the door opened. She muttered under her breath, then said loudly, "Come on in, Belle. There's plenty of room here at the counter."

Belle Ramsey stopped just inside the door. Her dark auburn hair and deeply tanned skin formed a sharp contrast to Sophie's fairness. While no hothouse flower, Sophie Truesdale was fragile appearing compared to Belle, who wore rugged trail clothes and had the look of someone used to physical work in the hot sun. The differences between the two women went deeper than their appearance.

Belle ignored Sophie and said, "I need a word with you, Pike."

Under less tense conditions, he would have offered to buy her a cup of coffee so they could talk over whatever riled her so. Sophie's withering look drove him away. He put a few coins on the counter and nodded in Sophie's direction. She slid the money off and stashed it in an apron pocket as if it was too hot to touch for long. Her mumbled words might have been a "Thank you, come again," but he couldn't tell.

That irritated him even more.

He followed Belle onto the boardwalk. As she turned toward him, the setting sun caught the long scar on her face put there by her cousin Doak Ramsey. Somehow it enhanced her good looks rather than detracting. Pike had appreciated that more than once, but he wasn't in any mood for such thoughts now.

"Did I rescue you from . . . her?" Belle looked past Pike into the café. Pike glanced through the window and saw Sophie working far too hard to wipe the spot where he had been sitting cleaner than a whistle, as if he had contaminated the counter.

"Good to see you," Pike said.

"I heard that Sam Crow brought in some dead rustlers. Rumor has it you were responsible for cutting their horse thieving short."

"I had a hand in that," Pike admitted. "Fiddler helped."

They began walking slowly down the street. Pike was more distracted than usual as Belle pressed close, their hips sometimes brushing. But it irritated him more than anything else.

"Fiddler? You have him out riding guard for you?"

"He wanted to come along and give me a hand." Pike paused. "There's a whole passel of gossip around town. First word of the horse thieves, and then a couple of youngsters poked around where one of our old stills was because of gossip by somebody named Freddie that we'd fired up the old family business."

"Have you?" Belle asked.

"Nobody believes the Shannon family's got no plans to start again. Sophie didn't believe me when I denied it. You don't sound like you believe me, either."

"Where there's smoke, there's fire," she said.

"The smoke's not coming from a Shannon still. Why are there so many rumors flying around all of a sudden?"

Belle shrugged. "Everyone's bored. There's nothing else to do. So?"

Pike looked at her, wondering what she meant.

"So when's the first batch going to be corked and ready?"

For whatever reason, the entire town, including people who knew he wouldn't lie to them, thought he was ready to light a fire under the old copper pot.

"Good evening, Miss Ramsey," he said formally. She called after him as he spun and walked off, but he paid her no attention. The way everyone insisted he was working to make moonshine again made him consider actually doing it. If for no good reason they thought he was lying, maybe he ought to make at least a batch or two.

Pike mounted and rode past the courthouse. By then he had cooled off. No matter what Sophie Truesdale or Belle Ramsey thought, he wasn't going to break the law. He had spent too many years looking over his shoulder, wary of the snapping, snarling pack of law dogs on his trail, to ever go back to such a life.

But a sip of fine Shannon bootleg would slide on down the gullet real fine about now. He felt he deserved that much.

CHAPTER 5

Fiddler sat on the front porch of the Shannon house, running his fingers up and down the instrument's strings. Somehow the music failed to come. Whenever he was blue, playing raised his spirits. Not now. It had been two days since he had fought it out with the horse thieves and found the boys searching for a nonexistent still.

"Not a drop to be had," he grumbled.

"What's that, Fiddler?" Pike's sister, Vanessa, came from inside the house. She pulled up a stool and sat beside him. "A bit of rain would cool things off, that's for sure."

Nessa was a lovely young woman, sure of herself to the point of cockiness, and a perfect fit in the Shannon family. Of all the children, only she had inherited her pa's flame-red hair. Light from the setting sun turned it into gently dancing flames that added to her indisputable beauty. She wore her favorite green dress that outlined her lush figure.

Fiddler saw that she had inherited as much from her ma as she had from her pa. He closed his eyes for a moment, resting the tired old things. Mary Shannon was still a beauty. She must have been the spitting image of her daughter when she was younger.

"I'd settle for a thunderstorm," he said, though he had

been thinking of moonshine. "Or just about anything that'll give a bit of excitement."

"Pike hasn't found that last rustler, has he?"

"No. I offered to help him hunt for the scoundrel, but he said he worked better all by his lonesome. That's true. Nobody needs me getting in the way."

"Why are you feeling sorry for yourself, Fiddler? You help out a lot around here," Nessa said. "Why don't you play a tune? That always lifts your spirits. I know it does mine."

"Don't want to," he said glumly. "And you don't need your spirit lifted. If it got any higher, you'd up and float away. You have a new beau?"

"Nothing like that," she said.

"You have things to do around here that make you feel good. Proper things, not made-up chores."

"You keep Mama happy. That's a full-time job."

He mumbled his reply. She grabbed him by the shoulder and pulled him around.

"You take that back this minute."

"Well, I feel like I've been put out to pasture. There's nothing I can do for you."

"Ask Torrance, then. He's in the office working on balancing the accounts ledger."

"Torrance doesn't need my help with that."

It was true. Torrance Shannon was a clever man, able to do all the bookkeeping necessary for the ranch to show a profit. What Pike did with the horses, Torrance handled with the banks and suppliers and . . .

"You're just feeling sorry for yourself. You're one of the family, Fiddler. Some of us had to be born into it. We've adopted you, you silly old fool." Nessa bent over and planted a kiss on his domed forehead. She got up, took an appreciative, deep breath of the twilight air, then ducked back inside the house.

Fiddler wiped his lips with his sleeve, wishing he had a drop of liquor to clear away. This was the first time in months and months that he wanted a drink, *really* wanted one. He knew where that road led, but it mattered less to him all the time.

"It's wearing me down," he said.

"Life? Is that what's wearing you down?" The bass voice rumbled and rolled like the thunder Fiddler had yearned for earlier.

"You make a habit of spying on a fellow?" Fiddler grumbled without looking around.

"Only when my granddaughter tells me to come out and cheer you up. Nessa sounded a tad worried about you." Dougal Shannon settled down on the stool Nessa had vacated.

"I don't need your pity."

"Ain't pity," Dougal said. "If you forced me to tell the truth, I'm out here to co-miz-er-ate with you." He drew the word out, as if biting into a bitter persimmon. "The boys have things running smooth-like, and what they don't do, Nessa does. The three of them are running the ranch better'n I ever could."

"You're right about that. They're too good," Fiddler said. "That doesn't leave anything for us to do."

"You are speaking the Gospel truth, Fiddler, that you are." Dougal put his hands on his knees and leaned closer. "So what are we gonna do about it?"

"I've been thinking about leaving," Fiddler said.

"Mary wouldn't like that one little bit. Who knows why, but she's taken quite a shine to you. Since Elijah was killed, you're the only ray of sunshine in her life."

Fiddler snorted.

"It's true. You don't see it. She's proud of her brood, but what she feels for them is different. You give her a look back at when she was happy being with a man. That's different from being proud of Torrance or worried about Pike."

"You left out Nessa."

"That girl gives her an ache she can't ease. Lookin' at your younger self can be a chore. The best thing for Mary would be seeing Nessa married off."

Fiddler stirred uneasily. He had thought about asking Mary to marry him, but he knew his own temperament. What he felt was the need to see what was over the horizon. Settling down wasn't for him. Taking those vows would ruin everything he had.

Or what little he had.

"Those boys I caught the other day. The ones looking for a still. Maybe they had the right idea," Fiddler said. "If anything would keep me occupied, making a few jugs of moonshine now and then would be it."

"Pike'd never allow it. I know my grandson. He can be all stiff necked. Right now he's making amends for close to ten years of raising Cain. He thinks following the law to the letter's the way to do it."

"Might be he doesn't want to ruffle Sophie Truesdale's feathers too much. I can't blame him on that score. She's a very attractive young woman. I know she's been spending time with that Holloway boy, but it's possible Pike still has feelings for her."

Dougal nodded in agreement, then said, "She's got a will to match his, too. You might say she's a bit mule headed."

"No more than Belle Ramsey. That lad does have them flocking around. Makes me long for the old days," Fiddler said.

Dougal snorted. "You never had women like that sniffin' after you. Not unless it was before you took to the bottle."

"I can't help but think about firing up that still again. It's like we owe it to the people of Warbonnet County to give them decent moonshine."

"Pike wouldn't agree. And you know what Torrance would say in that learned, long-winded way of his." Dougal stared out across the rolling hills toward the pasture where the rustlers had tried to steal prize Shannon breeding stock.

Fiddler had to laugh as he heard Torrance's outraged voice ringing in his ears. He and Pike locked horns constantly, but in this they'd be in complete agreement. Starting the old family business again was out of the question.

"You want me to give you a hand tomorrow when you go into town for supplies?" Fiddler asked.

"No need. I can handle it. You might want to count the head of horses just to be sure none of them have wandered off or been rustled." Dougal heaved himself to his feet. "Time for me to help Nessa."

"You and her want me to—?"

"No need. Set yourself back and take it easy. If you've a mind, play something to take your mind off being so down in the mouth."

Dougal went inside. The door clicked with a finality that sent goose bumps popping up on Fiddler's flesh. It was so final.

So final that they didn't need him for even the simplest task. He picked up his fiddle and began playing "Johnny, I Hardly Knew Ye."

It did nothing to cheer him up. It was meant to match his dour mood.

CHAPTER 6

"Sure you don't want some company?" Fiddler shifted from foot to foot, looking up at Dougal as the other man climbed onto the wagon the next day. "Loading all those supplies can wear out an old man's back."

"And your back ain't just as old as mine?"

"Well . . . not quite."

Dougal Shannon laughed. "You take it easy. I'll be back 'fore you know it."

He snapped the reins and got the two mules pulling hard. The wagon creaked and groaned as loud as Dougal's joints, then wagon, mules, and driver rolled far enough down the road so that Fiddler no longer heard.

The cloud of dust mocked him, though, as he stood there deep in thought for a considerable time.

The only logical reason Dougal had for telling Fiddler not to ride along was that he had something to do in town and wanted privacy doing it. Fiddler had heard that a new widow woman had moved in out by the schoolhouse. It wouldn't surprise him if Dougal took the long way into town and just happened to pass by, maybe to talk a spell, maybe for something other than talking. From the gossip

Fiddler had heard, the woman was pretty as a spring day and friendly.

Mighty friendly.

Fiddler didn't blame Dougal for that, if he was planning on such a stop. He only wished he felt differently about being the only one on the Shannon ranch to be floating on the air, drifting aimlessly like the puffy white clouds above.

He set out toward the barn and wandered down a road behind it. Although he had been down this way a hundred times, somehow he had ignored an old wagon pulled off to the side. Idly, he went to it and climbed into the seat, imagining a team hitched up and ready to take him across Texas to parts unknown. Once or twice he bounced on the hard wood seat.

"Sturdy enough," he said. Considering that it had been sitting untended for who knew how long, the wagon was in decent condition. He swung around and stepped into the rear. The bed was enclosed and only a few cracks let in light. Making it watertight against a full-blown Texas gully washer wasn't likely, but repairing the roof enough to ride out most storms was possible.

"A first-rate medicine wagon just like I drove way back when," he said with a note of awe in his voice as he peered at the vehicle.

He pushed open the rear door and sat on the edge, swinging his legs as memories flooded back. Doctor Collins had given him a ride for the better part of two months when he was hardly older than the youngsters who'd been hunting for the Shannon still.

"Those were fine days. The doc selling his snake oil and me shilling for him." Fiddler reared back and called in his raspy voice, "*I got a sore leg, Doc. Will that fine medicine of yours cure me?*"

As plain in his mind as if it had occurred yesterday,

he saw himself leaning heavily on a crutch and hobbling forward from the crowd that always gathered when a medicine wagon came into town. Any town on the frontier. They were all the same, full of folks desperate for any sort of break in the monotony of their day-to-day lives.

None of them ever seemed to notice that the poor crippled boy asking for a cure wasn't anybody they had ever seen before.

Now, Fiddler jumped down from the wagon and assumed a pose as if answering his own question, thumb hooked under his suspenders and one foot thrust forward like a politician launching into an oratory.

"Why, yes, son, it will. Aches and pains disappear like magic after a single dose of Doctor Collins's Powerful Pain Potion. Here, my boy, take a sip. Not too much! You don't want to get too healthy. Your friends would all be jealous of your shining vigor. And there's no telling what the ladies would do to the specimen of masculine potency you'd become!"

Fiddler smiled as memories flooded him. He'd take a sip of the so-called pain potion, make a face, then cry out in delight as he threw aside his crutch and danced a little jig.

"I was quite a performer. Better than those folks who trod the boards in San Francisco, Doc always said."

He walked around the wagon a few more times, inspecting the axles and wheels. With minimal work and a coat of paint, the old wagon was a spitting image for the one Doc Collins rolled around Texas in.

"I wonder whatever became of him." The dark cloud lowered around him again. He hadn't left the snake oil salesman. Doc Collins had abandoned him one night in San Marcos. By the time he had stopped feeling frightened and started being angry instead, there wasn't any chance of finding the traveling salesman.

"But his potion surely did go down smooth." Fiddler climbed onto the driver's box. Doc Collins faded as he imagined himself driving the wagon around. Making the snake oil wasn't hard. He had whipped up more than one batch for the peddler. All it took was a little of this and some of that to make it bitter. What medicine wasn't bitter?

Then fill the rest of the bottle with moonshine.

"Moonshine," he said in a low, reverent tone. That was the secret. That was the secret to a lot of his trouble.

"Where's that paint you got for the barn?" Fiddler asked Dougal. "You didn't go and use it all up, now did you?"

"Don't get so worked up. I still have enough for you to slosh on the side of your wagon," Dougal said, eyeing the vehicle rather dubiously. "This past week you've put in more time fixin' it up than if you'd built it from scratch."

"I'm not much of a wainwright. There's no rush and I'm taking my sweet time with this project. It's been rather enjoyable."

Fiddler put his fists on his hips and surveyed his handiwork. It was better than new, he thought.

"Unless you're planning on using the wagon for something useful, you have all the time in the world."

Fiddler shot a sharp look at Dougal. The man goaded him.

"Who says I won't be doing something useful? I can haul freight for folks too busy to do it themselves."

"It's sturdy enough," Dougal allowed, "but finding customers will be hard. Most folks have their own wagon. If Pike wants anything hauled around here, he uses the big wagon."

"I intend to take small jobs," Fiddler insisted. He let Dougal ramble on about how such a business wasn't profitable. With a can of red paint and the smaller tins of white and green he had scrounged, the wagon would be decked out in style.

But not yet. Not too soon. He wasn't much of an artist, but Doc Collins's wagon hadn't been all that snappy. It called attention to the spiel and not much else. How well he sold the snake oil mattered more than lettering on the side of the wagon.

Before Fiddler was ready for that, he had a few other chores to take care of. He waited for Dougal to get tired of teasing him and wander off before hitching a mule up to the wagon. Out back of the barn rose a small hill of full grain sacks he had gathered over the past week.

"Whoa, hold on," Fiddler called to the mule. The lop-ear turned a giant eye in his direction, as if demanding that he make up his mind. Were they moving or were they standing?

He secured the reins on the brake handle and circled to the rear of the wagon. He took a quick look around to be sure no one was spying on him. Before, he wanted them to notice. Now it was different. He was a man with a mission.

Nobody on the Shannon ranch would approve of what he intended to do.

Fiddler grunted as he wrestled the bags of grain into the wagon. Doing so much physical work turned every single joint into a burning pit and each muscle into a mile of aches. He'd never felt better. Finally, he was doing something.

The grain sacks were piled on either side of the wagon bed. Then he looked around, trying to act as if he didn't have a care in the world. This was the most secret part of his trip today. It took a few minutes for him to confirm that he wasn't being watched. He yanked back a tarp and began loading crates of equipment into the wagon.

It took the better part of twenty minutes. Fiddler was left

sweaty and tired and happier than he'd been in a coon's age. The mule brayed when he urged it into motion, but it finally relented and began dragging the heavy load across the yard, down to the road and . . . to a special place.

If the two youngsters had come this way a couple of weeks later, they'd have found some curious goings on in the woods. The double-rutted road wasn't quite as overrun by weeds. Wagon wheels had crushed the plants springing up in the bottom of the ruts. And curiously, the newly pioneered road ended in a wall of vegetation.

Fiddler pulled back on the reins, secured them, and went to the towering bushes. He reached into the thick greenery, fumbled for a moment, then found the latch. He stepped back and swung open a gate. It had been camouflaged with brush from all around. It took a few minutes for him to drive the wagon through, close the gate, and then continue driving deeper into the woods.

A clearing opened where he could pull his wagon close to a tumbledown shack. He expertly maneuvered around so that he didn't have to lug the sacks of grain too far.

By now, he was regaining some of his youthful muscle. And if he lied to himself, it made no difference if he was as spry as when he was twenty. He felt years younger. Finally, he was working toward a goal. Fiddler kicked open the door and heaved the grain sack inside.

He hadn't forgotten how to set up a still. A low fire under a copper pot kept things from cooling down while he was gone. If the fire had gone out, reheating the pot and getting the slow drip of moonshine from the coils into a jug would take a couple more days.

Humming, he set to work. The last batch had produced two gallons. With that much 'shine, he had enough makings for a hundred bottles of snake oil. He glanced across the shack to a table creaking under the weight of bottles and greens and even tubers waiting to become . . . what?

He hadn't come up with a catchy name for his snake oil yet. There was time, though. Another few days would give him twice the moonshine already prepared. With such an inventory, he was sure to make the potion the best anybody in all of Texas had ever sampled.

"Sampled," he said, sighing. The smell made his mouth water. The sight caused his stomach to clench. The wet, slick feel across his fingers burned his very soul.

He had not let a single drop pass his lips. The temptation was great, but he knew if he weakened just once there'd be a second time and another and another. Four gallons of the pungent 'shine wouldn't be enough to quench his bottomless thirst.

Fiddler stirred the pot some more, broke apart clumps, and let the heat do its work. While this batch distilled, he'd hunt for more herbs and maybe some berries to give color to the bottled snake oil.

He stepped out of the shack, stretched, and then froze. Something felt wrong. He relaxed and tried not to be too obvious as he glanced around the woods on either side of the road. Nothing moved. That was the real warning. The unnatural quiet crushed down on him.

"No sound," he told himself, "isn't a good sign." Someone had scared all the animals as they prowled about and spied on him. He went to the wagon and rummaged around in the rear. He yanked a shotgun free and whirled around, the barrel aimed into the dank, cool woods.

Nothing moved. Fiddler lowered the Greener and began singing loudly. He pulled a sack from the rear of the wagon, slung it over his shoulder, and with the shotgun in hand set out. A dozen paces into the trees, he stopped singing and kept walking. Each step was shorter than the one before until he came to a complete stop.

Fiddler listened for sounds and this time heard one that wasn't normal for the forest. No coyote or rabbit made the creaking sound of old boots walking toward the shack. He checked the load in his shotgun, then retraced his steps as quietly as he could.

The door of the shack stood half open. He had closed it to help keep the smell of cooking mash trapped inside. Using his foot, he kicked the door open all the way. He thrust the shotgun barrel inside and yelled, "Hands up high or you'll get ventilated!"

A dark figure bending over the cook pot slowly unwound and turned, hands in the air.

"You wouldn't shoot me, would you, Fiddler?"

"Dougal! What are you doing snooping around here?"

"Point that firestick somewhere else," Dougal said. "Your shaky old finger might twitch and do something we'd both regret."

Slowly, Fiddler lowered the shotgun. He didn't say anything, just waited for Dougal to answer his question.

"I noticed the grain missing after I fetched back a dozen sacks from town last week," Dougal said. "So much missing could only mean one thing."

"I'm working the still again," Fiddler finished with a note of defiance in his voice. "What are you going to do? Tell Pike?"

"I could do that," Dougal allowed. "Or I could turn you in to the law. Which is worse, being on Pike's bad side or rotting away in jail?"

"Don't fool around with me," Fiddler snapped. "You caught me fair and square. What are you going to do?"

"I figured out what you were doing before I came out

here to be sure. I've already decided. I'm going to blackmail you, Fiddler."

"Blackmail? I don't have a penny to my name!"

Dougal Shannon grinned ear to ear. "It's not money I want."

"Then what?"

"When you pull out, wherever you're goin', I want to ride along. This ranch is as wearisome for me as it is for you."

Fiddler clutched his shotgun just a little tighter as he thought about what Dougal had just said. Of all the options he might have imagined, this one seemed the least likely. But it appealed to him, Fiddler realized.

He shoved out his hand and shook Dougal's. "Partners," he said.

Dougal's smile grew even wider as he pumped Fiddler's hand.

CHAPTER 7

Pike lifted the last rail into place, stood back, and wiped sweat from his forehead. The morning's work had gone well. The pasture fence was once more secure. That wouldn't keep a feisty horse from jumping over it, but it offered a powerful suggestion to even the orneriest critter not to try. For most horses, that was good enough.

For horse thieves, though, it wasn't much of a challenge. He swiped his bandanna across his forehead once more and looked around the pasture. Three dead rustlers was one thing, but the fourth had escaped. By now he could be drinking tequila in Mexico, but Pike doubted it. Whether the Shannon family had anything more to worry about from the man was a matter he and Torrance debated endlessly.

His brother insisted the outlaw had hightailed it, maybe not to Mexico but far enough away that the Shannons had no call to remain vigilant. Pike thought his brother was too caught up in his books and failed to understand human nature. The remaining rustler's pride had been stung. The way he had slunk away after nearly drowning as he hid in the stock pond would make him all the more inclined to get revenge.

The horses didn't care who owned them. If they had plenty of grain and grass and water and the chance to run free, they were content.

The outlaw was a bother, but nothing Pike intended to lose much sleep over. He hiked back to the tree where he'd tethered his dun. The sturdy horse cropped at grass and barely seemed to notice as Pike took the reins and stepped up.

What did cause the horse to jerk its head around was the rumble of wheels along the dirt road on the other side of the fence. Pike stood in his stirrups and watched as Fiddler's bright red wagon rattled along.

Fiddler had worked like a fiend on that wagon for close to three weeks now. Pike rode inside the fence, watching the wagon sway to and fro. The wagon looked like a small barn because of its color, but Pike noticed some darker lines. He trotted faster to catch up and get a better look.

He frowned when he read the outlined letters. It was as if Fiddler intended to paint his name on the side and tested the water with light brush strokes before committing himself. Pike slowed and let the wagon pull ahead. Fiddler hadn't seen him. For some reason, Pike wanted to keep his discovery of those letters a secret.

"It's not like I'm spying on him," he said to himself. Then he tugged on the reins and galloped across the pasture. He'd be at the house fifteen minutes before Fiddler since the road wound around before deciding to go to the Shannon house.

He finished tending his horse and was walking to the house from the barn when Fiddler pulled up. Pike went to greet the man.

"You're up early, Fiddler," he said. "That's not like you."

"I had work to do, Pike." Fiddler looked away and added. "Hauling. I had a load to move and wanted to get it out of the way."

"Are you hiring yourself out?" Pike wondered who would pay Fiddler a thin dime for such work. The wagon wasn't built to move bulky freight, and smaller loads weren't hired out. Most folks had their own wagons for that.

"I am. I decided to make a few extra dollars."

Pike heard the quaver in Fiddler's voice. The man looked away when he spoke and showed all the signs of not telling the whole story—or maybe he was outright lying. That possibility put Pike on guard. Fiddler had no reason to lie about how he used the wagon, or even why he had spent so much time and effort repairing it.

"Who?"

"What do you mean, Pike? I got to do some more . . . work."

"Who's hiring you? That's not a hard question, is it?" He stepped closer and tried to make out the letters Fiddler had sketched on the side of the wagon.

"Here now, give an old man a hand climbing down."

"You don't need my help," Pike said. "You're as spry as ever."

"Then keep the mule from tearing off on its own. That critter's been acting up something fierce."

"Almost like it's got a mind of its own," Pike said dryly. "Who's paying you to haul a load?"

"Don't know why that's any of your business," Fiddler grumbled, and finally said, "I was hauling grain for Karl Erickson. He's been laid up and his son Beau is a ne'er-do-well. He can't rely on him for a single, solitary thing. So I've been helping him out until he gets back on his feet."

"There's no need to get so touchy," Pike said.

"I've been working hard," Fiddler insisted.

"That's the truth, Pike. He has been." Dougal came up and looked at the faint outlines on the side of the wagon.

Pike started to ask about the small can of paint his grandfather carried, but Dougal hastily set it inside the wagon and turned his back on it. If he hadn't known better, Pike would have thought Dougal was hiding something. But it was only paint.

"How's the repair on the wobbly wheel coming?" Dougal asked.

"Wheel? Oh, yes, it's about fixed. I was getting ready to take a drive to see how it's spinning." Fiddler climbed back into the driver's box and took the reins.

"I'll come with you." Dougal settled next to Fiddler. The two exchanged a whisper too low for Pike to overhear. Louder, Dougal said, "I can be a real help if it begins to wobble."

"Wobbly wheel, yeah," Fiddler said.

Pike watched them drive away. He puzzled over their behavior. They acted like schoolboys caught throwing spitballs in class.

He considered trailing them. In spite of Fiddler's loud assertion that all they intended was to check out a wheel that wasn't showing any sign of being shaky, Pike wondered what they were up to.

He returned to the barn. His horse whinnied in resignation when he saddled up and rode out. He reached the main road and trotted toward town. To get to the truth, he needed more information.

Pike rode straight to Erickson's seed and grain store in Warbonnet. The owner swept the boardwalk in front. He looked up from his chore and waved to Pike.

"What can I do for you, Pike? You can't be wanting more grain, not yet."

"Good afternoon, Mr. Erickson. You're looking fit. I heard you were laid up."

"I had a touch of gout a week back, but it's better. Got me some dark cherries from Miss Truesdale that cleared up the pain. She's quite a gal, Miss Truesdale."

"She helps the doc out. I reckon she's learned most of what he knows."

"That's 'cuz he doesn't know much," Erickson chuckled. "I'd listen to her until the cows come home if she keeps telling me to eat more of her fine pie."

"Why's your boy not doing the sweeping for you?"

Erickson stared at Pike curiously, then said, "Beau's got a job cutting trees. As much as I want him to take over the store one day, he's got a bee in his bonnet about becoming a lumber baron. I swear, he does twice the work of anyone else in the crew, and they're all hard workers."

"Glad to hear he's doing well."

Erickson leaned on his broom and stared at Pike, obviously waiting for him to say something more.

"All that talk of pie's made me hungry," Pike said. "I'll try Miss Truesdale's cherry pie on your recommendation."

"You don't look like the sort to have gout," the store owner said. "If you need more grain, I can get it loaded for you. Just send Fiddler by again."

"How much work's he been doing for you?" Pike hated himself for asking. This was too much like calling Fiddler a liar to his face.

"For me? Nothing, unless him carting those sacks out to your place counts as working for me. But unless there's a huge load, I don't deliver. Folks like you have wagons already."

Pike bid the grain store owner good-bye and turned toward the far end of town where Sophie's café sat alone, proud and doing a good business for the time of day. He hesitated before going inside. He and Sophie hadn't parted on the best of terms, and he wasn't exactly sure why. A quick breath, a move to brush trail dust off his clothing, and then he went in.

The only place left inside was at the counter. He settled down as Sophie came from the kitchen. Her eyes widened a little seeing him, then narrowed.

"What do you want, Mr. Shannon?"

Her icy tone took him aback. Responding the same way got him nowhere. He didn't have any reason to feud with her.

"Karl Erickson said you have about the best cherry pie there is. He wouldn't lie to me, so give me a piece of that fine pie, if you please."

She harumphed, cut a piece from a full pie, and dropped it in front of him.

"May I have a fork, please?"

"I suppose so." She dug around under the counter and put one down in front of him with a loud click.

"It looks good," he said, still trying to find something to soothe her.

"Don't choke on it."

"Oh? Is it chokeberry pie?" His feeble joke caused her to stamp a foot and storm off into the back.

Pike's temper was fraying. He rounded the counter and followed Sophie into the kitchen.

"Get out of here. You're not welcome in my kitchen." Her lips thinned to a razor slash. "You're not welcome in my café!"

"What's got your dander up? I haven't done anything but be polite."

"You know what's wrong, Pike Shannon. There are many things you do that I can tolerate, but not lying. You . . . you *liar*!"

She reached for a pan. He stepped away since it looked as if she intended to throw it at him. She caught herself before rearing back for a decent attack. Instead, Sophie waved it around in front of her.

"You have some nerve showing up here. You know what I think about liquor and . . . and moonshine!"

"You're a member of the temperance league," he said. "I think you're wrong about forcing all the saloons to close and shutting down the sale of liquor in the entire county, but I respect your stand."

"Oh, do you now? Do you, Pike Shannon? You liar!" Her self-control shattered. She swung the pan at him.

He blocked it, his big hand circling her slender wrist. She struggled with impressive strength but had no chance against a man used to roping horses and lifting bales of hay all day. When she stopped fighting, he released her.

"You'll have to explain what you're talking about. I don't know. I really don't."

"There you go, lying through your teeth again." She stamped her foot. "You don't know a thing about a running still? Not a thing?"

"That rumor's been floating around for weeks. That's all it is. A rumor." He snorted. "It almost got two boys in trouble because they believed it."

"You *are* running a still. You *are* making more moonshine. That's not a rumor. People riding past your ranch all tell the same story. The smoke, the smell—and you deny that Mr. Erickson's not supplying you with the grain to make the moonshine? He's not a dull man. He knows!"

Pike stared at her, words not coming. Pieces fit together. He hadn't wanted to believe it, but Fiddler was running a still.

"Fiddler," he started.

"Don't you blame it on that old man. All he's doing is

acting as your errand boy. Nobody works a still on your ranch without the great Mr. Pike Shannon knowing. Or are you admitting you're stupid, that Fiddler put one over on you?"

Pike would have let her know that Fiddler had done that very thing. Being duped by a good friend was painful, but not as painful as lying to Sophie, who had been a good friend to him in the past even if they *weren't* romantically involved anymore.

"I have half a mind to turn you in to the sheriff. You're flouting the law. You—you—" She sputtered as she tried to get the words out past her anger.

Before she ordered him out again, he touched the brim of his hat, then left without a word. Arguing with Sophie Truesdale wasn't going to get him anywhere. If he wanted to settle accounts with her, he needed Fiddler to confess to her what he had done.

CHAPTER 8

Fiddler threw a bucket of water on the fire under the boiler. A huge hiss filled the shack. The puff of steam forced him to back outside. The sizzle and pop quickly died down. The still was shut down. Stacked outside were jugs holding the output for the last week.

"Eight gallons," he said, shaking his head. If he had run the still day and night, there'd have been considerably more, but he didn't need that much.

Fiddler licked his lips and picked up the jug closest to hand. He lifted it to his nose and sniffed. His nostrils flared. Old memories rose like spirits from the grave. His mouth even began watering, as if he was getting ready to sample a fine meal.

"Nope, not gonna happen. Nope, not at all." He put down the jug before old habits forced him to take a swig. As much as he told himself it'd be just a teeny taste, he knew better. He knew where giving in led, too. That was a part of his life best left behind.

He'd spent too many nights in a jail cell for being drunk.

The wagon was parked a ways off. He looked it over with some satisfaction. The red barn paint made it stand out, but the white and green lettering he'd added proclaimed this to be a real medicine wagon.

The top line read: FIDDLER'S EUROPEAN POTION; the bottom: CURES WHAT AILS YOU. He had wanted an eye-catching illustration. A delightful lady beckoning seductively would have been nice. Or a lady holding a bottle of the concoction and winking broadly would have been as good at delivering the message he intended.

His artistic skills weren't up to the chore. "Who'll care?" he asked himself. "The devil's juice in every bottle will sell it."

He picked up the nearest jug and stepped up into the back of the wagon. His workbench along one wall was littered with ground-up roots and crushed leaves. With ridiculous care he set down the moonshine and began mixing his "European" potion.

"A little of this and a pinch of that." He hummed to himself as he worked. Bottle by bottle he added about an inch of his ground mixture. Then came the part that delighted him most.

He popped the cork, poured in the 'shine, and shook up the bottle. The mixture turned an amber color. Adding a drop of berry juice changed the color to a wicked looking blue.

"Perfect. Who wouldn't want to take a sip of this?" He inhaled the vapors coming off one bottle with real appreciation. The addition of the moonshine completed the formula. It hardly mattered that he had already forgotten the portions. Fiddler wasn't even sure what herbs and ground-up roots he had put in, but the liquor was the most important ingredient. The rest only gave justification for the sale.

If Warbonnet County and surrounding counties had gone dry, that was a shame. Selling a patent medicine wasn't a crime. If the buyer drank a bit too much, that wasn't Fiddler's fault. He smiled. If they wanted to buy a second bottle, that was his pleasure.

That and making the pitch.

He had missed the excitement of being away from the Shannon ranch too much not to feel a chill down his spine thinking of the places he'd travel and the new places he'd see.

Working slowly, he sealed each bottle with a blob of melted wax. He put his brand into the slowly cooling wax to show who had sold the potion. Twenty bottles stretched along his worktable, ready for the crowd to press close and demand to be cured of what ailed them.

He leaned back to bask in the glow of doing something again. Fiddler jerked around when he heard a noise outside. The shotgun leaning by the door was loaded and ready to chase off intruders. He grabbed it and poked his head out. Movement in the woods south of the road sent him scuttling through the wagon to climb into the driver's box.

He looked around to be sure he wasn't surrounded. It might be those pesky young'uns come back to sneak a sip of moonshine. The still hadn't been running before. It was now.

Fiddler climbed down and cautiously glanced around the back of the wagon. Something rustled branches in a large bush. He drew back the hammer on the shotgun and pointed it straight into the thicket.

"Come on out or I'll blow you to Kingdom come!"

The leaves rustled some more, high up about where a standing man would push branches aside. But no one emerged.

"I'm counting to three, then I open fire!"

"Hold your horses, you old reprobate. I'm not done relieving myself."

"Dougal! I ought to shoot you for sneaking up on me.

You know better than that." Fiddler lowered the shotgun and eased the hammer down.

"I wasn't sneakin'. I came up and felt the urge. You know how it is when you get to be our age. Nature don't give you much warnin'!"

"Is that the way it's going to be when we pull out? You needing to go commune with nature every ten minutes?"

The branches parted and Dougal Shannon appeared, working to fasten the buttons on his fly. He wiped his hands off on his overalls and came closer.

"You did a real good job with the lettering," he said as he peered up at the side of the wagon.

"You're not the one I have to please." Despite that comment, Fiddler felt a small glow of accomplishment that Dougal approved of his handiwork. "As long as the crowds buy a bottle or two, that's what matters."

"This is advertising," Dougal insisted. He tapped the side of the wagon. "Do it right and they'll believe you know how to mix medicines." He peered into the wagon. "You have enough ready to sell?"

"Got a couple crates' worth. With this batch, that makes fifty bottles."

Dougal went to the shack and waved away the steam leaking from inside.

"All shut down? Are you going to take apart the still?"

"No call to do that. All the fires are out and the hot parts are cooling down nicely. It'd take a day or more to tear down the equipment."

"You intending to come back and make more?"

"If sales are good enough." Fiddler blinked. He hadn't thought too far ahead. "I probably am coming back. This is just . . . I don't know what to call it."

"Running away from home," Dougal said. "That's what it feels like."

"Yes, that's it," Fiddler allowed. "I'm too old to run away with the circus. Besides, there's no circus passing through right now. Going back to what I know is just as good."

"I'll be back sooner or later," Dougal said. "I want a bit of excitement, too. Torrance likes life as dull as dishwater. It surprises me that Pike is going along with him."

"Pike is trying to walk the straight and narrow. An admirable goal, I'll grant you." Fiddler made a face. "But boring as it can be, unfortunately."

"You have the look of a man ready to hit the trail," Dougal said. "Are we going right now?"

Fiddler took a deep breath and answered, "There's no reason to hang around any longer." He peered at Dougal. "You sure you want to come along? You have it easy here."

"So do you," Dougal shot back. "That's the problem. Life for both of us is too dang comfortable."

"My gear's in the wagon. Are you going up to the house to fetch anything?"

"I've got everything I need in my saddlebags." Dougal hurried off and returned leading his horse. The saddlebags bulged and a large bedroll had been strapped over the horse's rump. He tied the reins to an iron rung on the side of the wagon and dusted off his hands. "Let's hit the road, partner."

Fiddler felt a pang of guilt about leaving without saying good-bye to Mary, but if he tried to explain what was eating him alive, she'd never understand. Worse, she had a way of making him do what she wanted. He'd end up staying and become even more miserable.

"I'm not sure where we're heading," Dougal said. "Where do you have in mind?"

"North," Fiddler said. "We'll go north and see what we can find."

He snapped the reins and convinced the mule to begin

pulling the heavy load. As apprehensive as he was about not telling anyone he was going, the thrill of a new adventure burned brighter. He had a future again, one filled with exploits to make his heart race.

CHAPTER 9

"I haven't seen him, Pike. Why are you asking? He must be around here somewhere."

Nessa Shannon looked up from her work. A pile of frayed rope stretched halfway across the room as she repaired it. Her nimble fingers kept working the hemp strands back into the rope to strengthen it even as Pike fumed.

"I've got a bone to pick with him," he said. Telling her of his suspicions about Fiddler firing up a still would get nowhere until he was certain. She would insist on knowing everything, and all he had for the moment were suspicions and a few of Fiddler's lies to go on. As irritating as anything else, he believed Sophie Truesdale's accusations rather than giving Fiddler the benefit of the doubt.

"Ask Torrance. He's in the office working on the books."

"What's the problem now? He said he'd closed them for the year, though it's five months until New Year's."

"His fiscal year is different from our calendar year. Don't ask me to explain that since it doesn't make any sense. He's talking about selling a couple of studs come spring to raise more cash. Find out which ones, will you? That sorrel we bought from the ranch over east in the Piney Woods is asking to be ridden. It's best not to prod

Torrance about cutting one out for my own use. You know how he is when I get attached to a particular horse. 'This is business, not pleasure.'"

Nessa turned back to her repair work.

Pike knew what she meant. Everything he mentioned to Torrance turned into an argument. If Nessa wasn't able to plead her case for keeping a particular horse, Pike doubted he was in any better position to do so. Torrance would find something else to grouse about, and they'd end up shouting at each other.

He stepped into the downstairs hallway. His mother worked in the kitchen, and, as Nessa had said, their brother hunched over the ranch's account books, mumbling to himself. Pike had no intention of asking what Torrance had found wrong. There was always something.

And if Fiddler was running a still, selling moonshine would be more than "something." Torrance would blame Pike, and their simmering feud would become a full-blown contest of wills. It was almost enough to make Pike consider climbing onto his horse and riding out, as he had done ten years earlier for much the same reasons.

Only now he was a decade wiser. Hiring out his fast gun had been exciting at first, then became a deadly chore. Every job he took on, some of them not quite legal, carried life or death as a conclusion. He was good enough that he had always ridden away after the gun smoke cleared. Pike was smart enough to know that, out there somewhere, a faster gun waited for him. When their paths crossed, he'd be the one moldering in a shallow grave.

He had given up that concern for running the Shannon spread. Right now, he was beginning to doubt he'd made the right decision.

He stepped onto the porch and looked around. Quiet. Oh so quiet. It got on his nerves now when for the months he had been back that silence had provided a sanctuary—except for a few times when he'd tangled with men who rode on the far side of the law.

A small smile crept to his lips. Every time that had happened moonshine was at the center of the fight. As much as his life had changed, that single problem hadn't. Deep down, Pike had to admit he enjoyed the process of moonshining as much as sipping at the potent result dripping from the copper tube.

He spent the next twenty minutes checking the bunkhouse, barn, and outbuildings. The smith hammering away at a new set of shoes for Nessa's horse hadn't seen Fiddler. It finally occurred to Pike to ask after his grandpappy. The smith hadn't seen Dougal all day, either.

That left Pike with an uneasy feeling. Fiddler and Dougal both might be tangled up in the newly illegal activity. Chewing out a friend of the family was one thing, but ordering his own grandfather around was a horse of a different color.

He returned to the barn and saddled his mare. As he rode off, he saw the deep ruts left by Fiddler's wagon. While Fiddler might have headed into town, Pike had the feeling his destination was somewhere else.

The still.

Riding slowly to give himself time to think proved a good idea. The wagon tracks veered away from the main road and cut across a pasture. Pike followed the newly cut impressions faster now. He galloped when he had a firm idea where Fiddler had headed.

When he found the wall of freshly cut brush tied to the gate, he knew he had found the still. It was the same location his pa had used before running afoul of Doak Ramsey. Pike came to the still minutes after getting a deep whiff of wood smoke. He sat astride his horse and stared at the old shack. Tiny wisps of white smoke seeped from inside.

The wagon tracks beside the shack were deeper leaving than arriving.

"How much moonshine have you concocted, you old reprobate?" He shook his head as he dismounted and opened the rickety door.

As he expected, the still had been used recently. The copper pot was still warm to the touch, but the fire under it had been extinguished some time earlier. The embers gave off enough smoke to fill the interior and leak out the scent that had alerted him. But the entire moonshine production had come to an end.

Pike scouted the area. A couple of broken jugs were the only evidence that the 'shine had ever been stored. Deep indentations in the soft earth along one outside wall showed Fiddler had produced at least five jugs of the liquid gold. A pile of empty grain sacks marked ERICKSON'S SEED AND FEED gave Pike an estimate that Fiddler hadn't gone wild making the moonshine.

"For his own use," he said sadly.

Fiddler had resisted the lure of liquor ever since Pike had returned to Warbonnet County. He and Fiddler had shared a jail cell for a night. When Dougal had bailed him out, Pike insisted they spring Fiddler, too. The man had been grateful and had shown it with loyalty and friendship ever since. The Shannons had come to think of Fiddler as one of the family.

Thinking that he had succumbed to drink again filled Pike with a mixture of sadness and anger over such a betrayal of his faith in the man's basic goodness.

He started to mount and ride after Fiddler. The wagon tracks were so visible a blind man could follow. Then he settled down. While not being anywhere to be found was no proof Dougal Shannon was in cahoots, Pike had to believe that was true.

"Fiddler and Dougal," he said, shaking his head. "That's quite a pair. Where have you gotten off to?"

He picked up the empty grain sacks and went into the shack. Dismantling the still and stuffing the coils and pots into the sacks took the better part of the afternoon. When he finished, he stared at the small mountain of equipment. If he had a lick of sense, he'd destroy it all. The good people of Warbonnet County had voted to become dry. Even having an unproductive still might be breaking the law.

Pike lugged the sacks off into the woods, found a place easily remembered, and buried everything there. Someday the voters would return to their senses and want to taste a drop of 'dew on their tongues again. When that happened, Pike need only dig up the equipment and get to work.

With the still dismantled, he could tell Sophie he had taken care of the problem. But how far should the apology go?

"I can't tell her I ran off Fiddler. She'd never believe I banished a friend. Then, too, eventually, she'd ask where Dougal was." Pike knew the woman who lived and breathed temperance would never believe he had exiled his own grandpappy for working on the still.

He mounted and rode away from the now-empty shack. It was best not to mention any of that to Sophie. Let her come to her own conclusions. The way gossip spread like wildfire in Warbonnet, she'd know the still was shut down and that Fiddler was responsible before he'd have time to ride back into town.

She'd either believe he was doing the right thing or continue to blame him. Either way, she'd make up her own mind. Arguing with her pushed her away and only caused them both aggravation.

As he rode back to the house, his thoughts turned to

Belle Ramsey. She wasn't as touchy about the subject of moonshining, but they hadn't parted on speaking terms. And Pike had no idea why not.

Getting rid of the still and Fiddler leaving erased part of his problem with the two women. Pike only needed to wait awhile to see what the view was like after the dust settled.

Chapter 10

"It's always so peaceful this time of day," Nessa said. She sipped at a glass of lemonade as she and Pike looked across the yard to the distant pasture where a dozen horses frolicked.

"Is that the sorrel you want?" Pike pointed to the stallion leading the others in their mindless racing. He admired the sleek lines. He saw why Torrance had bought the horse, and it was even easier to see what drew his sister to it.

"He's about the fastest horse I've seen. Maybe I should talk Torrance into racing him. We could make extra money winning a few claiming races."

"That's too much like gambling for Torrance," he said. Pike sipped at his own lemonade. His ma had made it. He could tell because she'd put too much sugar in it. Her taste was off just a mite, or maybe she thought her children preferred it so sweet that an inch of undissolved sugar like a candy mountain piled up on the bottom of the glass.

Pike had liked it that way when he was ten. Now he preferred a drop or two of moonshine in it.

That got him to thinking about his latest trip into Warbonnet. He'd made a point of not telling Sophie Truesdale that he had destroyed the still. It had to be better if that good news—for her—made its way through someone else's gossip. Pike had been disappointed when she passed him on the street, pointedly ignoring him.

Maybe things were never going to work out between the two of them, especially now with Curtis Holloway in the picture. He could live with that. But he still valued Sophie's friendship, and he didn't like it that she thought badly of him. He liked even less that she had refused to believe him when he told her flat out that he hadn't taken up moonshining again.

He stared into the gathering night. The insects buzzed, and in the distance frogs croaked as they hopped around the edges of the stock ponds scattered around the ranch. He felt like those frogs, jumping from one place to another, from one woman to another. After returning to Warbonnet County and meeting Sophie and Belle, he had spent months trying to choose between them. Each appealed to him in a different way.

If not for that trip down to Pecan County and everything that had happened during that hazardous journey, he might still be trapped in that morass of indecision, Pike realized. In a way, he was mighty glad Sophie had taken up with Curtis. It had saved him from having to make up his mind and meant that he could turn his attention unreservedly to Belle.

But now Belle wouldn't even give him the time of day, and Pike still had no idea why. Whatever he had done was serious enough for her to turn her back on him.

Pike suddenly sat up straighter in the chair. Something had broken into his reverie, and he was glad to push those pointless thoughts away. Over in the pasture, the horses galloped away from the fence along the road. Someone was coming toward the house.

"There's only one rider," Nessa said. "I saw his silhouette when he turned into the road leading up here."

Pike considered fetching his six-gun. His holster with the Colt hung on a hook just inside the door. Nobody rode out this way in such a determined fashion so late in the day unless it meant trouble.

"It's that boy. What's his name?" Nessa went to the edge of the porch and waved.

"Jimmy McCall," Pike said. He stood beside his sister as the boy galloped to a spot half a dozen yards away before yanking hard on the reins. A gritty cloud rose.

Pike waved his hand to disperse it as Jimmy swung down from the saddle. The boy should know better than to create such an annoying dust storm.

"Mr. Shannon, Miss Shannon, I got a telegram. Mr. Throckmorton paid me a dollar to bring it to you right away." He patted his pockets. A moment's panic passed when he found the folded envelope. He tripped on his way up the stairs.

"Settle down," Pike advised. "You're here. What's so all fired important that it has to be delivered tonight?"

"I ain't read it, Pike, sir. I know better after—after Mr. Throckmorton cautioned me that this is 'bout the same as reading somebody's US Mail letter." He held it out, not sure who to give it to.

Pike resolved the dilemma by taking it from the boy's hand.

"Pike, give him a tip," Nessa said. "He's come a long way."

"I missed dinner," the boy said.

"Go on into the kitchen and get yourself something." Pike tore open the envelope. A single sheet of foolscap fluttered out when he upended it.

"Our ma is still there." Nessa half turned, intending to escort Jimmy in. Then her curiosity got the better of her.

"There's no need to wait out here for a reply. Tell her I said it was all right for you to eat your fill after such a long ride from town."

"Thanks, Miss Shannon. I missed dinner," the boy repeated to emphasize how hungry he was. He disappeared into the house.

Pike held up the sheet to catch a ray of light escaping from a kerosene lamp in the front hall. He read the telegram, then read it a second time as grim trenches appeared in his cheeks.

By now Nessa was bursting with eagerness to find out the contents. She burst out, "Well, what is it?"

"It's from Dougal," he said.

"Well, it's about time. I've missed him, but I'm still mad at him and Fiddler, too, for lighting out and never so much as waving good-bye." She sucked in her breath, then let it out slowly. "What is it, Pike? What's wrong?"

"They went up north to Kiowa Springs. Dougal doesn't give details, but he says Fiddler is in bad shape. He's not sure he'll live much longer."

"That's terrible!" Nessa took the telegram and read it for herself, as if her brother might have held something back. She returned it to him when she satisfied herself he had told her everything in the message.

Pike took a deep breath and tried to calm the worried thoughts racing through his mind. He said, "Considering what a penny pincher Dougal is, it has to be serious for him to spend the money on a telegram."

"He did say Fiddler was seriously hurt, but he never said what happened." Nessa chewed on her lower lip in worry. "We should go to Kiowa Springs right away."

"*I* should go. There's no call for you to do anything but look after that sorrel," Pike said, trying to keep his voice light. His heart, however, had turned to lead. What had Dougal and Fiddler gotten themselves into?

If they had been arrested for peddling moonshine, Dougal would be locked up in a cell awaiting trial. If . . .

Pike shook his head. He had nothing to go on. Fiddler was hurt, and he was family. Not by blood but by adoption.

"I should tell Mama," Nessa said.

"Go on," Pike said, relieved she had volunteered. She knew how he would deliver the sad news. She was more inclined to soften the contents of the telegram than Pike.

"Are you leaving in the morning? You should get a good night's sleep and a decent meal before hitting the trail."

"The boy rode like the wind to deliver the message. Getting to Kiowa Springs as quick as possible is the least I can do."

Nessa stepped over to her brother and hugged him.

"You be careful, Pike. I know, I know. That's crazy advice and nothing you're likely to pay any attention to. But if we lose you along with Dougal and Fiddler, it'd be a disaster."

Pike thought on how their pa had been murdered and his older brother, Tyree, had died after being kicked in the head by a mule. One by one the Shannon men were dying.

He pushed his sister away and told her, "I'll do whatever's necessary."

Their eyes locked. She heaved a deep sigh and said, "I'll fetch your gun. You don't want to forget that."

That was the last thing Pike Shannon would leave behind.

CHAPTER 11

Two days of hard riding to the north brought Pike into Kiowa Springs an hour after sundown. The town was larger than Warbonnet. It had grown up next to a cavalry outpost that had been abandoned when the frontier, and the ongoing fight against the Indians, had moved farther west.

However, by that time the army's presence had calmed down the danger in the area enough that a number of ranchers had moved in and established good-sized spreads. Those cattlemen needed a place to buy supplies and conduct other business. The presence of the springs that had given the settlement its name helped it to grow, as well.

These days, the cross streets were almost as heavily built up as the main street through the center of town. A goodly number of buildings were empty, but the stores that showed any activity seemed to be doing a lot of business.

Pike passed a gambling den and wondered if they served liquor under the table. Like Warbonnet County, Kiowa Springs was dry. That didn't keep a steady flow of men from going into and out of the Royal Flush.

Pike kept riding. He could check the place for Fiddler and Dougal later on, if he needed to. His first idea was to locate their medicine wagon. A quick turn around the plaza in the middle of town failed to reveal the wagon. Might be a good idea to meander up and down the side streets, Pike decided, looking for empty lots where a moonshine salesman might draw a crowd.

Nothing.

As he rode, he kept an eye out for a doctor's office. If Fiddler was hurt as seriously as Dougal said, a doctor must have been called. When Pike saw a sign decorated with a caduceus, he knew his search was over. He recognized the symbol as having been used by the US Army Medical Corps.

He dismounted and looped the dun's reins around a wrought-iron hitching post, then went up a stone walk to the building's small porch. He rapped on the door. No answer.

"Hello? Is anyone here?"

Doctors often made rounds and left their office. Thinking Fiddler might be in a back room while the doctor was gone, he opened the door. Pike stared at the empty room. It wasn't just empty, it was abandoned. All the furniture had been removed. A cabinet stood open. Nothing but dust on the shelves showed the doctor hadn't worked here in a long time. Still, Pike wanted to be sure.

He made a quick tour of all the rooms. Judging by a discarded newspaper in a back room, the doctor had left two months earlier.

The sawbones could have just moved to a different surgery, Pike mused. And if the doctor had indeed left Kiowa Springs, there might be a veterinarian who also tended people. Pike stepped outside and looked around.

Night was falling, and Kiowa Springs hadn't installed any gaslights. Soon the town would be as dark as a cemetery and almost as quiet.

The most noise came from the direction of the gambling

house. Realizing he had a long search ahead of him through deserted streets if he didn't get some clue where Fiddler might be laid up, Pike made his way back to the Royal Flush.

Back home, he always considered gossip and the people who spread it to be pains in the neck. Now that might be a quicker way of finding Dougal and Fiddler than continuing his futile search in the dark.

Long experience caused him to hesitate outside the double swinging doors, hitch up his gun belt and make sure his Colt rode easy in its holster. Only then did he push through and step into what should have been a saloon.

The first thing he noticed was that no barkeep walked behind the long mahogany bar. There was a shiny mirror on the wall, but no bottles lined the shelves under it. A faro table ran to his right. The woman wearing a low-necked red silk blouse and revealing a little too much bare skin worked to take the money from a half dozen gamblers—or, Pike decided, admirers. They paid less attention to their bets than to the dealer as she bent forward.

Green-felt-topped tables filled the rest of the room. All of them were crowded with men playing cards. The table nearest him had four men playing whist. Beyond them, at the next table Pike thought the trio used a pinochle deck.

He looked up when a cheer rose at the back of the room. Someone had hit it big on a roulette wheel. The only game not currently being played was chuck-a-luck. The cage hung untouched and the table where the rig had been installed was empty.

"You looking to get lucky, mister?" The woman who came up alongside Pike moved like a cat. She had red hair, but not a shade that nature had given her. She was slender to the point of being skinny and no longer young, but it was hard to judge the age of women in her profession. It was a life that ate up the years.

He shifted slightly to avoid her, but she didn't take the hint.

"We got all kinds of games of chance." She winked broadly. "And some of the games in the back room are a lead pipe cinch. A man like you would be welcome."

"That sounds mighty inviting," Pike said, stretching the truth a considerable amount. "First, I need to find the town sawbones. I went to an office across town, but it was empty."

"That's Doc Fowler's old place. He pulled up stakes and moved to Dallas. Kiowa Springs hasn't had a doctor for nigh on three months."

Pike made a noncommittal sound. If the doctor was gone, the next best choice was the veterinarian. In some towns, the vet was a better choice. Vets had better bedside manners. The ones who didn't get bit or kicked by their four-legged patients tended to be the gentlest.

"You don't look like you need a doctor. I can restore anything you've been missing out on the trail." She paused. Her eyes narrowed. "Or do you need a doctor because of some disease you picked up at another . . . crib?"

A commotion broke out at the rear of the gambling parlor. A burly man dressed in bib overalls growled like an animal and picked up another, smaller man. From the look of the gent hoisted into the air, he was a shopkeeper. His canvas apron flapped as the giant of a man began spinning him around and around.

Pike recoiled when the shopkeeper went flying. He landed on the chuck-a-luck with a loud crash. The man who had smashed him down thrust his arms over his head, clenched fists, and roared in triumph.

"For a dry town, there's a lot of carousing," Pike observed.

The woman gasped and took a step toward the fracas. She put her hand to her mouth to stifle an outcry when the one-sided fight turned even more vicious. The big man's fists came down like sledgehammers on the hapless storekeeper's chest, then he rolled the smaller man off the table. The storekeeper landed facedown. The toe of the big man's right boot slammed into his ribs and curled him into a pain-filled ball.

"Who's the two-ton fellow doing all the punching and kicking?" Pike asked.

"That . . . that's just Harvey feeling his oats. Don't pay him no never mind. Me and you can go in the back. I . . . I can show you a real good time."

The woman's choked voice told Pike that she had more riding on the fight than she wanted to show. The giant she had called Harvey loomed over his victim, pausing as if trying to figure out which part of the storekeeper's body he wanted to stomp or kick next.

"Is anybody going to help that gent?"

The woman stiffened and gripped his arm.

"Don't go getting involved. You don't want to cross Harvey or any of his clan. They're all bad news."

Pike watched the shopkeeper get his feet under him and painfully start to put distance between himself and his attacker. Harvey reached out with a long, muscular arm, caught the collar of the shopkeeper's shirt, and jerked him back.

"Not so fast, you little pissant," Harvey boomed. "You're not gettin' away that easy."

Pike would have horned in on this fight, but the woman clung to his arm.

"It's not worth it, mister. There's more'n just Harvey. You're new to town so you don't know. You interfere and they'll take it out on John."

"John's the storekeeper?"

"How'd you know that?" She shook her head. "Never

mind. Let lil ole Ruth—that's me—show you what Kiowa Springs has to offer."

"That's a mighty impressive show back there," Pike said.

"You just got to town. Take some friendly advice. Don't meddle. Keep riding. You can be a couple miles outside town by midnight. There's nothing for you here."

She clung even more fiercely to his arm. Her fingers cut into his flesh as she watched the man Harvey pounded on take another punch to the belly.

"Now you can get outa here," Harvey said as he shoved John away from him and toward the batwings.

Pike pulled free from Ruth's grip. As the injured man staggered past them, Pike turned and followed him into the street. He caught the shopkeeper just as the man was about to collapse on the boardwalk.

"Are you all right?" Pike steered the man to a bench in front of the gambling hall.

"Don't bother with me. You don't want them mad at you, too." The words came out in a strained voice that revealed how much pain the shopkeeper was in. He winced as he sat, then arched his back and grabbed it. "I done sprained something back there."

"I can get you to the doctor, if you need a sawbones." Pike had forgotten for the moment what the woman had told him about the doctor abandoning the town for Dallas.

"The doc's the only one with any sense. He hightailed it months back. I should have gone with him. I should leave now, but they'd track me down." John looked up at Pike. "You're new to Kiowa Springs. Take some advice. Ride on out. Don't look back."

"You're the second one to make that suggestion in the last five minutes."

"New here and already you've got friends looking out for you."

"Your name's John?"

The man's eyes widened. "Who told you? Was it Ruth? She knows better. She'll find herself in a world of hurt." He tried to stand but his legs gave out. He cried in pain and clutched his chest.

Pike saw that John had turned a pasty color. Shock was setting in from the beating. He wasn't a doctor by any means, but he had seen enough injuries in his day to recognize symptoms of a busted rib or two.

"If there's not a doctor in town, where do folks go to get patched up? You need looking after."

The man shook his head. He had turned white as a sheet from pain, sweat beaded his forehead, and he shook like a leaf in a high wind.

"Miz Brewster was a nurse. She's about the only one still around who knows anything about doctoring. But she's got patients now."

"Does she now? Who might they be?" Pike held his breath.

"The snake oil peddlers. What happened to them's what'll happen to you if you don't leave." The shopkeeper closed his eyes and moaned softly. "It's what'll happen to me if I don't knuckle under." He coughed, spat a dark gob, and seemed to fold in on himself. "Got to please 'em. End up in bad shape if I don't. Got to."

He shuddered and stopped talking.

Pike thought for a moment that the man had died. He pressed his fingers into John's throat and felt the irregular thump-thump of his heart. He wasn't dead but was approaching it.

"Where do I find Miz Brewster?"

The man didn't open his eyes. He lifted his arm and his

fingers curled around. Using his index finger like a gun barrel, he pointed down the street.

"Boardinghouse . . . Edge . . . edge of town."

"Come on. I'll take you to her."

The man resisted with surprising strength as Pike tried to lift him off the bench.

"No! Don't sic them on her. They're mad dogs." He thrashed around, making it difficult for Pike to get a solid grip.

"Mister, do as John says. Don't move him." The soiled dove had followed them out of the gambling hall. She pulled Pike's hand away. "I'll see to him. Harvey's in his cups and won't notice. With any luck he'll die of alcohol poisoning before morning."

"I can help," Pike started.

"I gave you good advice. I heard John give you the same advice. Ride on out of town. This isn't your fight. If you get involved, Kiowa Springs'll be where you're buried."

The woman knelt beside John and whispered to him. He got to his feet. With Ruth's arm around his shoulders, they stumbled around the corner of the building. She was half a head taller than he was, Pike noted. They made an odd pair.

Pike was tossed on the horns of a dilemma. It wasn't in his nature to let a bully have his way. He wanted to help John, but this trouble wasn't why he had come to Kiowa Springs. Fiddler and Dougal needed him more, and they were family.

He glanced around the corner of the building. Part of his decision was made for him. The two had vanished. Finding them wouldn't be too hard, but if Dougal and Fiddler were anywhere, it would be at Miz Brewster's boardinghouse getting tended.

Pike stopped at the doors leading into the Royal Flush

and looked over the batwings. Harvey might be drunk, but he hadn't passed out. He was engaged in a fistfight with a man closer to his size. From their appearance, they might even be brothers. Pike frowned when he remembered what the woman had said about Harvey being in his cups.

"There's booze being sold somewhere in town. Harvey knows where that is." Pike snorted. Probably everyone in town knew. Something like that always became an open secret.

Pike mounted and trotted in the direction the shopkeeper had pointed. In less than five minutes, he saw a neat white fence around a house. Two windows were lit, but he didn't see a sign telling him this was a boardinghouse. He circled the house, looking for Fiddler's wagon. A small stable out back had five stalls filled. None held Fiddler's mule.

He tethered his horse near a watering trough and walked around to the front. Pike stood and listened hard for several minutes. People moved around in the house, but who it might be was a mystery.

The only way to find out was to ask. He knocked on the door. The sounds inside died down. When the door opened a fraction, an older woman peered out. Her expression was one of annoyance at being disturbed.

"Ma'am, sorry to bother you," Pike said as he pinched the brim of his hat, "but I'm looking for Miz Brewster."

Her face lit with surprise. "I don't know you. Why are you asking after me?"

"Are you tending two boarders by the name of Dougal and Fiddler? I'm Pike Shannon, and Dougal's my grandpa."

"You look something like him."

Pike put a friendly smile on his face. "More like him than I did my pa. He had red hair. What little hair Dougal's got left is snow white, but it was dark like mine when he was younger."

Pike wasn't too surprised when the woman opened the door to let him in. What did surprise him was that she held a four-shot Colt House Model behind her skirts and acted as if she knew how to use it.

"You're the one he sent the telegram to. I can see why he wanted you by his side."

Before Pike asked for the entire story, a nearby footstep made him look around. Dougal propped himself against a door leading into the dining room. His grandpappy's appearance shocked Pike, but he tried not to show it.

"You must have tangled with a twister," Pike said. "Folks don't look as bad as you do unless they've been spun around a few dozen times and then spit out."

"It's good to see you, too, Pike. You always had a way to make a body feel better." Dougal heaved a deep sigh. "You always tell the truth, too. No spoon of sugar to help it go down."

"You get yourself back to bed, Dougal Shannon," Mrs. Brewster ordered. "I told you not to wander around until you're stronger."

If Dougal was the better off of the two, Pike wondered if Fiddler hadn't already given up the ghost. He asked.

"No, he's still alive. Not kicking too much, but alive. He'll pull through." Dougal sounded tired beyond his physical condition. His words came out bone-weary and soul-seared.

"The only reason I'm hoppin' around the way I am is because of your fine chicken soup, Ada," Dougal said. "It works real healing miracles."

"Unlike that witch's brew you and Fiddler sell," the woman snapped.

Pike saw that the woman was one of those, like Sophie Truesdale, who favored temperance.

"There are so many cures to what ails me," Dougal said. He smiled broadly and perked up.

Pike glanced at Ada Brewster. With a certain air of reluctance, as if she couldn't help herself, she returned Dougal's smile.

"Who's responsible for all that?" Pike pointed at Dougal's bruises and cuts. From the way he hobbled when he walked out of the dining room, he had taken considerable punishment to his body and legs.

"The family that runs this town," Dougal said, "doesn't take kindly to competition. That's what they claimed Fiddler's potion was."

"They're making moonshine?"

Pike saw Ada Brewster's reaction. She might favor Kiowa Springs being dry, but the men running the town clearly didn't care about that and continued to run their still.

"Big Belly Ledbetter," she said as if the name burned her tongue. "He's the pa. He's got two sons and who knows how many cousins and nephews."

"Not that many," Dougal said. He winced as he moved his right arm. "But enough to whup up on Fiddler and me 'cuz we're old-timers."

"They had no reason to do that to you," Pike said. "All this Big Belly Ledbetter had to do was ask you to move on." He saw the play of emotion on his grandfather's face. The situation became clearer. "He *did* tell you to keep moving and Fiddler balked like the old mule that he is."

"Something like that," Dougal said.

Pike guessed it was exactly like that. Fiddler had mouthed off and told Ledbetter what he could do after ordering him and Dougal out of town.

"He's got the law in his pocket," Dougal said. "There

was a small disagreement over how long it would take us to leave."

"You're still alive." Pike wondered why Ledbetter and his boys hadn't killed them outright.

Ada Brewster read the question in his mind. "He said he was only roughing them up because they're so old. He thinks that's respecting age. I don't know about his upbringing, but his granddaddy ran Kiowa Springs before I came here."

"He has some respect, then," Pike said. But from the extent of Dougal's injuries, Ledbetter didn't have an overabundance of veneration for old folks.

"He took our wagon. If he'll give it back, we'll leave. And the mule. He took that lop-eared monster, too."

"Not until you're healing better." Ada Brewster pointed to a bedroom. "In there. You've had too much excitement for one day. You need to rest."

"Yes, dear," Dougal said, laughing. He hobbled away and disappeared into a room.

"I want to see Fiddler," Pike said.

"He's in the next room. Don't you go waking him up. He needs his sleep."

"Yes, ma'am," Pike said dutifully. He opened the bedroom door and looked in. Fiddler lay on the bed curled up into a ball. A ray of moonlight slanted through the window and lit his face.

Pike's fingers twitched, and he tapped the side of his holster. He'd seen his share of men on the losing end of a fight. Fiddler was in about the worst condition of any of them. Even if he had waved his shotgun around, the old man wasn't up to a bare knuckles fight.

He closed the door, being careful to do so silently. Mrs. Brewster motioned him into the kitchen and pulled out a chair for him at the table. Gratefully, Pike sank into it. He had traveled too far too fast not to be dog tired.

"Dougal says good things about you," she said. Without asking, she dished up a bowl of beef stew. Pike was so hungry he didn't mind that she served it cold. Along with sourdough biscuits, he was sure this had to be the finest meal he'd ever eaten.

"When they're up to leaving, I'll get them back to Warbonnet; they've had their adventure." Pike pondered how rude it would be to ask for a second helping.

"They won't go without that wagon. I don't understand why they're so attached to it, but it's like an echo when they talk about getting it back. One says wagon and the other's already agreeing." Ada Brewster set a glass of water on the table in front of Pike. He drank it down.

"It's their property. I'll get it back." He sopped up the last of the stew with a final piece of biscuit.

"Forget it. In a week Fiddler will be strong enough to go back with you. Don't tangle with the Ledbetters. Everyone who's tried has come to a sorry end." She heaved a deep breath. "Some of them have been found, all beat up like Fiddler and Dougal. The rest? Big Belly knows how to hide a dead body better than anyone who's ever lived in Kiowa Springs."

As Pike started to tell her he wasn't a greenhorn at dealing with men like the Ledbetter clan, loud voices outside the front door brought him to his feet.

"Irene!" Mrs. Brewster cried. "My daughter. And that's Big Belly's oldest with her!"

CHAPTER 12

"You saved his life, Irene," Ruth Carstairs said. "I was in such a state. I never had to patch anyone up."

Irene Brewster looked from the gambling hall girl to the man sleeping peacefully on the narrow bed. John Garston had two broken ribs and bruises all over his back where Harvey Ledbetter had smashed him into the gaming table.

"I learned enough doctoring from my ma to take care of simple injuries," Irene said. "She saw worse than this in battle, I'm sure. Men with their legs blown off. Bullet wounds that tore away bloody chunks of flesh. Men without—"

"Yeah, thanks." Ruth looked sick at the list of injuries Ada Brewster had endured and nursed. "All I care about's John. He's a good man and shouldn't be beat up like this. If we had a decent marshal in town . . ." Her words trailed off.

They both knew Kiowa Springs needed a real lawman, but as long as the Ledbetter family ran things that would never happen. No matter how terrible the crime, if it was committed by a Ledbetter, the marshal looked the other way.

"When are you going to marry him?" Irene asked.

"When is he going to make me an honest woman?" Ruth's laugh was brittle. "Anyway, I like working at the Royal Flush."

"As a . . . a lady of the night? You don't have to do that. John cares for you. And you must for him or you wouldn't risk getting into trouble by hiding him like this."

"They'd kill him," Ruth said.

"They'll kill *you*," Irene said forcefully. "The good people of Kiowa Springs need to do something about them." She looked as if she wanted to spit, but that was unladylike. "If we can't stop their violent ways, we should at least stop them from making moonshine. The last good thing we did in town was to outlaw liquor."

"What else can I do for him?" Ruth wrung her hands. "He looks so peaceful sleeping like that."

"When he wakes, be sure he takes a little water. Not too much. It might cause him stomach upset. I don't know what damage might have been done inside other than the busted ribs." Irene pulled back the cover and ran her fingers lightly over the bandages around his chest. "He'll be sore and moving will be hard, but the broken ribs didn't puncture a lung."

"I couldn't have gotten him to my room without that drifter's help."

"He's probably come to work for Big Belly," Irene said sourly. "No one else with any sense comes here."

"Those snake oil peddlers came here," Ruth said. "The ones your ma is tending."

"As I said, no one with a lick of sense comes to Kiowa Springs. I have to get home. Mama might need some help. They were beat up pretty bad. Being so old, they came even closer to dying than poor Mr. Garston."

Irene hugged Ruth. She wished the soiled dove would leave the Royal Flush. She was smart and still good-looking. Letting men use her was wrong, but Irene suspected her friend stayed at the casino because they furnished her with illegal moonshine.

Demon rum. It ruined even the best people.

She opened the door a crack and peered out. Noise from the Royal Flush rolled like summer thunder. For two cents she would sneak into the storeroom and empty every keg of illegal liquor. Irene knew that if she did, the Ledbetters would never rest until they tracked her down and did terrible things to her. Worse, dishing out their revenge wouldn't stop with her. They'd put her ma in their sights, too.

Seeing no one in the alley, she slipped out and let the sultry night engulf her. Irene rushed past the Royal Flush and moved like a ghost along the boardwalk, heading home. She let out a startled yelp when she ran into a solid mass.

"Lookee here. What have we got?" Harvey Ledbetter towered over her. He looped his thumbs into the straps on his bib overalls and pushed out his huge belly.

"Excuse me. I didn't see you." Irene tried to step into the street. Harvey moved to block her.

"I was just gettin' some air. Why don't me and you go into the Flush and—"

"Don't bet on it," Irene said. "Now, let me by."

"You ain't gonna miss out on havin' a good time with ol' Harvey, are you? It's my duty to see that you enjoy yourself."

He grabbed her arm and lifted her onto her toes.

No matter how Irene struggled, she wasn't able to move. The giant of a man wrapped his bulky arms around her and pulled her close.

"Gimme a kiss. You know you want to."

Irene put her head down to avoid the man's mouth. She twisted one way, then the other but wasn't strong enough to break free. With the quickness of a lightning bolt, she whirled in his arms, her chest pressed into his. She brought her knee up as hard as she could.

He grunted and released her. She stumbled back and looked for a spot to run. Her choices were limited.

"You should not have done that." He reached for her again.

Irene blinked. She wasn't sure what happened, not at first. One instant Harvey Ledbetter was coming for her, his arms outstretched and about to close around her like a bear trap.

The next he was lifted up from behind and thrown aside like a wad of paper. He landed hard in the street and rolled over a couple of times before he came to a stop on his back. He pushed himself up on his elbows. Shaking his head to clear it, he peered at her with such malevolence that Irene backed away.

"I'll get you for that, you little bi—"

A rumble like thunder or the sound of distant drums interrupted him. "Shut your stupid mouth, boy."

If Harvey was a mountain of nasty gristle, his pa Big Belly Ledbetter was twice as high and twice as mean. He hadn't missed any meals, and his belly bounced over his broad leather belt, but his powerful arms, thick with muscle and nearly as big around as the trunks of small trees, showed he wasn't a man to tangle with. The Ledbetter patriarch had picked up his son and thrown him ten feet without any strain.

"But, Pa, she—"

"She didn't hurt you none, kicking you there."

"I scrambled his brains, that's all," Irene said angrily.

"Are you sayin' what I think—"

"Harvey, hush up." Big Belly Ledbetter turned to Irene. "I got a message for you to take to those snake oil hawkers." He moved with surprising agility when she tried to dodge around him.

Irene saw that Harvey was struggling to his feet. The look he gave her convinced her she stood a better chance with his father.

"You mean the two old-timers you beat up? Tell them

what you want yourself, unless you're afraid of what they might do if you actually face them."

"Pa, she's sayin' we jumped them from behind," Harvey said as he climbed to his feet. "She can't get away with tellin' lies about us!"

Big Belly silenced his son with a cold glare. It didn't warm any when he turned back to Irene.

"You watch your tongue, missy. Tell them I want them out of town by Saturday. The only reason they weren't run out earlier is that I don't like seeing old men all laid up like them."

"You beat them up. You and your boys." Irene realized she pushed Big Belly to the limits of his patience. He had a bad temper that built to the boiling point right now.

"They tried cutting into my business with their bottled poison. I run the liquor in town. I don't let any strangers roll in and sell their moonshine. 'Til Saturday, then they'll know what it's like to really hurt."

Irene saw how close to ending up like Fiddler and Dougal she was. As much as she wanted to argue with Ledbetter, self-preservation took over. She kept quiet.

"Come on, Harvey. We got some serious gambling to do. That new roulette wheel's begging us to give it a spin." Big Belly Ledbetter strutted off. Harvey trailed after him, looking back over his shoulder at Irene.

She shivered. If looks could kill, she was a goner.

Irene walked faster. The streets were deserted at this time of night. Most families were safely hidden behind locked doors. The only socializing in town was done at the Ledbetters' Royal Flush. More than once she jumped at a moving shadow. She never realized there were so many stray cats in town.

She heaved a sigh of relief when she saw her home. Her mother had left a light burning in the front window. Irene wasn't sure why she was still up, unless her two patients had taken a turn for the worse. If that was true, Irene dreaded having to answer her ma's questions about where she had been.

Ada Brewster didn't think much of Ruth Carstairs as a friend. Irene understood why. Ruth hadn't shown much inclination of reforming her sinful life, but a decent heart did beat in the woman's breast. How she had taken in John Garston was all the proof Irene needed to keep trying to make her see the light.

She opened the gate in the white picket fence but whirled around at a strange sound. For an instant she thought she stared into a dark cloud.

"Ledbetter!"

That dark cloud—Harvey Ledbetter himself—lumbered closer to her. A coarse, humorless chuckle came from him.

"Didn't think I'd be able to slip away from my pa that fast, did you?"

Irene balled her fists and readied for the fight of her life. There was only one reason Harvey Ledbetter had followed her home. She vowed to put up as good a fight as she could against him.

"You shouldn't have kicked me. It hurts." He moved closer. She took two steps back.

The front door was twenty feet away. Irene worried that Harvey Ledbetter was faster than he looked. Her only chance was to get inside the house and lock the door. Her ma kept a small gun in a drawer nearby.

"It was meant to. You tried to kiss me. I don't want that kind of attention from you." She backed off another step.

"One kiss. Then I'll go."

"Your pa told you to leave me alone. I have to deliver his message. If I don't, you'll be preventing me from doing what he wants." She groped for the words that would keep the giant at bay. Fear of his pa was the only threat she could think of.

"Give me a kiss. Then you can do what he told you." Harvey Ledbetter reached out for her. She got a little closer to the front door, but it felt as if it were on the other side of Texas.

He moved with an agility that caught her by surprise, seized her by the arms, and lifted her onto her toes. Being held like this, she wasn't able to repeat her attack from earlier. Irene stared up into the man's gaping mouth. A front tooth was gone, and his breath was bad enough to gag a buzzard.

"Pucker up," he said, pulling her closer.

A new voice cut through the night like a knife.

"Can you help me out, miss?" The voice rang like steel cold with a knife-sharp command to it. "I'm looking for directions."

Harvey Ledbetter dropped her. Irene fell to her knees, gasping. She brushed away tears from her eyes and looked past her attacker to the man mounted on a dun horse. He sat astride with his hand resting on his holster.

"Y-yes, I can tell you anything you need to know." Irene scooted back from Ledbetter.

"Who're you? You can't interrupt me and my girl." Ledbetter turned his back on Irene, giving her the chance to dart to the front door. She tugged at it. Her ma hadn't barred it. She pushed inside but hesitated before closing the door and securing the lock.

Ledbetter waddled over to the horseman.

"I asked you a question. Who are you?" Ledbetter reached up to grab the rider.

Irene had never seen a man draw and cock a gun so fast.

"I'm the one holding the gun," the rider said. "And you're

the one who's going to have a hole in his head if he doesn't back off."

Ledbetter hesitated. Any man would if he found himself staring down the barrel of a Colt.

But then his fury got the better of his common sense. He snarled, "You can't talk to me like that. I'll rip your heart out. I ain't afraid of you!"

Ledbetter grabbed at the rider, clearly intending to pull him from the saddle.

Irene wasn't able to see exactly what happened. Only the conclusion was obvious. The cowboy hadn't fired. Instead he swung his pistol in a short, vicious arc that ended on the side of Ledbetter's head with the sick crunch of metal smashing into bone. Ledbetter fell backward like a felled tree.

Conflicting emotions coursed through Irene. She wanted Ledbetter to be dead, but that was a terrible thing to wish for. When he groaned and stirred, new emotions warred inside her. She couldn't help it. She was sorry the massive brute was still alive.

"Have a good night," the rider said, but he pitched his voice loud enough to carry. He wasn't mocking Ledbetter. He was bidding her good night. With a move as fluid as his draw, he returned his revolver to its holster. A touch to the brim of his hat assured her he was wishing her farewell. He tapped his heels on the horse's flanks and trotted off.

For a moment, Irene stood there and watched him ride away, but then common sense took over. She closed and locked the door.

When she turned around, her mother stood there holding the small pistol that she kept in a drawer in the foyer table. Ada Brewster's hand was clenched tight around the bird-beak handle.

"Did that monster hurt you?" she asked.

Irene shook her head. "Not really. I was more scared than anything else."

Irene double-checked to make sure the door was secure, then joined her mother in the front room. They both kept an eye out through the curtains as Ledbetter got to his feet and staggered away like a drunk, all the fight knocked out of him for now. After several minutes when Harvey Ledbetter didn't come knocking, Ada returned the pistol to the drawer.

Irene realized what a narrow escape she'd just had. And she had no idea who had rescued her.

"Mama, do you have any idea who that stranger who helped me was?"

"Come on out to the kitchen, child," Ada Brewster said. "I'll tell you about it." As the two women turned, Ada muttered something else.

"Trouble, that's who he was."

CHAPTER 13

Pike only rode a hundred yards before pulling back on the reins and stopping his horse. He looked back in the direction of the boardinghouse, hoping that soon Fiddler and Dougal would be sleeping quietly. Although both were beaten and bruised, they were in good hands. Ada Brewster looked after them as well or better than a doctor. And if the sly glances between her and Dougal were any indication, she was going to give them the best care possible.

Mrs. Brewster had her daughter there now to help her, too, if need be. As soon as Mrs. Brewster had heard the voices and told him who they belonged to, Pike had slipped out the house's rear door, grabbed his horse, and circled around to take Ledbetter by surprise.

Pike hated to admit it, but he had taken a considerable amount of pleasure in buffaloing Harvey Ledbetter like that. He didn't know Irene, but he wasn't going to stand for any woman being treated rough like that.

One clout on the head wasn't going to cure Harvey Ledbetter of his troublemaking ways, though. His pa ruled Kiowa Springs with an iron hand, and Harvey figured he could run roughshod over anybody he wanted to. He had demonstrated that with the shopkeeper, John, and again with Irene Brewster.

The best thing Dougal and Fiddler could do was heal up enough to travel and leave the town far behind. They weren't equipped to handle the kind of violence that the Ledbetter clan could dish out.

The only problem was that Big Belly Ledbetter had taken their wagon to some spot to use against them. Knowing Ledbetter's type, Pike suspected Fiddler had no chance of getting his medicine wagon back without more trouble.

He nudged his horse into motion again and rode into the thick shadows under a clump of post oaks. Of all the people he had run across in Kiowa Springs, Harvey Ledbetter was the one most likely to reveal to him where the wagon had been parked. Big Belly was calling the shots. He had no reason to cooperate if Pike asked, but his son wasn't too bright. Pike might not have to work too hard to get Harvey to lead him to the wagon and its contents.

Figuring that Harvey would head back to the gambling hall, Pike waited in the shadows until the big man came stumbling along the street, rubbing his head. The way he moaned loud enough to be heard warned Pike he might need to clean his gun. The front sight probably had some blood on it.

Harvey stopped abruptly in the middle of the road and groaned, "What happened?" The huge man took a hesitant step and looked around in panic. "How'd I get here? My head!" He put both hands to his temples and winced as new pain shot through him so fiercely that he bent double and cried aloud.

Pike took little pleasure in the man's discomfort. If their paths had crossed at a different time and place, Pike would have just plugged Ledbetter and not thought twice about it.

"What's gone on here?" Harvey Ledbetter spun around in a circle and cried out in frustration.

From what he shouted into the still night, he had lost any memory of the last few minutes. Pike almost rode to the man to refresh his memory.

Ledbetter got his balance back and turned to glare toward Ada Brewster's place. Pike wondered what was going on in the man's head as Harvey just stood and stared at the house. He raised his fist and shook it in silent rage. If he had tried to return to the boardinghouse, Pike was ready to fill him with lead.

That wasn't necessary. Ledbetter turned and started stumbling away again. His gait became less wobbly as he walked back to the settlement's business district.

Pike knew where he was headed. The Royal Flush was as lively a place as he'd ever seen, especially one where no whiskey was being served—or none that he'd witnessed. The soiled dove had hinted he could get a shot in the back room—and more, since she was willing to reveal about everything.

He considered finding her. She had helped the shopkeeper after Harvey Ledbetter had slammed him into the table. That showed Pike she had some decency lurking inside. While finding another job in Kiowa Springs might have been hard for her, the way her eyes twinkled when she invited him into the back room warned of a wild streak. In Pike Shannon's experience, women working in such places and catering to any man with two bits in his pocket were not to be trusted.

If she told him where to find the medicine wagon, she might be as inclined to warn Big Belly Ledbetter what she had revealed.

He walked his horse slowly, alert for trouble. Spending two hard days on the trail had taken its toll on him, but sleep was as far from his mind as the crescent moon poking up over the horizon. Fiddler and Dougal were taken care of. Loading them into the wagon and driving out of town would complete the mission. Fast, quick, easy.

Pike remained mounted when he spotted Harvey Ledbetter going into the casino. Since Ledbetter was on foot and there wasn't a horse anywhere along the street, Pike went to the rear of the gambling house. Half a dozen horses were tethered there. One of them was bound to belong to Harvey Ledbetter.

Pike started to dismount and wait when a commotion inside the casino caught his attention. Riding off and not getting involved in another fight would show discretion.

"Torrance would approve," he said softly, then laughed. Torrance was the only one in his family who'd approve of avoiding trouble. He backed his horse away until they were both well in the shadows and then waited to see what was going to happen.

"I'll bust your fool head, boy!" The voice sounded like boulders tumbling down a mountainside. "What do you mean you don't know who walloped you?"

The scuffle spilled out the back door of the casino. A big shape sailed through the air, crashed to the ground, and scared the horses. In the dim light coming from inside, Pike made out a man with a huge belly who took a couple of stalking steps toward his victim. Even someone without any imagination would identify the huge man as Big Belly Ledbetter.

That identification was confirmed a few seconds later when Harvey Ledbetter pushed himself up a little and held out a hand toward the man-mountain advancing toward him.

"Pa, you don't have no call to whup up on me like this. I ain't done anything wrong."

"You let a stranger pistol-whip you, you fool," Big Belly rumbled. "Where'd he go?"

"How should I know? He 'bout knocked me out with his gun. I can't hardly remember a thing. My head is still spinnin' and—"

"You don't know if he's in cahoots with the two old geezers at Brewster's boardinghouse?"

"No, sir," Harvey said, trying to stand. His pa shoved him back into the dirt. "Aw, Pa, don't treat me like this. I don't deserve it."

"If you had half the brains of your brother, you'd be a genius." Big Belly Ledbetter stood over him, fists clenched. He reared back to unload a punch, then evidently thought better of it. "Get Augustus."

"Why? Gus don't know any more than I do." Harvey cringed when Big Belly started for him again. "He ain't that smart, Pa. And—"

"I want the two of you to stand guard over that medicine wagon," Big Belly said, ignoring his son's protests. "If the owlhoot who clobbered you has come for the pair at Brewster's place, he'll want to claim the wagon."

"Can I kill him, Pa? Should we ambush him?"

Harvey finally climbed to his feet as he asked those questions. His eager voice hardened Pike toward the Ledbetters even more. They were nothing more than bullies and back shooters.

"If you do, be sure nobody finds the body. Now git. I can't stand the sight of you no more."

Big Belly made shooing motions with his hand, then went back into the casino.

Harvey Ledbetter untied a horse's reins from the hitching post and swung up into the saddle. His weight caused the horse to miss a step. Its rider viciously whipped it with the reins as they started off. Pike forced himself to watch silently from the shadows. It was criminal mistreating an animal like that, but he needed Harvey.

For a little while longer, anyway.

Ledbetter took off like a shot. Pike trailed him at a distance great enough that the man wasn't going to spot him. If anything, he was in such a hurry he'd never have noticed Pike even if he rode a couple feet behind.

To Pike's surprise, the man only rode a short way down the street. He halted in front of a hotel and bellowed up at the windows on the second floor.

"Gus! Get your lazy bones out here. Pa's got a job for you. Gus!"

A light flickered in one of the second-story windows. Pike edged closer. A man wearing a union suit opened the window and poked his head out.

"Quit your caterwauling, Harve. You'll wake the dead."

"You'll be the dead one if I tell Pa you disobeyed him. He wants us to stand guard over that wagon."

"The ugly one painted all red? You do it. I want to sleep."

"I'll tell him who burned the last batch of mash. He was madder'n a wet hen at losin' an entire two gallons of 'shine."

"That was your fault!"

"You were supposed to watch the still, but you and that red-haired Wilkins hussy snuck off into the woods. You know what Pa thinks of her. When he finds out you ruined a batch because the two of you were—"

"Get on along," Gus shouted. "I'll be there when I climb into my pants and strap on my gun."

Augustus Ledbetter ducked back and slammed the window. His brother cackled like a hen and rode on. Again Pike was taken by surprise at how short a distance he went before dismounting. Harvey led his horse down an alley. Pike found a hitchrail some distance away, then walked back, wary of what he might find. The Ledbetters sounded as if they laid traps for the unsuspecting all the time. Pike wasn't going to blunder into a clumsy ambush.

He grinned from ear to ear when he saw Fiddler's wagon. It stood in the middle of a weed-overgrown vacant lot. Buildings on three sides had the feel of being deserted. Pike listened hard, but if Fiddler's mule was staked out here, it kept quiet. As noisy as the beast always was, Pike knew its braying would be heard blocks away.

Skirting the area, he kept a sharp lookout for Harvey Ledbetter. The man had come here but was nowhere to be seen. One by one Pike peered into the buildings. Two were deserted stores. The third had been used as a warehouse. Some crates remained inside, barely visible in the poor light.

Curious, he checked the door and found it unlocked. Fumbling through the darkness, he found a stack of crates and tried to move one of them.

It was heavier than he expected. Working his fingers under the top where it wasn't nailed down properly, he heaved. Nails tore out of dried wood with a creaking sound.

The scent that hit him was intoxicating. A half dozen jugs inside had been padded for travel using ripped and wadded newspaper.

He lifted one jug out, pulled the cork and inhaled deeply. This reminded him how he had missed the sharp scent of moonshine since Warbonnet County had gone dry. Tipping the jug back, he let a few drops wet his tongue. Pike gagged. He dropped the jug back into the crate, shaking his head as he shoved the cork back in the neck.

"Nobody's going to confuse that with Shannon 'shine," he said softly. The Ledbetters might be running a still, but their product was terrible. The worst dreg from Fiddler's batch was a country mile better than this swill.

Pike made his way through the storehouse, counting as he found one crate after another. The Ledbetters had stacked fifty gallons of their rotgut. The only reason for so much, considering Kiowa Springs was dry, had to be that they were supplying the entire countryside. Big Belly had quite a business going here.

Fiddler and Dougal had blundered into a sorry situation. There wasn't any way to know before driving into Kiowa Springs that they intruded on another moonshiner—and what he considered his exclusive territory. If the county hadn't been dry, competition would have kept Ledbetter under control. As it was, beating up old men barely added to the criminal charges against him. Keeping his still running was worth the added risk.

"What's one or two more crimes when it comes to breaking the law?" Pike turned grim as that thought came to him. He had ridden a dangerous trail for close to ten years. At first, hiring out as a guard or courier had been the extent of his work.

Being a fast gun opened up chances for more lucrative—and illegal—pursuits.

He was glad to have returned to Warbonnet County and his family. Such a life on the trail caught up with a man sooner or later.

A board creaked behind him. Pike spun, went into a gunfighter's crouch, and had his smoke wagon out in a blurred move. He homed in on where the sound had come from. Only shadows. No movement. Moving cautiously, he slipped behind a stack of crates and hunkered down. The darkness did as much to hide him as it did whoever had entered the storeroom.

A man grunted, then cursed. A crate fell from the top of a pile and crashed to the floor. Pike popped up like a prairie dog to take a quick look. All he saw was the fallen box laden with the moonshine jugs.

If someone had tried to move the crate, why hide? Pike knew he was being stalked. He slipped along a wall, concealed by a stack of crates. Playing cat and mouse wasn't his intention. He wanted to get away without exchanging lead.

A new curse from the far side of the room made him tense. He had followed Harvey Ledbetter here and then the man had vanished. Hiding in the room was curious, but Pike had no idea what thoughts went through Big Belly Ledbetter's son's head. From the way his pa talked, not much went on between Harvey's ears.

But they had talked about another of the clan. Augustus. The man who had poked his head out the hotel window. Facing two of the moonshiners in the dark, in a room they knew well, was a sure way to get filled with bullet holes. Pike kept moving quietly toward the door where he had entered.

A burst of speed got him through the door—and earned him several bullets whining through the night as guns blasted behind him. He dodged to the side and pressed his back against the building's front wall. If the would-be killer bulled through the doorway after him, Pike intended to reduce the odds against him by one.

Long seconds passed. No one followed. Either his attacker was smart enough to realize the danger of a deadly trap waiting to be sprung, or he intended to set one of his own and lure Pike back into the building.

Pike looked around the vacant lot next to the building. The wagon stood lit by faint moonlight. Rapidly moving clouds overhead cut off the silvery moonbeams now and then. He judged the distance and bided his time. A billowing cloud hiding the moon gave him his chance.

A quick dash brought him to the medicine wagon. He ducked beneath it and lay on his belly. His gun pointed at the storehouse door. Nobody came through. Inching forward, he stood.

He almost died.

Slugs ripped away at the wagon on either side of his head. Pike dropped again and hunted for the shooter. Foot-long orange flame leaped from the muzzle of a revolver. He had missed the man on his first scout. What he had thought was an empty store had sheltered the gunman.

Pike rested his hand against the wagon wheel. Another muzzle flash betrayed his attacker. Pike returned fire. A loud cry of pain told him he had hit his target. But the cursing continued. He had wounded the man, not taken him out of the fight.

He swung around as he caught movement from the corner of his eye. Whoever had been in the storeroom with the shipping crates finally came out to join the firefight. Pike emptied his gun at the moving dark shape. He saw the man double over and heard low moans of pain. But the gunman stumbled on. If Pike had had another couple of rounds, that stumble would have been right into a grave.

With practiced ease, he knocked out his spent brass chamber by chamber. In less time than most men could clear leather, he was again loaded for the fight.

Frantic whispers told him the two gunmen had joined forces. Making out their words wasn't possible, but he had a pretty good idea what they said. First one and then the other complained about how he had winged them. That meant both were still in the battle. Pike slipped to the other side of the wagon and looked up. Getting to the roof would give him an advantage of shooting from higher ground.

Fiddler hadn't seen any reason to put rungs on the side of the wagon. As much as Pike could have used them now, he had to agree. Paint had been more important than climbing to the roof. Pike jumped and tried to grab the edge to pull himself up. After the second try, he gave up. The two men looking to fill him full of lead weren't going to stay put, no matter how badly wounded they were.

From all he had seen of the Ledbetter family, they were a nasty bunch. They might be bullies, but he had intruded on their territory. Like hungry wolves, they'd protect what they considered their exclusive domain.

Pike edged around and climbed onto the driver's box. The curtain separating the driver from the rear of the wagon had been ripped down. He slithered like a snake into the back. The Ledbetters had thrown all of Fiddler's herbs and roots onto the floor. The jugs of moonshine he used to give his elixir some kick were missing.

He went to the rear door and opened it a crack. Two men stood a couple of yards behind the wagon. They huddled close enough to whisper to each other. Pike pushed the door open another inch to get a better shot.

For an instant, he thought his Colt had misfired. The report came an instant before he pulled the trigger. Then pain seared through his head and he fell backward. He sprawled across the chemicals strewn on the floor and stretched out, staring up at the roof. He tried to sit up. His legs twitched but otherwise didn't budge. The shot had paralyzed him.

Loud cries outside died down, replaced by the crackle of a fire chewing away at the wagon's dry walls. The flames danced in front of his face as the roof became engulfed. Again he tried to sit up. This time smoke filled his lungs. He choked. He choked and passed out.

Chapter 14

Irene Brewster sat on the edge of her bed, wringing her hands. Only a few minutes had passed since the nearly disastrous encounter with Harvey Ledbetter in front of the house. Irene was still fully dressed, and her mind was whirling. Nothing was right.

She stood up and left the room, moving through the darkened house with the ease of long familiarity. She knew her mother had turned in and might be asleep already, so she was careful not to make much noise. She went to the hall table and quietly opened the drawer. The small-caliber pistol her ma kept there gleamed in the dim light of a lamp turned low in the parlor. With a shaking hand, she picked it up and clutched it to her breast.

Knowing it was foolish, she opened the front door and looked for Harvey Ledbetter. She had no desire to shoot him, but he was becoming increasingly dangerous. His off-color remarks to her were now more pointed every time she encountered him. He even dared to touch her.

"And he tried to kiss me." She shuddered. It was a terrible fate being stalked by the likes of any Ledbetter, but he was the worst of the family. Big Belly had a wife who kept him in line, but Harvey had no one to rein him in when he got in too amorous a mood.

Irene swallowed hard. She knew Harvey had stumbled away already. If she was honest with herself, she hoped to catch a better look at the stranger who had rescued her. There was no reason for him to still be nearby, but Irene hoped he might be, anyway. He had risked his life to pry her loose from Harvey's clutches. She wanted to thank him. She should thank him. Properly.

She wanted to know his name and where he came from and more about him. Her head spun. When she realized how attracted she was to a complete stranger, she blushed. This wasn't like her. Anyway, he was gone.

And then he wasn't.

Irene had started to close the door when the familiar figure rode out from the shadows under some trees up the street toward the main part of town. She hesitated. It was so forward to call out to him. She did anyway.

"Wait, I want a word with you!"

Irene rushed to the road when he never even glanced in her direction. She cleared her throat. Her voice had been a mite weak, reflecting her reluctance to be so presumptuous. This wasn't the way her mama had raised her, and simply trying to attract the man's attention had been so . . . forward.

He rode slowly, and beyond him, silhouetted for an instant against the lights from the main street, was the big, unsteady figure of Harvey Ledbetter. Her stomach tied into a knot when she realized what was happening. The stranger was following Harvey, making sure he didn't return to the Brewster house. He might not realize how much trouble he could be letting himself in for, though.

Moonlight reflected off the barrel of the four-shot Colt House Model as Irene held it up. Her mama had taught her to use the pistol. She had practiced until she could hit four bottles, one after another, with the full load.

But that was make-believe. Shooting a man, even a pig like Harvey Ledbetter, was different.

"But what if I'm saving a man's life? Or using the gun in self-defense?"

As she argued with herself, she almost ran back into town.

She kept the stranger in sight for most of the way, then his horse outpaced her. Irene slowed and wondered if she should return home. She needed sleep after tending John Garston. Considering how Harvey Ledbetter had broken the man like a twig erased any doubt about what to do.

She had to warn the stranger. It was her duty. If she patched up Ledbetter's victims, it was right and proper for her to keep someone from getting all busted up in the first place.

Clutching the bird's-head grips even harder, she almost ran toward the Royal Flush. Where else would Harvey Ledbetter head at this time of night? If the stranger trailed him, he'd be there, too.

Several minutes later, she was panting when she stepped onto the boardwalk across the street from the gambling den. Her nose wrinkled with disdain as she stared at the crowded place. Gambling wasn't as terrible as drinking, but she knew that went on inside, too. Big Belly Ledbetter owned the place, and everyone knew the Ledbetter family operated a still somewhere to the north of town.

If you were one of his friends, or had enough money, buying a drink of moonshine was as easy as falling off a log.

Irene looked around and almost gave up, when she spotted the stranger far down the street turning into an alley. She squeezed between a bookstore and a bakery and came out in an alley running parallel to the main street. If she guessed right, the stranger was headed for a lot surrounded by buildings that Ledbetter owned. But she wasn't sure, because she couldn't see him anymore. She couldn't see much of anything back here.

"Oh no!" The exclamation escaped her when she heard a sudden eruption of gunshots somewhere not far off. She envisioned the worst. The stranger had ridden into an ambush. He had called out Harvey Ledbetter and been beaten to the draw. He—

"No," she said, calming down. "There's no way any of the Ledbetters outdrew him." She remembered the easy way he'd handled his gun. That liquid grace told of long practice. No one moved like that who hadn't also practiced firing. She was a decent shot. Irene believed the stranger was a dead shot.

She shivered again. Everything pointed to him being a hired gun. There wasn't any reason for her to get involved if he had a feud with Big Belly and his clan. Let them shoot it out, if the gunman had been paid to kill the Ledbetters.

Irene half turned to go home. More gunshots convinced her to go to the man's aid. He hadn't been cut down. The reports made it sound as if the Battle of San Jacinto was being fought all over again.

The closer she came to the fight, the more cautious she became. Finding an overturned carriage to hide behind, Irene peeked out. The dark lot was dominated by Fiddler's medicine wagon. She had wondered where Big Belly had parked it after beating up the two men her mother nursed.

The sporadic gunfire trailed off and then stopped entirely. She edged closer, using the corner of a building to hide her from the men shooting it out around the wagon. For a moment she had a hard time figuring out what she saw.

The wagon rocked a bit back and forth as if someone moved inside. Then a new flurry of gunfire tore hunks of wood off the wagon and all movement stopped. Irene clutched her Colt. She almost added to the bullets flying around when two dark figures came from inside a storeroom across the lot. They exchanged whispered words, then split. One man hurried to another abandoned store and slipped inside. The other gathered weeds and piled them under the wagon.

Irene watched, not sure what they were doing—or what she should do. As she hesitated and considered taking a potshot at the man piling up the weeds, the other returned with a small barrel on his shoulder.

This time she heard their words clearly.

"It's a waste of good 'shine," the weed man said.

"We can make more, Gus. Get ready with that lucifer." The one toting the barrel heaved it high into the air and let it fall. The liquid contents splashed all over the weeds and side of the wagon.

She identified both men now. Harvey Ledbetter had spilled the moonshine. She approved of anything that got rid of another gallon or two of the vile destroyer of men's lives. Then Irene changed her mind about that. Augustus Ledbetter dropped a lit match onto the weeds.

The flare illuminated both of them as if they'd stepped into sunlight. The flame touched the moonshine on the wagon's side and set fire to the wood. Both men yelped at the sudden fire. They disappeared down a street leading to the vacant lot.

The flames engulfed the wagon. Irene watched, mesmerized by the leaping blaze, then remembered someone had been inside the wagon.

Being burned to death was a terrible way to die. She let out a cry of anguish and ran to the back of the wagon. The door swung back and forth, fanning the fire. Inside she saw a man sit up, choke on the heavy smoke, and crash back.

Irene never hesitated. She shielded her face with her arm, leaned in, and grabbed both of the man's feet. Putting her foot against the back of the wagon gave added leverage.

A huge yank dragged the man through the debris inside the wagon. He coughed again and began struggling. Somehow, together, both her tugging and his kicking caused him to squirt from the wagon like a picnicker spitting out a watermelon seed.

Irene fell away and hit the ground so hard the impact knocked the breath from her lungs. For a moment, she stared up at a nighttime sky filled with gathering storm clouds and obscured by billows of smoke. The fire threatened to set her ablaze. When she tried to get away, her arms and legs refused to obey.

Then she was flying.

"Stop fighting me." The voice came in her ear. Her vision was blurred from the smoke, but she felt strong arms holding her. Blinking hard, she finally saw how the stranger carried her from the fire.

"Put me down," she said. Her raspy voice cleared as the smoke finally left her lungs. "I can walk just fine."

She cried out when he dropped her. Irene looked up from his feet, astonished. Then her anger took over.

"I saved you! How dare you treat me like this?"

"And I saved you. You were gasping like a fish out of water. If I'd left you, you'd have been fried like a catfish."

"You didn't have to drop me like a sack of suet." She refused his hand to help her stand.

"I'd say you were more like a sack of grain."

Irene stared him in the eyes. He was several inches taller and broad of shoulder and thick of chest. For a hired killer, he wasn't at all ugly. Uneasily she realized it was just the opposite. He was a handsome man, even all smeared with soot and dust and not a few cuts on his face oozing blood.

They held the stare for a moment too long. Irene stepped back.

"I hope you at least consider me to be a bag of expensive grain."

"Oats," he said firmly. "That makes you about the most important thing in the world to my horse."

Irene felt another surge of outrage, then had to laugh.

"You're the first man who's ever used such a backhanded compliment on me." She wiped her still-watering eyes. "It *was* a compliment, wasn't it?"

"Only a fool insults a woman who just saved him from being fried like a strip of bacon. That makes us quite a pair, doesn't it? A hunk of bacon and a slab of catfish. We're quite a meal."

He grinned as he herded her from the lot and down another street. His dun nervously pawed the ground.

"You've rescued me twice from the Ledbetters," she said. "I still owe you."

"The name's Pike Shannon. Pleased to be of help, but don't consider yourself beholden. I only did what was called for."

"Shannon? My mama's taking care of Dougal Shannon. Are you his grandson? He sent a telegram but all he said to us was that he wanted you to come escort him and Fiddler home."

"Charity runs in your family," Pike said. "Your ma didn't have to take care of Fiddler and Dougal." He smiled just a little. "She has to know my grandpappy might be a hard one to pry loose."

"I've seen how he looks at Mama," Irene said. "And I've seen how she looks at him." Almost guiltily, she looked sidelong at Pike. Attractiveness ran in his family, and the Brewster women weren't immune.

Uneasily, she went on, "We should take a side street to get

back to the house. Big Belly Ledbetter has eyes everywhere. The men he doesn't own outright he has cowed."

They walked to the boardinghouse in uneasy silence. Pike led his horse, and Irene scolded herself for stepping around every time the dun got between her and Pike. Being close to him made her feel safer, even if her original guess that he was a hired gunman still bothered her.

She finally blurted out, "Do you kill people for a living?"

Pike pushed his hat back on his head. His eyebrows rose in surprise.

"What makes you ask that? I'm not a gunslinger. I raise horses. I don't suppose Dougal got around to mentioning that since he was so busy making calf's-eyes at your ma."

"That's something I noticed," Irene said, shaking her head. "Ma's not looked at another man since Pa died."

"It must be something in the Shannon blood," he said.

Before Irene answered that with a jibe of her own, the front door of the boardinghouse flew open and Ada Brewster stepped out onto the porch, wearing a dressing gown cinched tight around her waist. She put her fists on her hips and glared at them.

"I couldn't believe my eyes when I saw you weren't in bed, Irene," she said. "You get in here right now. It's not safe out in the street."

Pike hung back. He wasn't sure if she meant him, too. Irene grabbed his arm and steered him inside.

"Into the kitchen," Irene said. "I need to clean those cuts." She made a face. "You've got a few burns, too."

"I thought your ma was the nurse . . ." Pike began.

"Kitchen. Now," Irene insisted. She moved between her mother and Pike to keep him moving without the other woman's interference. As she stepped into the hallway, she handed her ma the gun.

Ada Brewster clucked her tongue but said nothing. She returned the pistol to the drawer in the hall table.

Irene firmly pushed Pike down and began examining him.

"I'll have to cut your shirt off. Some of the cloth is burned into the wounds."

"The shirt's seen better days," Ada Brewster said, sniffing. "And it stinks of smoke." She fixed Irene with a hard look.

"Wood smoke, Mama. Wood smoke and gun smoke. Why not see if one of Pa's old shirts will fit him? It might be tight across the shoulders, but he needs something."

"I've got a spare out in my saddlebags. I can—"

Irene shushed him and began gently peeling the cloth from his body. When he was stripped to the waist, she began tending the cuts and burns. She wondered how he kept from flinching as she applied rubbing alcohol. That had to sting something fierce.

"What are you going to do now? Are you and those two snake oil peddlers going to leave town?"

"Ledbetter has to pay for burning their wagon. And he certainly has to pay for the beating he gave them. From what I've heard, the marshal is in his hip pocket."

"You heard right," Irene said. She began applying gauze and tying it into place. Pike slowly looked like a mummy she had seen in one of her schoolbooks. "The Ledbetters make all of the moonshine in Kiowa Springs, and they won't stand for any competition."

Ada Brewster came back into the room and held out a shirt for Pike.

"Here, let me help you. Don't you dare stretch too much and open those cuts I just tended." Irene held the shirt so he could get his arms into the sleeves. She had been right.

The shirt was tight across the shoulders. The sleeves were an inch too short, too, but it was better than nothing.

"Big Belly wants to be the only moonshiner, is that it? He'll run anyone out of town cutting into his market?"

"Or kill them. He's a gross, vicious pig," Ada Brewster said. "His sons are no better."

"Worse," Irene muttered.

"I'll have to find a way to deal with him myself," Pike said.

"You can't take the law into your own hands, Mr. Shannon," Ada said. "That's not right."

"Until the citizens get together and do it, I don't see any other way."

"One man against Big Belly's entire family? You wouldn't stand a chance."

Irene saw the smile lift the corners of Pike Shannon's mouth. He was a handsome man, but this was a cruel smile. If anyone stood a snowball's chance in hell of running the Ledbetters from town, he was seated right in front of her.

CHAPTER 15

"I need to know more about how Ledbetter runs things," Pike said as he sat at the kitchen table with Irene the next morning. She looked mighty pretty in this domestic situation, but he pushed that thought out of his mind for the time being. "Who can I ask?"

"I know as much as anyone," Irene said.

Pike tried not to laugh. The kind of business he needed to ferret out wasn't anything Irene Brewster would know firsthand. He doubted she had ever been inside the Royal Flush. From what Pike had seen, the gambling den was the center of Ledbetter's more honest businesses. But Irene looked down on any mention of moonshining. Pike needed to know everything Ledbetter did, since, if the Royal Flush was his public face, the still turning out 'shine was the real source of his money.

"The illegal goings-on are what I need to know about," he told her. "Can you tell me where his still is?"

She made a face. "If I knew, I'd have burned it to the ground a long time ago." She frowned at him, as if realizing something for the first time. "Is that how you destroy a still? Burn it down?"

"An ax works better," Pike said.

"Oh. I didn't know that." She took a deep breath and let it out slowly as she considered his question. "If you dare to ask anyone, they would have to trust that you won't tell Big Belly they told you his secrets." She leaned forward on the kitchen table and pushed aside the breakfast dishes to get down to serious talk. "If you ask the wrong people, Big Belly will know before you can snap your fingers."

"None of the Ledbetters have gotten a good look at me. Harvey could have in the Royal Flush, but he was too busy beating up John Garston to pay attention to anything else. With my new shirt"—Pike looked down at the one Ada Brewster had given him—"there's not much chance of them identifying me at all."

No one at the shoot-out before they burned Fiddler's wagon had a good look at him. He smiled as he recollected laying his pistol barrel alongside Harvey Ledbetter's head. That blow had knocked loose at least some of Harvey's memories. Pike had seen that happen to men kicked in the head by a horse or who had their head struck in other ways. A small patch of their life simply wasn't there for them anymore.

But those memories usually returned eventually. Even if that happened with Harvey, Pike still ought to be in the clear; the only time they'd been close to each other was in the dark street.

"They might not have ever gotten a good look," Irene said, "but asking questions is what will alert them. Big Belly is suspicious of everyone."

Pike said, "I've seen how he treats his own boys. I get the feeling he wouldn't turn his back on them."

"For good reason. Harvey is the one to look out for, but Augustus is meaner than a stepped-on prairie rattler." She took a deep breath. "You need me to do the asking for you."

"If they're as dangerous as they seem, you're putting yourself in danger even letting me stay under your roof."

"Mr. Shannon—"

"Call me Pike," he cut in.

She brightened from her dark mood. "All right, Pike. You said it last night. The citizens of Kiowa Springs need to stand up to the Ledbetters. I'm willing to recruit them."

"You leave that peashooter in the hall drawer," he said sternly. "It's a .41 caliber and deadly at close range, but it's got a reputation for firing all four rounds at the same time. And it's hard to hang on to with that grip."

"You might raise horses, but you also know your way around guns."

A moment of revulsion crossed her face. She didn't like guns much more than she liked moonshine, Pike thought.

"Where do we start?" he asked. He wanted to avoid questions about his past since he had been everything she despised, a moonshiner *and* a gunfighter. "I need to find Ledbetter's still. Somebody in town must know where he's hidden it."

"This early in the morning, the gambling den will be empty. Anybody who works there later on this afternoon and in the evening will be at home sleeping." Irene pursed her lips. "Let's go before any of those lazy, worthless Ledbetters climb out of bed."

As they went toward the center of Kiowa Springs, Pike tried not to be too conspicuous, but he walked with his hand near his Colt. After all the Ledbetter family had done to him, Fiddler, and Dougal, not throwing down on them the instant he spotted them would require a considerable amount of self-control. He wasn't sure he was up to it.

"Down here." Irene looked around, then ducked down the alley beside the Royal Flush. She knocked on a door at the rear of a building adjoining it.

When no one answered, Irene called out, "Ruth, it's me. Irene Brewster. Let me in."

Pike hung back. The door opened an inch. He saw an eye peering out. When the door opened farther he recognized the pretty soiled dove from the Royal Flush. She had tried to entice him into the back room, and he had turned her down.

"How's Mr. Garston doing?" Irene asked.

Ruth stared at Pike and muttered something. She tried to close the door, but Irene was too quick. She stepped forward and prevented the door from closing.

"It's all right, Ruth. He wants to help."

Pike tried to eavesdrop on the furious whispering between the two women. Whatever Irene said finally caused Ruth to relent. She stepped back and let them inside the tiny room.

Pike had no trouble deciding that Ruth was a soiled dove, if there had ever been any doubt. He had been in his share of cribs where girls took men for a quick tumble. He could have reached out and touched the walls on both sides of the narrow room. The space was hardly long enough for the single bed where John Garston lay. Any possessions Ruth had must have been shoved under the bed. No other storage was possible.

"How is he doing?" Irene perched on the edge of the bed and put her hand on the man's forehead. He stirred but didn't awaken.

"John had a fever last night, but I gave him plenty of water and put a wet rag on his forehead. After that he rested better." Ruth answered Irene but never took her eyes off Pike.

"He's a friend," Irene said, seeing the other woman's uneasiness. "Really."

"We talked for a few minutes yesterday evening when I rode into town." Pike watched how Ruth reacted.

"I remember," Ruth said. "How could I forget fresh meat? We don't see that many strangers in Kiowa Springs."

"Handsome strangers, you mean?" Irene's question came out sharper than Pike expected.

"Yeah, handsome. You are the best-looking man in this miserable town."

"I'd like to make it less miserable," Pike said. "I intend to run the Ledbetters out of Kiowa Springs."

"They don't run," Ruth said. "Are you up to gunning them down?"

Pike paused a moment, then nodded. "If I have to."

Ruth's expression changed. Suspicion disappeared and something like awe replaced it.

"From your looks, you're the one to do it." She stared hard at the Colt swinging at his hip.

"Does anybody else run a still around here? Who do the Ledbetters consider competition?"

"Nobody. I don't know anybody else." Ruth pressed back against a wall and crossed her arms, as if daring him to call her a liar. She answered too fast for this not to be a lie.

"John Garston here," Pike said as he put things together in his mind. "Does he just give you moonshine he's bought . . . or does he run a still himself?" Before Ruth said a word, Pike finished his thought. "He reeks of 'shine. I smelled it on him last night. A man in his cups smells the same, but there's something more."

"Pike, what are you saying?" Irene looked angrily at him. "Mr. Garston runs the feed and grain store. He's one of the few upstanding citizens in town."

Pike ignored her as the picture formed in his head. "There's another smell on his clothes. Woodsmoke. Must be oak. It burns hotter and longer than other, softer wood.

That makes it best for fueling a still and keeping it running without feeding the fire too much."

"You got it all wrong," Ruth insisted. "That's against the law. John's no moonshiner."

"Ruth," he said softly, "he gives you all the moonshine you want. Isn't that so?"

"You mean Mr. Garston pays Ruth for her . . . her services in moonshine?" Irene's shock turned her pale.

"I suspect there's more to it than that." Pike looked intently at the dove. "You wouldn't buck the likes of Big Belly Ledbetter to take care of John just to keep your supply of 'shine flowing."

"I love him," she said in a choked voice.

"And I love her," came Garston's raspy whisper from the bed. "You leave Ruth alone. You got no call badgering her."

"We'll all come out ahead when I deliver some much-needed justice to the Ledbetter clan. I intend to start by destroying their still."

"Not mine," Garston said, trying to sit up in bed.

"Mr. Garston, I can't believe you are flouting the law!" Irene exclaimed. "Serving liquor—making it!—is completely illegal. The citizens of Kiowa Springs voted for prohibition."

"So did other counties," Pike said with some distaste. Making 'shine illegal caused more lawbreaking than letting moonshiners produce reasonable amounts. He saw that Irene was a dedicated promoter of temperance, but not as much as Sophie Truesdale. She wrestled with the idea that the man she had tended ran a still.

"If Pike stops the Ledbetters," Irene said to Garston, "will you voluntarily cease all illegal production?"

"No, John, don't agree to anything." Ruth faced Irene. "I can't repay you for getting John through the rough spots.

Harvey hurt him something fierce. But you can't force him to give up the still as your payment."

"We're not going to do anything like that," Pike said before Irene could shoot back a furious reply. He saw it building inside her like a storm. "Do you know where the Ledbetter still is, Garston?"

The man shook his head and closed his eyes. In a weak voice he said, "The family're the only ones who know. I tried to find out. Augustus is the weak link in that chain. He wouldn't give me even a hint."

"Harvey is the one responsible for running the still," Ruth said. "Big Belly would think it was too much work. And John's right. Augustus is too stupid to do much of anything. Harvey is the one working the still, and his brother is the muscle."

Pike had other questions, but the crunch of gravel outside alerted him to an unwanted visitor. He pressed his index finger against his lips to shush the others.

He expected it but still jumped when a loud knock came at the door.

"I know you're in there, Ruth. You got the grain fellow with you? I need a couple bags." The single rap became a heavy pounding that threatened to knock the door off its hinges. Pike wasn't surprised. He recognized the voice immediately.

Harvey Ledbetter.

Pike touched his Colt and moved to stand behind the door. He motioned for Ruth to open up. She swallowed hard and then did so, peering out through a space no more than an inch wide.

"You got no call making such a ruckus this early in the morning, Harvey. What do you want?"

"I told you already. What are you, deaf? I need a couple bags of grain. Is Garston in there with you? Get him out of bed. His store's all locked up. If he don't come along this very minute, I'm fixing to break into the storeroom and take what I want."

Irene fumbled in Garston's vest pocket and found a key ring. She handed it to Ruth, who stared at it as if she had no idea what to do.

"Tell him to take what he needs," Pike whispered.

"Is that Garston? Get his scrawny ass out here so I can talk to him."

Pike pressed his face against the door and looked out the crack between the door and the jamb by a rusty hinge. The space wasn't large enough to thrust a gun barrel out, but shooting through the wood worked as well.

"He's all laid up from when you slammed him into the chuck-a-luck table last night."

"Yeah, thanks for remindin' me of that. He's gotta pay for the damage. Busting up gambling machines we can use made my pa all angry."

"Take an extra bag of grain to pay for it," Ruth said as she opened the door just wide enough to hand the keys through to the hulking man outside. "John said you can open the store and get what you need. His wagon's parked out back. You can use it as long as you return it before sundown."

"I'll keep it as long as I please," Harvey said, "and I might decide not to bring it back at all."

"Help yourself to the jawbreakers in the jar on the counter, too," Ruth said.

"I like the red ones." Grinning, Harvey tossed the keys into the air and caught them. He stomped off through the alley toward the street.

Ruth closed the door and leaned against it. She shook like a leaf in a high wind.

"Choke on the candy, you—"

"It's all right, Ruth. This is working out just fine," Pike said.

"He'll steal my grain," Garston said. His wrath gave him strength. He sat up and tried to push past Irene. She gently pressed him back into the bed.

"Consider it a cheap price to pay for getting rid of the Ledbetters," Pike said.

"Why does he want grain?" Irene asked.

Pike, Ruth, and Garston all looked at her. She opposed moonshine and clearly had no idea how it was made.

"You stay here. By the time I've gotten to my horse, he'll have the sacks loaded. He's heading straight for the Ledbetter still. I'd bet a hat on it," Pike said.

Irene started to chide him for such a sentiment, then she broke out in a grin.

"I'm not betting against you." She inched around Ruth and pressed against Pike. In a low voice she said, "Be careful."

Then she surprised him with a kiss full on the lips.

CHAPTER 16

Pike glanced over his shoulder as he left Ruth's room to be sure Irene stayed there. She was a fiery one. He appreciated that, but she wasn't like Belle Ramsey. Belle could ride all day and shoot from horseback with her carbine and never miss.

He frowned as he ran for the boardinghouse and his horse. Why he compared the two women was a good question. Belle was back in Warbonnet County and, like as not, still mad at him about something. He had never figured out what that was, but it put her in a powerful bad mood.

He caught his breath, then saddled his dun. A quick check told him his Winchester's magazine was full. Fighting off the entire Ledbetter clan wasn't his intention, but it never hurt to be prepared. As he swung into the saddle, he saw Dougal peeking out from between blue-and-white-checked curtains in the kitchen. He acknowledged his grandpa with a wave, then put his heels to the horse's flanks.

Having Irene tag along would have been dangerous. Pike had no intention of arguing with Dougal because he knew his grandpappy would want to come along and settle scores, too. He hadn't taken the news of the medicine wagon being burned down to the axles too well. Pike doubted he had told Fiddler yet. In his condition, Fiddler hardly needed more to upset him.

Pike rode toward the Royal Flush, not sure where Garston's store was situated. Harvey Ledbetter had turned west. That was as good a direction as any. He had to smile when he spotted the grain and seed store only a short way down the street from the gambling house. The horse wanted to stop and sniff at the intriguing aromas coming from inside the store. Pike forced it to go a hundred feet farther, then navigated the space between two stores.

In less than ten minutes Harvey Ledbetter drove a wagon around from the rear of the store. As he passed Pike without noticing him, he cursed the mule pulling the wagon. The way he used his whip on the poor beast almost destroyed Pike Shannon's resolve to follow unobtrusively.

For two cents, he'd beat the living daylights out of Ledbetter in the middle of the street.

"I would never treat you like that," Pike said, patting his dun's neck. The horse was skittish, still attracted to the smell of grain coming from those bags in the rear of the wagon.

From what Pike saw, five bags of grain weighed down the wagon so much that a back wheel wobbled. Ledbetter paid no attention to it. Pike hoped the wheel would stay on, because the last thing he wanted to do was help the man repair his wagon so he could keep on trailing him to the still.

Pike rode slowly, letting the moonshiner pull ahead by a quarter mile or better. He enjoyed the scenery along the road, though it wasn't much different from home, mostly rolling hills covered with live oaks and post oaks and underbrush with lots of briars and brambles. Tiny creeks cut across the landscape here and there with cottonwoods growing along the banks.

Pike's mind drifted to what it would take to fire up a still again. He enjoyed the process almost as much as he did sampling the 'shine dripping from the pipe. There was always a feeling of achievement when the still successfully produced its first drops. Seeing others enjoy his product created a special pleasure, too.

"The money's not bad, either," he said aloud, laughing. There wasn't any reason to lie to himself about that. Good 'shine brought in good money.

He hadn't sampled much of the moonshine Fiddler had concocted, but from what little he'd tasted, it was first-class, county-fair-blue-ribbon quality. Fiddler had learned well when the Shannon family had run a still day and night.

Pike's memory of the delight from those days faded. It wasn't as if Sophie—or Irene—convinced him it was wrong. Running the still because it was against the law gave it a special thrill. Nobody got hurt. Making 'shine wasn't like robbing a bank. The Shannon family had always worked hard to deliver the best liquor they could. Unlike some of the others running a still just for the money, nobody sampling Shannon 'shine had ever got sick or turned blind.

He crested a low hill and cautiously looked ahead down the road. Ledbetter and the wagon were nowhere to be seen. Pike twisted around to be sure Harvey hadn't gotten behind him somehow. The road stretched empty as a banker's promise all the way back to Kiowa Springs.

Pike slid from the saddle and walked slowly, studying the dusty road. The heavy wagon hadn't left much in the way of ruts, but the marks were fresh. The hot Texas winds hadn't wiped them away yet.

Using his hand to shield his eyes against the sun, he

studied the sky. Clouds built up to the southeast. A storm was headed his way, maybe by twilight. Judging by the leaden underbellies of the clouds, this promised to be a real frog strangler.

"And there are the wagon tracks," he said softly. Harvey had driven over the ditch alongside the road, hardly leaving a mark, but ten feet farther along crushed weeds marked his tracks. Not a hundred feet distant a wall of oak hid any shenanigans going on deeper in the forest.

Pike looked for the telltale plume of smoke rising from the fire necessary to distill moonshine, but either the Ledbetters weren't operating today or Harvey needed the grain to start a new batch.

Rather than follow right away, he scouted along this stretch of road. He found several places where a wagon had come from the woods. These ruts cut down into the grass, showing a heavy load had left the forest. He closed his eyes and imagined a stack of crates all jam-packed with jugs of 'shine. The still somewhere in the forest had produced all the liquor in the storeroom off the vacant lot where Fiddler's wagon had been reduced to ashes.

"They burned Fiddler's medicine wagon," he said softly. "Turn about is fair play. I should have poured out all their moonshine back in town." He told himself there'd be time to do so after he chopped up their still. Irene Brewster might even help him break open the casks in that storeroom and pour out Ledbetter moonshine into the weeds.

His horse snorted and jerked about nervously. Pike led the mare into the woods to get out of sight. He doubted Ledbetter would be leaving the woods so soon. There hadn't been enough time for him to unload the grain, much less take on a new load to cache in town.

Pike drew his rifle from the saddle scabbard when he spotted what his horse already had scented. A boar rummaged around in the undergrowth. Taking down an animal this big and strong with a single shot was unlikely. If the feral pig charged, every round in the Winchester might not be enough to drop it. Worse, the gunfire would alert Harvey Ledbetter.

"Better him hearing than me being gored," Pike decided. He lifted the rifle and took careful aim. A shot between the eyes would be chancy, but he would risk it if the boar charged.

Pike waited tensely for a long moment, his finger ready on the trigger. Then the boar snorted, turned, and walked away.

Pike let out a breath he hadn't known he was holding. Taking his finger off the trigger and lowering the rifle, he watched the thick undergrowth for any more movement in the brambles. There wasn't any reason for the pig to lie in ambush for him. He was pretty sure a pig's brain didn't work that way. A full-out charge served its purpose just as well. After a few more minutes, Pike was convinced the beast was gone. He led his dun forward until he found a spot to tether the horse.

From there, he sniffed and let his nose guide him to the still. A sudden clap of thunder made him jump nervously. He hadn't realized how taut his nerves were. Through the green leaf canopy overhead, he watched storm clouds piling up to tumble over and claim another blue patch of sky.

Rain would make his approach easier. Ledbetter wasn't likely to hear him if a rain started pounding at the trees. Already a wind kicked up. The soft rustling through the leaves turned into a more ferocious noise. As much as he wanted to avoid being drenched, he had a mission to complete.

Pushing through the wall of vegetation, he found himself at the edge of a small clearing. Smack in the middle stood a shack. A stove pipe sticking up through the roof puffed out black billows. Mingled with the rancid smell came one he knew so well.

Moonshine.

Garston's wagon stood beside the shack. The bags of grain were missing. Ledbetter had already lugged them inside. Pike circled the clearing and got a better idea what it would take to destroy the still. Even more, he wanted to set fire to all the 'shine Big Belly Ledbetter had produced. The storeroom in Kiowa Springs hinted at the operation's output—the Ledbetter family distilled better than ten gallons a week, if Pike's guess was right.

At least that much was stored outside this shack, sitting there in jugs placed against one of the side walls.

Pike ducked back into the forest when Harvey kicked open the shack's door and came out with a heavy crate. It was so ungainly he had trouble loading it into the back of the wagon. Grunting with effort, he tried to lift it into the bed but failed. When the crate slipped out of his hands, he had to jump back hurriedly to keep it from crashing down on his feet. Pike didn't hear the sound of jugs breaking when the crate landed behind the wagon. Harvey must have packed them in there pretty good.

Pike knew he could destroy them, though, given the chance.

"Gus, get your lazy bones out here and help," Harvey yelled. "I can't hoist the hoochinoo into the wagon by my lonesome."

"What the hell are you talkin' about?" Augustus Ledbetter asked from inside the shack. "Hoo-what?"

"That's a special name the Injuns way up north have for what we make. That's their name for moonshine," Harvey smugly declared.

"You're all the time throwing your book learning into

my face. It ain't my fault I never learned to read, what with the way Pa worked me and let you go do as you pleased."

Augustus Ledbetter came out of the shack, carrying a crate, too. Far stronger than his brother, he hefted the liquor easily. When he dropped it in the wagon bed, the vehicle sagged under the weight.

"Are you plum loco?" Harvey snapped. "You're gonna break the axle doing that, not to mention takin' a chance on busting the jugs. Set it down *easy* like. Now help me with this one."

"You ought to steal a bigger wagon." Augustus Ledbetter worked his fingers under the far side of the crate on the ground and waited for Harvey to help. He began cursing when Harvey impatiently waved him to finish adding to the payload already in the wagon bed.

"There wasn't any call to steal a wagon," Harvey said. "That worm Garston told me to use it. Like he gave me the sacks of grain."

"He's a sneaky one. I wouldn't put it past him to poison the grain so we'd end up brewing poison." Augustus looked up at the smoke curling from the stovepipe, then to the sky. "It's fixin' to rain something fierce. You'll get drenched if you head back now."

"Pa wanted some fresh moonshine. He's throwing a whale of a party tonight. He wants all the gamblers to be soused."

"That makes 'em easier to cheat," Augustus said, grinning broadly. "Most are too dumb to know they're being robbed blind anyway, but this lets us clean them out and never break a sweat."

Harvey Ledbetter jerked his head and then wiped at his face.

"The rain's commencing to start. If I get stuck in a mud bog, it'll take forever to get to town."

"And you'll be soaked to the skin. That'll be the first bath you've taken in a month of Sundays."

The brothers went into the shack as they continued wrangling with each other. Pike pulled the brim of his hat lower to shield his eyes when the rain began to pelt down harder. He knew where the Ledbetters were holed up. He needed a way to bring a touch of justice to them for what they'd done to Fiddler and Dougal.

And everyone else in Kiowa Springs.

He boldly walked across the clearing to the wagon. Neither of the brothers had bothered to unhitch the mule or see to protecting the animal from the storm. Pike scooped up a rag that lay on the seat, hopped into the wagon bed, and then jumped across to the roof. He landed with a loud thud.

"What in tarnation was that?" Harvey demanded from under Pike's feet, loud enough to be heard through the roof.

"The storm's getting worse, that's all," Gus answered. "Might've been a branch fallin' on the roof. Why are you so jumpy, Harve?"

"There's something going on in town. Pa knows what it is, but he's not telling. It's got something to do with them two snake oil peddlers we roughed up."

"Old lady Brewster's nursing them. They ain't fit enough to get out of bed, much less cause any mischief."

"They looked mighty sneaky. Are you sure?"

The two argued while Pike slowly made his way across the rickety roof. He took the rag and stuffed it into the stovepipe. It took only a few seconds for the brothers to come boiling out of the shack, choking and coughing on the smoke that had backed up from the stove.

"Drop your iron," Pike called down to them. He didn't expect them to put up any fight when he held the high ground and had a Winchester in his hands.

However, the Ledbetter boys were sorely lacking in

common sense. Both clawed at the holstered revolvers on their hips. Pike fired over their heads, but close enough to make both brothers dive to the ground behind the wagon. Then he started shooting into the crates loaded onto the back. Splinters flew and glass shattered. The smell of moonshine wafted up from the crates. Both Ledbetters began to curse in rage as their precious 'shine drained out and dripped through cracks between the boards of the wagon bed.

Pike waited for them to pop up so he could put some lead into them. But one stayed under the wagon, and the other came out into the open just long enough to dive behind a woodpile used to feed the fire. Pike snapped a shot at him, but the bullet kicked up dust right behind the scurrying Ledbetter brother.

After that, he had to divide his shots between the pair, swinging the rifle back and forth to go from one to the other. The brothers worked in unison better than Pike would have thought possible. One fired to draw his attention. When he shifted his aim, the other opened fire, forcing him to spin back in the opposite direction.

Worse yet, the rain was hammering down harder now. Tiny wet fists punched at Pike's hat brim. He slid back along the roof to avoid the shots from the Ledbetters. His heel caught on a warped board and sent him down hard. He sat and pulled his foot free.

Pike reached out to the stovepipe to pull himself up. He jerked his hand away from the metal when a spark jumped from the pipe to his hand. He had seen blue haze dancing around weathervanes during a storm and knew they attracted lightning. By getting too close, he had burned a small spot on his left palm, as much from the electrical shock as from the heated metal trying to exhaust the smoke trapped under his feet. Rolling away, he reached the far side of the shack and dropped to the ground. From here it wasn't more than a dozen yards to where he'd left his horse. It was time to retreat.

It galled him to admit that he had been outsmarted by Harvey and Augustus Ledbetter. They charged around the shack from opposite directions and caught him in a crossfire. Only now he was off the roof and exposed.

Worse, he might as well have been on stage with a spotlight shining on him. The lightning forking across the sky lit up the forest so vividly he worried that his shadow would be burned into the grass.

Augustus drew a bead from around the corner of the shack. "Get them hands into the air. Surrender!"

"Shoot him!" shouted his brother as he came around the other corner. "There's no reason to let him live. Shoot him! We don't need no prisoners."

"You're right, Harve. Pa would ask why we let this varmint ruin an entire load of moonshine."

Pike dropped to one knee and began firing at Harvey Ledbetter. If he was the leader, taking him out of the fight gave him a better chance of escaping.

"Get him, Gus. Get him!" Harvey slipped in the mud and fell. If he hadn't, Pike would have ended his miserable life then and there. As it was, the slug whistled harmlessly over Harvey as the big man thrashed in the mud like a hog in a wallow.

Pike swung back to fire again at Gus. The hammer of his rifle clicked down on an empty chamber. Augustus Ledbetter whooped in glee and braced his revolver against the side of the shack. Even if Pike had had a round ready in his rifle, he didn't have a clear shot.

A new flash of lightning revealed a startling sight. Crashing out of the brush behind Gus Ledbetter, the feral pig poked its snout up into the air, as if sniffing the rain.

Pike slapped leather, drew his Colt, and began firing at the pig. A beast that big could be injured by a handgun. Killing it was almost impossible. Infuriating it was easy.

The pig charged Gus. The man turned and added a few more rounds to the minor wounds Pike had already inflicted. Then came a din that drowned out all the storm's fury. Gus and the pig crashed to the ground—fighting, rolling, kicking, biting, and snapping at each other.

Pike hightailed it for his horse. He yanked the reins free, vaulted into the saddle, and plunged deeper into the forest, away from the still. He looked back and saw that a mud-drenched Harvey Ledbetter was trying to help his brother, but that just wound up with both of them fighting for their lives against the boar hog.

Pike hoped the pig won.

CHAPTER 17

Pike dodged through the forest, changing directions several times. He hadn't expected the Ledbetter brothers to get away from that maddened hog, let alone to be so eager to chase whoever had shot up their still.

Nor had he seen any saddle mounts around the clearing where the still was located. They must have had the horses tied somewhere in the woods nearby. But there was no mistaking the swift rataplan of hooves closing in on him as the rain rhythmically beat on the leaves overhead.

As he rode, he reloaded his rifle. He looked for a decent spot to fort up but hadn't come across one so far. Harvey and Augustus Ledbetter knew these woods better than he did. They would be on top of him in minutes.

Looked like it was time to risk something they would never expect.

Pike slid the Winchester back in its saddle boot. He kicked his feet out of the stirrups and drew his legs up. The rain made the saddle slick, but he managed to stand up on it. Balancing precariously like a trick rider, he judged distances, reached up toward the tree limbs above him, and jumped.

The dun trotted on without its rider. Pike hung by his

hands for a second before he was able to pull himself up and hook a leg over the branch he had grabbed. He kicked hard, curled around the branch with his belly pressing into the rough bark, and lay flat along the thick growth. Moving cautiously, he drew the Colt and watched his back trail. His keen eyes spotted the Ledbetters before they had a chance to come across him. He had gotten out of sight barely in time.

Gus trotted forward from a thick clump of bushes, pointed to the wet leaves, and called, "He's this way, Harve. I got 'im."

"You got him or his tracks? He's been trying to confuse us."

"He's not good enough to confuse me. We know these woods better 'n anybody else, and that includes Pa."

Pike would have let them ride on if they would. He was no bushwhacker.

But fate worked against him. A good-sized chunk of bark that he had dislodged from the branch when he pulled himself onto it chose that moment to fall and hit Augustus Ledbetter squarely in the noggin. Gus jerked his head back and looked up, his eyes widening as he spotted Pike in the tree. He yelled and jerked his rifle up. The weapon cracked and sent a slug ripping through the leaves a few feet to Pike's left.

Gus had opened the ball, so Pike squeezed the Colt's trigger. He had aimed to take Augustus from the saddle. A gust of wind blew a small branch in front of his target. The bullet meant for Ledbetter's heart veered enough to rob Pike of a killing shot. He had to be satisfied with only winging his target.

Augustus let out a shriek of pain and fell from his horse. He thrashed around on the ground, kicking up a curtain of leaves and detritus as the rain fell harder. Pike shot through the momentary cloud of water and soggy foliage. The man screeched even louder.

"He shot me, Harve. He shot me *twice*!"

"Quit your caterwauling or *I'll* shoot you!" Harvey roared. "Where is he?"

Pike answered the question with a bullet in Harvey's direction. The bullet blew splinters off a tree by the man's head. Sticky sap got into Ledbetter's eyes. He cursed and clawed at his face.

"He blinded me. He's a devil. Get him, Gus. Shoot him. I can't see!"

He spun around and around, his horse beginning to buck to unseat the panicky rider. Pike held off taking another shot. If Harvey tumbled from his crow-hopping horse, Pike thought he'd have a better shot.

Luck turned against him. Both Ledbetters scuttled through the mud and disappeared into the brush. Pike heard them yelping and cursing more as briars clawed at their flesh. He didn't have a clear shot at them anymore.

"How'd you get away from that boar?" Pike shouted. "Were you too putrid for it to eat you?"

He wanted to rile the brothers. If he got them mad enough, they'd rush him. He knew the type. When cold calm was necessary, they'd explode like a stick of old dynamite and make mistakes.

Pike scooted along the limb to get a better shot at the trail, just to make sure nobody else was coming along it. His instincts warned him the Ledbetters might not be as stupid as they looked. A small roll to the side let him fall to the ground. He wanted to be back on his feet where he could move around.

He reacted fast and got his feet under him before he hit. Immediately, he sprang forward and fell belly-down on the ground. The Colt came up in time for him to get a shot off at Harvey, who had wiped the sap from his eyes and circled to the right.

Bullets flew back and forth for a frantic couple of heartbeats as Pike and Harvey exchanged shots. Pike got the better of the skirmish. Harvey retreated and took cover in the dense woods.

Pike didn't know how badly Gus was wounded, but the other Ledbetter brother wasn't out of the fight. He opened fire again, the shots coming uncomfortably close to Pike.

Pike wiggled backward, got a tree trunk between him and his attackers, and then ran for all he was worth in the direction his horse had trotted. One slug whined past him, but it was high and far off target. Both the rain and the thick vegetation hid him from accurate fire.

A ravine with a sluggishly flowing stream cut through the forest. He took another chance. The two on his trail weren't likely to think he'd come after them again. In their minds they had run him off. He'd be theirs for the catching, not the other way around.

Pike slipped down a muddy bank and once more covered the trail with his gun after thumbing fresh rounds into it. He waited only a minute before both Ledbetters came crashing along the trail.

But it was their riderless horses that galloped out. They were trying to trick him, Pike realized. They knew about this ravine and had guessed that he might try to take advantage of it.

He twisted back to his left at a sound. One of them had slid down the ravine farther downstream to sneak up on him. The man was slathered in mud and constantly swiped at his eyes. The other brother came at Pike from upstream. Sounds of him sloshing about in the stream were hidden by the rain and the rush of rising runoff water. The two of them were so muddy he couldn't tell which was which as they charged along the ravine at him.

A bullet tore past Pike's ear just as he triggered a shot at one of the attackers. The man flopped backward and yelled, "He done shot me again, Harve! I'm dying!"

Pike doubted that. No one with a fatal wound created such a ruckus. Augustus Ledbetter had a way of claiming worse injuries than he actually suffered. Pike took another shot but missed by a wide margin, his aim thrown off by the pouring rain.

He couldn't stay where he was. Pike dug in his toes and kicked his way up the muddy embankment. Shots rang out, but he didn't feel the smash of any bullets hitting him. He reached the top, stumbled out of the ravine, and looked down at himself. He was totally covered in mud, too. The rain worked to wash away some of it, but he was more like a clay statue than a human being.

Pike swung first left and then right, sending a bullet in each direction. Gus Ledbetter was nowhere to be seen, but he caught a glimpse of Harvey ducking back. This fight was even now. That would change in a hurry if both men again got position on him and attacked.

If he stayed any longer, there was a good chance the Ledbetters would end up plugging him. Stumbling along, he reached a large tree and ducked behind it.

Pike let out a piercing whistle. From somewhere nearby, he heard his dun answer with an aggrieved snort. He ran as hard as he could in that direction until he saw the horse standing under some dripping trees. Pike grabbed the reins and vaulted into the saddle. His jump almost carried him across the horse's back. Even the seat of his britches was slicker than glass from the buckets of mud he had rolled around in.

Head down so the rain rolled off the brim of his hat in a

steady stream, he made his way out of the trees and back to the edge of the embankment. Below, Harvey tried to help his brother out of the stream. As Pike suspected, Augustus didn't look like he was really hurt that bad. They only succeeded in washing off some of the mud by splashing around in the water. This was likely the cleanest either of them had been in a while.

They hadn't seen him yet, and they were cussing so loud they probably hadn't heard his horse. Pike tugged at the reins and hightailed it away from there while he had the chance. He found a game trail that led to a road. Any hint of direction was wiped away by the pouring rain. Then lightning flashed across the sky and gave him a look at a rise in the road.

He had stopped there on his way to the still when he was hunting for Harvey's tracks, he recalled. Riding faster now, he saw a sign with chipped paint letters assuring him that he was headed toward Kiowa Springs.

By the time he reached town, the rain had washed away all the mud on his clothes as surely as hydraulic mining tore gold out of a hillside, although he was still soaked to the skin, of course.

He passed by the Royal Flush. Big Belly Ledbetter stood just inside the swinging double doors glaring at the world outside. Pike paid him no attention and kept riding through the sheets of rain still hammering down.

After tending his horse in the shed behind Ada Brewster's boardinghouse, he tried to squeeze out as much water from his clothing as he could. He'd just get wetter when he dashed to the house, but maybe he wouldn't drip quite as much on Mrs. Brewster's floors.

It hadn't been a productive day, he thought bitterly. He had shot up Big Belly Ledbetter's latest run from the still, but the equipment remained intact. He had pinked Gus

Ledbetter a couple, maybe three, times, and might have winged his brother.

Even so, he had sent a message to Big Belly that somebody in Kiowa Springs intended to disrupt, if not destroy, his moonshining operation. And since Harvey and Augustus had, once again, not gotten a good look at him, they couldn't tell their pa who he was. Big Belly still would have no idea who his nemesis was.

So yeah, maybe the day hadn't been all that successful.

But it would be. Soon.

Chapter 18

Big Belly Ledbetter stood just inside the Royal Flush, staring out at the sheets of rain pouring down. He shifted from one foot to the other to avoid a drip coming through the roof. Everything around him was like that. Leaking and inexcusable.

A solitary rider passed by outside. Big Belly gave him a quick once-over. A stranger. With the storm dumping enough water to drown the entire town, he'd be lucky if he didn't wash away. The rider was only passing through from the look of him. Right now he hunted for shelter.

Big Belly almost called out to him to come into the gambling den. The thunderstorm had scared off the usual customers. Big Belly spat. They were all cowards, afraid of the dark and wet and lightning.

"Those worthless young'uns of mine are the same. Scared of the dark and suspicious of the light." He wiped off rain that had splattered onto his face. With a sweeping motion he cast the drops aside.

Everything was falling apart. Everything was wrong. He knew it but wasn't able to figure out what had caused all his woe. Before he could crush the cause under his boot heel, he had to put a name to it. The pair of drifters peddling their snake oil hadn't been the start of his trouble. They were just a symptom. Others in Kiowa Springs thought they could run their own stills and cut into his business.

Big Belly went to the long bar and fished around behind it until he found a crockery jug sealed with a blob of melted wax. His jagged thumbnail made a single circle around the neck of the jug to cut through the wax. A flip of the same finger sent the plug flying. He swung the jug around and rested it on the outside of his elbow, hoisted it, and let the potent moonshine pour into his mouth. He choked and spat some out. Then he took another long pull.

It burned his gullet and puddled warmly in his belly. A third sampling made him feel a tad more hospitable toward the world. Then he saw the back door swing wide.

"Don't you track mud in here, you worthless skunk," he roared as he saw Harvey about to come in. "What do you think this is, a barn?"

"Aw, Pa, it's wet outside. And we're soaked to the bone."

"Don't track mud in. Don't you dare drip mud onto the floor, either." Big Belly Ledbetter shoved the jug back under the bar and waddled to the back door where his two sons huddled just outside.

"If we don't come in and shut the door, the rain'll flood the place," Harvey said. "You don't want that, Pa."

"I don't want you two annoyin' me, is what I don't want." Big Belly grumbled. "All right, get inside and try not to mess up too much. Stand over there in the corner."

"Thanks, Pa. It's getting cold outside now that the wind's kicked up," said Augustus. "The rain washed off most of the mud. We was covered with it after the shoot-out."

Big Belly spun and faced his younger son. He shoved out his belly and bumped him so hard Gus stumbled and crashed into the wall. Big Belly followed and pinned him.

"What're you going on about? What's this about a shoot-out?"

"We don't know who it was, Pa. The storm hid his face," said Harvey.

"And he was as covered in mud as we was," Augustus added. "He might as well have worn a mask."

"And a duster," added Harvey. "Head to toe he was rolled in mud after he shot up that load of moonshine."

Big Belly turned on his older son. Harvey backed away, ready to bolt out the door and back into the storm rather than face his father's wrath. Ledbetter's face turned red as anger built to the boiling point inside him.

Bit by bit he ripped the story from his sons.

"I've never seen such a good-for-nothing pair in all my born days," he declared when they had finished telling him what had happened. "Somebody tried to destroy the still and did shoot up the 'shine, then you chased him and lost him?"

"Pa, he shot me," whined Augustus. "Three times. See? Here and here." He held up his left arm. His shirt sleeve had bloodstains on it in two different places, one on the forearm and one on the upper arm, but neither wound looked like it had bled heavily. "And if you look at my back, he—"

"Shut up. I ought to finish the job he started. You don't have any idea who shot you *three* times? What'd he look like?"

"We don't know who he is, Pa. Honest. He was off in the distance and then covered in mud and—"

Big Belly silenced Harvey with a furious stare. Without knowing it, he clenched his fists so hard the ragged nails cut into the palms of his hands. Blood dripped to the floor and was washed away by the puddles left by both his sons.

"There are at least two others running stills. They want to drive me out of business. Who was it? One of them?"

"Timmerman don't have the stones to do it, Pa. And Garston's all laid up," said Harvey. He brightened as he asked, "Do you want me to rough him up some? He's making time with that gal I've taken a shine to. That'll show her who—"

"Shut up," Big Belly roared. "It's not them, neither of them." He fumed, then spun and punched the wall so hard he drove his fist through it. The rain driving against the back wall washed away blood from his scraped knuckles. With a quick move, he yanked his hand back and stared at it.

Harvey frowned as he thought. "If it's not them, who can it be, Pa? There was a rumor of somebody over in Jenks Crossing running a still, but that's twenty miles off."

"It's somebody closer at hand," Big Belly said. "I shouldn't have been so generous to those snake oil peddlers."

"You shoulda tarred and feathered them," Augustus said.

"Shoulda hanged 'em," chimed in Harvey.

"For once you're both right. First tar and feathers, then hanging. That would have solved my problems before they reached this sorry state." Big Belly grumbled under his breath, "Can't believe an entire run of moonshine was lost. An entire week's work, gone, shot to hell. You know how much money that cost me?"

"Well, Pa—" Harvey started. He clamped his mouth shut when Big Belly glared at him. Another word and he'd be bleeding on the floor rather than dripping rainwater.

"Nobody else would cross me like this," Big Belly went on. "Gus, fetch that ax handle under the bar."

"Bar? You mean—"

"You know what I mean. In the big room. The place what used to be a saloon." He clenched his hands again, but his mind sailed far beyond his two dimwitted sons.

The two selling their moonshine from the back of the medicine wagon had to be at the heart of his problems. Before they drifted into town, everything had run smoothly.

He reached out. Augustus slapped the ax handle into his palm. Big Belly gripped it hard, pushed past his boys, and stomped out into the rain. He ignored the way he was soaked within minutes. His dander was up, and nothing mattered but protecting his moonshine empire in Kiowa Springs.

Sloshing through the mud, he walked to the front door of Ada Brewster's boardinghouse and rapped hard with the ax handle.

The old woman came to the door. Her eyes went wide when she saw him.

"Out of my way, woman." He used the wood stave to push her aside.

She grabbed it and tried to wrestle it from his hand. He was much too big, too strong, too determined. She was helpless against him.

"You can't come in here," she said. "You get back outside. You're tracking mud in."

He shoved Ada Brewster harder. She collided with a divan and lost her balance. She sat heavily, still sputtering for him to leave.

"Where're those two strangers?" he demanded harshly.

"Right here, you fat polecat." The cold voice was accompanied by the metallic ratcheting of twin hammers being pulled back and cocked.

Big Belly turned and faced Dougal Shannon. The old man held a shotgun and braced himself against a doorjamb. The shotgun's barrels didn't waver as they pointed at Big Belly.

"You can't go shoving a fine lady like Miz Brewster around like that," Dougal continued. "And you surely can't do it in her own house. You clear out or there's gonna be a heap of cleaning to be done in here. Guts all over the walls."

Big Belly roared and began moving forward, so mad that he was heedless of the danger. When his weight gained momentum, nothing could stop him. Dougal must have been so shocked by Big Belly ignoring the threat of the shotgun that he didn't pull the trigger. It was like a locomotive hitting a cow on the tracks.

The shotgun went flying and so did Dougal. He landed on his back in the hall leading to the bedrooms. Big Belly couldn't check his forward motion and fell forward, pinning Dougal to the floor.

"You fess up!" he yelled. "What have you done?"

Dougal cried, "Let me up and I'll show you what I can do!"

Big Belly gripped the ax handle in both hands and pressed it down across Dougal's neck. He leaned forward slightly. Dougal turned red and began gasping for air. He wasn't strong enough to force the stave off his throat.

"You better let him up. I'm nowhere near as good a shot as Dougal there, but then you're a mighty big target."

Fiddler held the shotgun Dougal had dropped when Big Belly bowled him over.

Ledbetter took it all in with a single glance. Fiddler's hands shook so hard the barrels darted all over the place. Chances were good he would miss, or worse, hit his partner.

"You better clear out of Kiowa Springs, both of you," Big Belly said. He rocked back and took the ax handle off Dougal's throat. He dropped his entire weight on his captive's stomach, torturing him almost as badly as the choking had.

"You can't bully us. We heard what you did to my wagon. You burned it up. You'll pay for that."

"How?" Big Belly watched Fiddler's reaction.

Fiddler thought, then said, "A hundred dollars. You'll pay a hundred dollars."

"For the wagon," croaked out Dougal. "Another two hundred for the lost product inside. And another hundred for a new mule. Four hundred dollars."

Big Belly levered himself to his feet using the ax handle as a cane. He scowled at the two men. The one he'd knocked down was hardly able to stand and the one who had ended up with the shotgun was too weak to aim. Pulling the trigger might be impossible due to his condition. Neither was in any shape to fight, due to the first beating Big Belly had given them.

"You leave right this minute, Mr. Ledbetter. I don't want to shoot a man, but I will." Ada Brewster had gotten a pistol from somewhere and clutched it in a steady hand.

Of the three, she was the most dangerous one at the moment. There wasn't any way she had ridden out to his still and tried to destroy it. She had the sand to plug Harvey and put a few holes in Gus, but he couldn't see her riding out in a buggy and carrying on a long, running gunfire in a rainstorm.

Besides, her clothes were dry. She hadn't been out in the rain. His short walk from the Royal Flush here had drenched him.

"Get them out of town fast," Big Belly said, waving his ax handle toward Dougal and Fiddler. Every move of the bludgeon caused an ominous swish.

He could tell that Ada Brewster wasn't scared of him. That was a mistake on her part. She could put all four rounds from that .41 in him and not stop him before he got in a few good licks. But she might get lucky and do some real damage to him with one of the slugs, so he fought back the urge to charge her and slap the gun out of her hand.

"You've been warned." He stomped out of the house and back into the rain.

The drenching didn't cool off his hot blood. Big Belly stewed as he returned to the gambling den. Lightning stretched across the sky, sporadically turning the town brighter than noonday. As quick as the light came it vanished. It was like his thought that Fiddler and Dougal were responsible for the attack on his still. That bright idea had faded fast when he saw them. They couldn't have done it, either.

He kicked open the back door and stomped into the room. Harvey and Gus were swilling some of their moonshine, passing a jug back and forth. Both fumbled to put the jug away and nearly dropped it. Harvey wound up with it.

Big Belly snarled and grabbed the jug away. He needed a drink. A long one.

He belched when he had downed enough of the 'shine to calm his nerves.

"You showed 'em, didn't you, Pa? Did you whup up on them worse than before?" Gus spoke more to fill the deathly silence than anything else. The only other sound was the falling rain.

"They weren't the ones who shot you two up and ruined my moonshine." Big Belly tried to keep his jumbled thoughts straight. When he left here, caught up in his rage, he had been sure the snake oil salesmen were responsible.

"Who done it, then?" Harvey asked.

"You said it was Garston or—" Gus started.

"It wasn't none of them. Nobody from Kiowa Springs, nobody what just rode into town. Maybe it's a will-o'-the-wisp flittering 'round out there in the forest." Big Belly took another long pull from the jug. The more he drank the clearer the world became.

"You said there wasn't any such critter, Pa," Harvey said. "If you can't touch it, it doesn't exist, you said."

"Shut up. Both of you. We need to figure out who's trying to put us out of business and stop him. When we catch him, I want him fed to the buzzards. To catch him, we need to lay a trap. I figure to bait it so he can't pass up such a juicy—"

Big Belly jerked around. Someone had crashed into a chair out in the main room.

He moved with surprising speed for a man of his girth. Someone had knocked over a chair. The batwings swung back and forth with a faint creaking sound. Someone had spied on him and then hightailed it. He let out a roar of anger and flung the ax handle with all his might. It missed a window by inches and knocked a hole in a solid wall.

When he found out who was bedeviling him, they'd pay. He'd make the varmint pay and pay and pay. With his life.

CHAPTER 19

Pike leaned back in the divan. He closed his eyes for a second. Only a second. No longer. Then he came awake with a start, hand going to his Colt at a small sound. Twisting around, he pointed his gun at the hallway leading to the kitchen.

He relaxed and pouched the iron.

"Sorry," he said. "You snuck up on me."

"I didn't want to wake you," Irene Brewster said. Her face was flushed, and she wrung her hands as if tying intricate knots. "That's not true. I wanted to but wasn't sure if I should."

Pike sat straighter on the divan and pointed to the other half of it. Irene hesitated, smiled as she came to a decision that this was all right, then hurried over and sat ramrod straight beside him. She folded her hands primly in her lap, pressed her legs together, and perched on the very edge of the cushion.

"Maybe you should change first," Pike said. He couldn't help but notice that her clothes were soaked and water dripped from her hair. What in blazes had she been doing out in that storm? "I've been in front of the fire long enough to dry my clothes, mostly."

She didn't move and seemed too worked up about something to take his suggestion. Since they appeared to have reached an impasse, he asked her, "What's bothering you, Irene?"

She half turned to face him. They were only inches apart. She didn't seem to notice—but Pike did—that whoever had designed the love seat had been an expert. Her nearness made him a trifle uneasy. If they had sat here to spark, they wouldn't be any closer than this.

"He's planning a war," she said breathlessly. The flush brought roses to her cheeks. Her dark eyes sparkled in the firelight. With a quick, nervous gesture she pushed her wet hair back from where it dangled across her eyes.

Pike had seen prettier girls in his day, but not many, and few with such energy and determination. She distracted him when he ought to be listening intently to what she had to say, and the way her shirt clung to her didn't help.

"War? Who're you talking about?"

"Who else?" She laid a cool, damp hand on his arm. "Sorry. I shouldn't get you all wet again."

"Don't worry about that. You're talking about Ledbetter, aren't you? What do you mean that he's going to war?"

"On the others who are running stills. Something happened at his still. He lost all his moonshine. He—" Her eyes widened. "Oh. It's something you did. You destroyed it!"

"It amounted to around ten gallons, by my reckoning," Pike said, chuckling. "That's what's got him stirred up, losing all that 'shine. Let him go after the other moonshiners. That means he doesn't suspect me."

"I hadn't thought of that. You can go back and destroy the still any time you want. That'll get rid of all the moonshine in Kiowa Springs!" She clapped her hands in delight, then abruptly sobered. "But that doesn't put them out of business for good, does it? They can rebuild."

"Quick as a fox," Pike said. "How'd you come to spy on him? He's not out on the street shouting this news for just anyone to hear."

"He was holding a family council in the back room of that horrid gambling den of his. I looked in. Nobody was in the big room, so I crept closer to hear better."

Pike looked at Irene with new admiration. Such spying took a lot of gumption.

"You took a big risk eavesdropping on such dangerous men. You shouldn't have done that."

"It was worth it to learn what Big Belly is up to. Somebody's got to stop him." She looked at him with admiration glowing in her eyes. "You destroyed all their vile moonshine?"

"The fresh batch," Pike said. "The storeroom near the spot where they burned Fiddler's wagon has quite a few gallons stashed away. Getting to it won't be easy now. They'll be on the lookout for trouble."

"Set fire to the building," Irene suggested. "You won't even have to go inside to do that."

"With so much alcohol inside, that'd start a fire big enough to burn down the entire town. You don't want to leave Kiowa Springs a pile of smoldering ash. Tell me what he's planning. How's he going to wage this so-called war?"

"Well," Irene said, turning to face him squarely. She leaned even closer and whispered in a conspiratorial tone, "He wasn't too specific, but he didn't sound as if he intended to destroy the stills."

"That makes sense," Pike said. "He kills the still owners and takes over their equipment."

"He'll double or triple his output if he does that. Kiowa Springs will be flooded with moonshine! That's terrible!"

"Not as terrible as killing the men running the other stills."

"There are two I know of. Mr. Timmerman and John Garston. I am so disappointed in Mr. Garston. And Ruth. She could talk him out of breaking the law, but she is addicted to potent drink. He gives her what she wants in return for—"

"Don't go guessing what's happening between them," Pike cautioned. "Saving lives is more important than gossiping about them."

"I never gossip. I know that the two of them, well, they are—"

"Is Garston still at Ruth's room? It's only a few steps from the Royal Flush's back door. He'd be the first one Ledbetter would go after."

"I'll warn him." Irene got to her feet and started for the front door.

Pike grabbed her by the wrist and swung her around as she stepped past him. Her eyes flashed angrily. She started to jerk free, then subsided.

"Stay here," Pike said in a tone that brooked no argument. "Change your clothes, go to bed, don't leave the house. I'll take care of this."

"You don't know Ledbetter! He's a killer. And he has a huge fortress outside of town somewhere. The stories people tell make it sound like he can defend himself against the entire US Army there."

Pike had seen more than his share of desperadoes. Big Belly Ledbetter wasn't any more dangerous than most of them. But Pike knew better than to underestimate Big Belly, especially since he had a couple of dumb but dangerous offspring backing him up. If Big Belly had a hideout somewhere away from Kiowa Springs, that would make it harder to stop him. Pike figured his best chance was to catch Big Belly in town before he had a chance to hole up.

"Where can I find this fella Timmerman? I'll warn him, too."

"He runs the apothecary. He has a room in the rear."

Pike nodded grimly. The owner of the grain store and a chemist. Perfect choices to operate a still.

"Get off to bed," Pike said. He barely kept from smiling at the way Irene blushed. Thoughts naughtier than running a still must be racing through her mind at the mention of bed.

She swallowed, bobbed her head in agreement, and hurried off. She cast a backward look at him as she went down the hallway. Then she ducked into the room next to her mother's.

Pike wondered if she would have taken such risks spying on Ledbetter and his boys if he hadn't been there. She wanted to impress him. He needed to tell her there was no call to do such dangerous things. Risking her life dragging him from the burning wagon had demonstrated her bravery and determination.

He made sure his gun rode easy in its holster, then went into the night. The rain had finally stopped. All he had to cope with were deep mud puddles. He sloshed along until he got to the boardwalk that led toward the Royal Flush. Light spilled from the open door, but no shadows moved about.

Pike hadn't intended on taking on the Ledbetters just yet, but maybe this was an omen. He pushed open the swinging doors and looked around. The Royal Flush stood empty. The only sound he heard was the slow drip of a leak in the roof. The rainwater spattered into a pool at the middle of the big room. The steady trickle missed a poker table by inches.

Nothing disturbed the dripping noise. Pike moved on cat's feet to the back room. Empty. Moving faster, he left the Royal Flush through the back door and went directly to Ruth's room in the next building. Pike drew his Colt when he saw the door standing ajar. His guts tensed at the realization that he might be too late.

Using his foot, he kicked open the door. He poked his pistol in and quickly saw that the room was as empty as the Royal Flush. Backing away, he tried to make out tracks around the door. The rain had turned the ground to one giant mud puddle unable to hold a footprint. He had no idea what had happened here. Ledbetter and his boys might have spirited Garston away to kill him away from town. Or the store owner might have hightailed it before the other moonshiners came for him.

Or Ledbetter might not be after Garston at all. Pike returned his gun to his holster and set off to find Timmerman. Finding him might reveal a lot more about Ledbetter's plans.

Walking down the middle of the main street, Pike swiveled from side to side hunting for the apothecary's store. He found it in the worst way. Gunfire drew him to a store a hundred yards away from the Royal Flush. Muzzle flashes showed through the plate glass window facing the street.

His sharp ears picked out the distinctive reports of two different pistols firing as he ran toward the building. Then a third joined the fight. He went to the front door and tried the latch. Barred. Not wasting time battering his way in, he darted to the side of the store. At the rear of the building, a bulky man fired wildly at something. The silhouette told Pike this was one of the Ledbetter boys and not Big Belly himself.

He took aim and cocked his Colt. The sound alerted Ledbetter. The shadow jerked out of the way just as Pike fired. Muzzle flame bloomed crimson in the darkness as rapid return fire drove him back.

"Pa, Pa! Some gunman's out front. He took a shot at me!"

Pike recognized Augustus Ledbetter's voice. He had wounded the man multiple times and now had missed the chance to end his miserable life. Gus had a guardian angel watching over him—or in his case, more likely a guardian *devil.*

A quick peek around the corner told Pike that Gus had taken cover behind a woodpile. Pike knew better than to rush forward without knowing where his enemies were hidden. He looked up. A canopy stretched over the boardwalk and gave access to the roof.

Shinnying up a post supporting the overhang, he pulled himself onto the roof. Within seconds, Pike was soaked again from sloshing through puddles all over the sagging roof. As careful as he was, the sound of his advance warned the Ledbetters. When Pike peered over the edge at the back of the store, he almost had his head blown off as a gun roared.

"I got him, Pa. I blowed his fool brains out!" Gus's voice came from directly under him.

Pike steeled himself, and with a lightning-fast move, he thrust his head out, saw where Gus stood, celebrating his supposed victory, and fired. It took less than a second. As he drew back, he heard Gus Ledbetter screech in pain.

"My shoulder. He shot me in the shoulder. I can't hold my gun, Pa!"

"Shut up," Big Belly Ledbetter snapped from somewhere nearby. "Get into there and finish Timmerman off."

"But, Pa, I can't hold a gun. I'm bleedin'! Bleedin' bad!"

Big Belly snarled like an angry grizzly. Pike heard wood splinter as the man kicked in the back door. Immediate gunfire answered the intrusion. Timmerman was still alive and putting up a fight.

Pike retraced his way to the front of the store, dropped onto the porch, then swung around. He kicked like a mule and knocked down the front door.

"Timmerman, I want to help. Don't shoot."

"Who are you? I don't recognize your voice."

Pike chanced showing himself. He expected to catch a bullet in the gut, but the apothecary held his fire. Pike slid inside the store. The scent of chemicals made him choke.

"It takes some getting used to the smell," Timmerman said, hearing Pike gasp. "Who are you?"

"Ledbetter wants to kill off his competition."

"He's not got a pharmacy," Timmerman said suspiciously from behind a counter where he crouched. No lamps were lit in the place, but enough light seeped in from the street that Pike could make out the chemist's lanky, middle-aged figure, as well as the revolver that Timmerman held.

"Your still," Pike snapped. "He wants to get rid of all competition distilling 'shine."

Hearing rapid footsteps, Pike lunged around the counter and tackled Timmerman. They crashed to the floor, Pike on top.

The chemist struggled, but Pike got off a couple of quick shots as Gus elbowed his way into the room, pushing aside a tattered hanging drape closing off the rear of the store. Big Belly had forced his son to continue the attack.

Pike's bullets drove Gus back, but then his Colt clicked on an empty chamber.

"Here," Timmerman said, shoving his pistol into Pike's hand. "You're better with a gun than I am."

"Reload this," Pike said, swapping guns. He felt the chemist fumbling at the leather loops on the gun belt that held spare rounds. By the time Pike had emptied Timmerman's pistol in a long peal of gun-thunder that held Augustus back, his Colt was ready for action again.

Once more they traded guns. Pike pushed up onto his knees. Through the ringing in his ears, he heard retreating footsteps on the other side of that curtain.

"Let's clear out," Timmerman urged, starting to get up to make a dash for the front door. "If they break some of those bottles, the place will fill up with poison vapors."

"No!" Pike grabbed him and yanked hard enough to spin him around. "They're waiting out there. Come on." He lurched forward, pushing aside the curtain.

The room beyond was empty except for a mussed bed and a large walnut wardrobe standing by the back door. Pike grabbed a handful of Timmerman's nightshirt and pulled him along.

"They circled around to ambush you if you left by the front door." Pike stepped out and took in the garbage-strewn alley. "Do you have some place to hide for a few days?"

"I'm not running from the likes of them!" Timmerman's outrage burned bright.

"I don't have time to argue. A few days, that's all. Hide. I'll take care of them by then."

"What if you don't?" Timmerman's belligerence hinted as to why he bucked the powerful Ledbetter family and ran his own still.

"I'll be dead. You can figure out what to do then. Now git!" Pike shoved the man so hard he stumbled a few paces.

"You plug those animals," the chemist said over his shoulder. "If you don't, I will!"

Pike motioned for the man to run. When Timmerman disappeared into the night, Pike went back into the apothecary. He had unfinished business with the Ledbetters.

CHAPTER 20

It was time to end this. Pike had at least two of the Ledbetters running around like chickens with their heads cut off, firing at anything that moved and some things that didn't. The third one, and any others who owed allegiance to the clan, could be taken care of when Big Belly Ledbetter was fit to be moldering in a grave.

But now it was time for Pike Shannon to finish what they had started.

He stepped into the main room of the apothecary and almost died. Bullets ripped at him from two different directions. Pike ducked and took cover in Timmerman's living quarters again. Big Belly had laid a trap for him, and he had walked into it with his eyes wide open. After warning Timmerman not to go out the front way, foolishly he had tried that very thing. He cursed as he made his way toward the back door.

Again he almost died. Two Ledbetters had opened up on him in front. The third gunman waited for him out back, probably Gus crouching behind the woodpile again. Pike cursed himself for underestimating Big Belly. The man hadn't become the power in Kiowa Springs by being stupid.

Pike had ignored that because he thought the man was nothing but a bully.

It turned out that he was a smart bully, and one who had trapped the only gun in town able to stop him. Pike crouched beside the bed, thinking hard. His best chance lay in escaping out the back, if that was Gus there. Taking on a single wounded gunman was safer than dealing with two.

But maybe that was exactly what Big Belly wanted him to think. Pike's gut tightened. A few seconds before he had thought the Ledbetters had retreated from the front of the store, but actually they had hidden, waiting for him to come to them. He had to be smarter now.

He heard whispers just beyond the back door. More than one of Ledbetter's clan waited for him.

He fired a couple of times out the back, then whirled around and emptied his Colt into the store's main room. Pike dived to the floor as this produced a hail of bullets from both directions. He had duped his enemies into firing at their own kith and kin.

Seeing this part of his plan working, he yanked open the wardrobe door, slipped inside, and pulled the door shut. Clothing hanging from hooks tangled with his arms as he struggled to reload, but he had to get fresh rounds into the revolver. Hiding here wasn't much of a refuge. He reloaded in the dark, then closed his eyes and settled his nerves.

The exchange of lead stopped. He was tempted to make a run for it but held back. Big Belly expected this lull to flush him out.

Pike was glad he waited. Seconds later more furious gunfire sounded. One round tore through the wardrobe door inches from his leg. Exercising supreme control, he didn't make a sound.

Then came unseen boots pounding on the floor and more gunfire. Seconds later Big Belly roared, "Stop shooting, you idiots! You're wasting ammunition firing at each other. If either of you could shoot worth a damn, you'd have filled each other with lead by now."

"Pa, where'd he go?"

Pike recognized Harvey's voice asking the plaintive question. His brother began arguing. Augustus had joined them from his hiding place behind the woodpile.

"Me and the twins never let him get by us. I swear, Pa. It had to be Harve who let him escape."

"Harve was with me," said Big Belly. "Nobody snuck past us. Either of us."

This set off a loud, angry argument between the brothers. Pike opened the wardrobe door a fraction and sneaked a look. He saw Augustus's broad back blocking the doorway into the shop. Big Belly and Harvey were in the main room. That left the pair Gus had called "the twins." Moving fast, he slid from the wardrobe and silently exited into the alley behind the store. Whoever the twins were, they weren't anywhere in sight.

He ducked when gunfire broke out inside the apothecary shop again. Loud cries told him he had moved at exactly the right time.

"Blow that wardrobe to splinters. He has to be hiding in there. Go on, you fools. Shoot!"

Big Belly's command was drowned out by a thunderous sound rivaling Santa Ana attacking the Alamo.

Pike broke into a run. They had trapped him and then foolishly let him escape. He wasn't well enough armed to take on what sounded like an entire army. By the time they finished shooting up Timmerman's store, the walls would look like wormwood and the wardrobe and its contents would be a smoking heap on the floor. He glanced over his shoulder and had to laugh.

Huge billows of white gun smoke rolled out from the

back door. Before Big Belly figured out where he had run, Pike turned down an alley and left the battleground behind. With long strides, he reached Ada Brewster's boardinghouse faster than if he'd been on horseback. He ducked in and closed the door behind him.

"You smell of smoke," Irene said. She sat on the divan, wearing a white muslin nightgown now and obviously waiting for him to return.

"You should lock your front door," he retorted.

"Are they coming for you? What are you going to do?"

"I need to get some things from my saddlebags. Are they out in the shed with my horse?"

He tried to step past her, but she stopped him with a palm pressed against his chest. She looked up, her dark eyes wide.

"In there," she said as she nodded toward one of the rooms opening from the hall. "I put your saddlebags in there. What do you need?"

Before Pike had a chance to answer, an insistent knocking came at the door. He lifted his gun, then returned it to his holster.

"That's got to be Big Belly or one of his boys," he said. "He's likely to be as angry as a stepped-on rattler."

"In," Irene said, pushing him toward the door she had indicated a moment earlier. "Get in there. Pretend to be sleeping."

He started to ask if she could handle Big Belly Ledbetter, then read the fierce determination on her face. Of course she was up to the chore. Pike stepped into the room and closed the door.

For a second he froze. This wasn't a spare room where Ada Brewster put up boarders. This was Irene's bedroom. Since the storm had passed, the moon had come out, and in the silvery light slanting in through the window, he saw the bed with its rumpled sheets, as if she had been tossing around restlessly.

Instinctively, he took a step back toward the door, feeling that he shouldn't be here, when he heard Big Belly roaring at the young woman. Pike knew starting a new fight in the boardinghouse would endanger Irene and her mother, not to mention Fiddler and Dougal. But there was something else he could do.

He kicked off his boots. Irene was likely right about him smelling like gun smoke. He stripped off his shirt and britches and tossed them out the window into a flowerbed. Pike shook his head. They landed in a puddle amid some bedraggled bluebonnets. There was no time to do anything about that. He had one more thing to do. He ripped open his saddlebags and pulled out his spare Colt.

Heavy footfalls outside ended abruptly when the door was kicked open. Big Belly filled the entire doorway, a six-gun in his pudgy hand.

"You," he barked. "Who're you?"

Pike sat up on the bed and used his foot to slide the saddlebags under a chair. He clutched the spare revolver and hoped Big Belly wouldn't see the butt of his usual pistol poking out from the saddlebags.

"Who're you?" Big Belly asked again. "What the hell's going on?"

"Mr. Ledbetter, please! He's a guest!" Irene protested. "You put that gun down this minute!"

"Shut up." Big Belly backhanded her and sent her stumbling down the hallway.

Pike boiled up out of bed, his Colt in his hand.

"You drop that smoke wagon, or I drop you," snapped Big Belly.

"You can't treat Miss Brewster like that, not in her own house."

"So what are you doing in her room dressed in nothing but your long johns? Hand me your gun or you'll die in her bed."

Pike put a sheepish look on his face and handed over the pistol. He tried not to grin when Big Belly did exactly as he expected. The moonshiner held up the weapon and sniffed at the muzzle. Then he opened the gate and spun the cylinder, checking each round. Big Belly looked up, puzzled.

"What's wrong? Other than I haven't oiled it recently. But then I haven't fired it recently, either. Haven't had a call to."

"Sir!" Irene pushed at Big Belly but couldn't budge him. She looked past him into her bedroom. Her eyes gleamed when she saw Pike in his underwear. Then she averted her eyes and tried to push Big Belly out again. It had as much effect as if she pushed against a mountain.

Big Belly took a deep whiff, then another. Then he tossed Pike's gun back to him.

"Who are you?" he demanded.

"Just passing through," Pike said. "You might say that I'm a friend of the family." He glanced toward Irene, who blushed.

"It's good to have friends," Big Belly allowed, sneering. "You staying long in Kiowa Springs?"

"I haven't decided," Pike said. "So far, the town's to my liking."

Irene covered her mouth with her hand and looked away. He imagined she was blushing furiously now. When Big Belly saw her embarrassed reaction, that completed Pike's alibi.

"Why don't you do as the lady suggests and leave? She and I have . . . unfinished business."

"I bet you do," Big Belly said. His nasty laugh would have caused Pike to call him out under different circumstances. As it was, he had swallowed Pike's story hook, line, and sinker.

Pike slid his gun back into the holster and waited until he heard the front door close. He hoisted the window and leaned far out to retrieve his shirt and britches. They dripped mud, so he hung them over the windowsill, but the cold wind made him shiver.

"Here, put them in this," Irene said. She held out a burlap bag. "You won't drip much on the floor. I can wash them later."

"That was quick thinking, letting me hide in here," Pike said, looking around. "Why didn't you pick a different room?"

"This one was closest," she said. Pike heard the lame excuse for what it was.

"You'd already stashed my gear in here."

"Never you mind," she said primly. "What are you going to do to that pig? Something terrible, I hope. He deserves any punishment you can deal out to him."

Pike said nothing. She was getting her dander up again.

"He's gone. No need to get worked up." Pike saw his words fell on deaf ears. Irene continued to conjure up tortures for Ledbetter and his entire family.

"He said he'd tell Harvey you were in my room. He was so foul-mouthed about it." She clenched her teeth and looked as if she would spit. Pike wondered if she had ever done anything so unladylike before.

"Big Belly checked my pistol, and it hadn't been fired." Pike pulled it from his holster and exchanged it for his usual weapon. This one felt more comfortable in his grip, but if the moonshiner had taken one whiff of this barrel, he'd have known Pike was the one in the shoot-out. "Since

Big Belly didn't bat an eye, he might have his suspicions about me but doesn't know we just shot it out or that I have anything to do with Fiddler and Dougal."

"He's suspicious of everyone, Pike. What are you going to do?"

He looked down at his long johns, then at her.

"First thing, I'll climb into my spare shirt and trousers. Then I have a little errand to run."

"Oh!" She took one last look at him and then hurried from the room, apologizing as she went.

He wanted to tell her there was no need to beg his pardon. Then he decided to let it go and just enjoy her reaction. He pulled on his boots, settled his gun at his side, and looked out the window. A pink glow in the eastern sky told him the sun wasn't far below the horizon. It had been a busy night.

Pike slipped through the window, avoided the flowers and mud puddle that had claimed his shirt and pants earlier, then carefully scouted the street in front of the Brewster house for any sign of Big Belly Ledbetter or a spy he might have posted. Seeing no one, Pike walked back into the center of town, looking up for overhead wires. He was pretty sure Kiowa Springs would have a telegraph office. The line would have been put in while the army post was still here. He found what he was looking for and a moment later peered through a dirty window into the office.

Even at this early hour, a telegrapher bent over his key, tapping out a message. Pike didn't know Morse code, but he recognized how adept the telegrapher had to be to send all the dits and dahs so quickly. Another quick look around told him that the coast was clear. He went inside. His nose wrinkled at the pungent sulfuric acid stench from the rows of lead-acid batteries.

This had been his night to endure foul chemical odors, first at the apothecary and now here.

The telegrapher looked at him with bloodshot eyes. “What can I do for you, mister?”

“Have you been working all night?”

“Somebody’s got to handle the traffic. You want to send a ’gram or pick one up? I’ve had a half dozen come in within the past hour.”

“I need to send a telegram.”

The telegrapher shoved a pad of paper toward him and dropped a stub of a pencil beside the paper. Pike hurriedly scribbled his telegram. The clerk squinted and slowly read the words, his lips moving. He looked up.

“Got it. And this is the recipient?”

“Torrance Shannon in Warbonnet County,” Pike said.

It was time to get reinforcements.

CHAPTER 21

"Why won't you tell me?" Irene Brewster glared at Pike across the kitchen table as she asked the question.

"You can't give away what you don't know," he said, finishing the last of the fried egg. He reached for another biscuit, but she pulled the pan away from him. Then she picked up his plate.

"I don't gossip. You went somewhere last night . . . or very early this morning, I should say. What did you do? I listened for gunfire, but the town was quiet after you shot it out with the entire Ledbetter family."

Pike looked longingly at the biscuits, then sighed and gave up. Irene was annoyed and wasn't going to let him have one. He wanted to keep the telegram he'd sent and Torrance being on his way as much a secret as possible. After what Big Belly had done to Fiddler and Dougal, it paid to be cautious.

"What are you smiling about?"

He shook his head, denying her a glimpse into his thoughts. Torrance might lose himself in his books and spend the livelong day adding up columns of numbers, but he was one tough hombre. After all, he was a Shannon.

"I've got a plan, and if I make a single mistake I'll end up dead."

"What are you going to do?" Irene leaned forward. For a moment she left the pan of biscuits unguarded. Pike snared one before she could stop him. She glared. "You're not going to get yourself killed, are you?"

"Would you give me the last biscuit if I said yes?" He polished off the one he had just grabbed.

She shoved the last biscuit toward him.

"Go on, joke about getting killed. At least you'll have a full belly."

"But not one as big as any of the Ledbetter family," he said. "Whatever happens, don't show any surprise."

"Are you dreamin' up another of your wild schemes, Pike?" Dougal came into the room. He walked without a limp, and most of his bandages were gone. A black eye was the worst of his injuries, at least of the ones showing. Pike noticed how his grandpappy sat down slowly as if his leg still bothered him.

"You might say that. I don't want you meddling, either." Pike looked from Dougal to Irene.

His comment set both of them off. They yammered at the same time, trying to drown out each other.

Pike stood up and reached for his hat, which sat on the table not far from his empty plate. "Time to go. Remember, whatever happens, don't get upset over it."

He reached the door as Dougal and Irene put their heads together and started talking in whispers. This wasn't a combination he was comfortable with. Dougal knew him too well, and Irene was likely to rush in where she wasn't needed.

He didn't want her getting hurt. She and her ma had lived in Kiowa Springs long enough to know how dangerous the Ledbetters were, but they had avoided serious problems so far. It was only Fiddler and Dougal peddling their snake oil that had upset the delicate balance in town.

Closing the door behind him shut off their hurried discussion. It did nothing to leave behind the feeling one, or both, of them would do something to endanger themselves. He almost wished he had told Dougal that Torrance was on the way.

Then he put it from his mind. Every ounce of daring he could muster up was required for what he had in mind. And Dougal was right about this being another of his wild, crazy schemes. Even he had to ask himself if this was going to work without him getting shot to pieces by the Ledbetters.

Pike went directly to the Royal Flush. It was too early in the morning for any gamblers to be at the poker table or the faro dealer to lay out her spread. But it wasn't too early for Big Belly Ledbetter and his two sons to be at a back table with a crockery jug on the table, not making any secret of what they were actually doing.

Pike didn't have to take a deep breath to pick up the pungent odor of moonshine as the three men worked as a family to down a half gallon of Ledbetter 'shine.

Big Belly never batted an eye, but both his sons drew their guns and pointed them at Pike as he approached. They cast wary frowns at him. He stopped a few paces from the table.

"That looks like mighty fine drinking," he said.

"The purest spring water in these parts," Big Belly said. "That's how Kiowa Springs got its name."

"Yeah," Harvey cut in, "this is Kiowa Springs water." He smacked his lips. "The best drinkin' water anywhere."

"Shut up, Harvey," Big Belly said. The words came out quickly, from long practice. "What do you want?" His piglike eyes bored into Pike. Pike had been in situations like this before. The slightest flinching on his part could be deadly.

"That's not a very hospitable greeting, not after you rousted me from a sound sleep last night."

"Oh, you were at Miz Brewster's place," Big Belly said. "I didn't recognize you with your clothes on."

"Him?" Harvey half stood and thrust out his gun. His thumb pressed down on the hammer, drawing it back. "He's the one what was in Miss Irene's bed?"

Pike never moved a muscle. For a moment they both were frozen like statues, then Big Belly swatted down Harvey's hand.

"You don't want to call him out, boy."

"I had the drop on him, Pa. And he was molestin' Miss Irene! You told me so yourself."

"If he was, she wasn't complaining about it none. Now sit down and keep your yap shut." Big Belly turned back to Pike, who hadn't moved a muscle. "What do you want?"

"I just got to town, and everyone says you run things. I want a job. If you're the man they say, working for you would mean working for the best there is."

"He wants you to hire him, Pa! That's rich. We don't need any gunslinger," Augustus said. He took a long pull from the jug, belched, and wiped his lips. From the way his eyes roved around, unfocused, he had started drinking before the other two Ledbetters. He was also sporting several bandages from the injuries he'd suffered in previous encounters with Pike—but he didn't know that.

"How good are—" Big Belly stopped short and scowled when Pike drew and cocked his Colt.

"I never saw him move, Pa," Gus said. "He was just standin' there and the gun showed up in his hand. It's like magic."

Pike lowered the hammer and returned the gun to his

holster, moving as if he were dipped in molasses now. That made his draw seem all the more remarkable. It was an old trick, but one that usually worked.

"You're fast," Big Belly allowed. "What makes you think I've got any call to hire a gun-wolf?"

Pike pointed to the jug between them on the table.

"Wherever that came from needs protection from the law."

"That's no concern of yours," Big Belly said. "Marshal Nance spends all his time enforcing other laws. Kiowa Springs might be dry, but not many folks here abide by that."

"A place like this gets rowdy. I can work as a bouncer."

"The Royal Flush ain't that kind of establishment," Harvey said. "Besides, we don't serve liquor here so there's never any trouble."

"My boy's right about that," Big Belly said. "A fistfight or two's all we ever get inside these walls. Drunken rowdies don't exist in Kiowa Springs since the good people voted to turn the town dry."

"Pa, maybe you can hire him to find whoever shot us up last night." Gus reached for the jug again. His pa snatched it away from him.

"You've had enough, boy. Your mouth is runnin' off something fierce." Big Belly smashed his fist down hard on Gus's hand when he reached again for the jug in spite of the warning.

"That hurt," Gus whined. "How am I supposed to handle a gun now with my hand all bruised?"

"You weren't doin' such a good job with your gun last night," Harvey said. "You tell us how to know the difference." He laughed at his younger brother's anger.

"Shut up, both of you." Big Belly looked Pike over from head to toe. "I get the feeling I know you."

"That's not likely. I just rode into town."

"No, I've seen you before," Big Belly insisted. His piglike face screwed into thought, then he brightened as the answer came to him. Pike prepared to throw down on him and his sons. "I remember now. I saw you ride in during the big storm."

Pike imagined he heard the man's brain thinking about everything he had seen the past couple days. He kept quiet. If he gave Big Belly a hint he wasn't what he claimed, there'd be lead flying all over the Royal Flush. Pike was confident he'd come out on top, but having a couple of bullets drill through him was a possible outcome, too.

Big Belly finally said, "I suppose we can use some help. Been some trouble around here lately. You fixing on staying around long?"

"As long as someone's paying me," Pike said. Those words had passed his lips more than once during the ten years he had drifted around the West. More often than not, he had left after blood was spilled and bodies littered streets in nameless towns.

"You've got the look," Big Belly said, nodding in approval. "Harvey, take this gent over to the storeroom. He can sleep there." Big Belly leered. "Unless he has a better bunk somewhere else."

"Room to spread my blanket's all I need. What'll I be doing?"

"Like you said, we've got some special merchandise that needs protecting." Big Belly tapped the jug. From the ringing sound, it was almost empty. "Not from the law, but from other folks who'd like to put us out of business. You and my sons will guard it to keep it safe until it gets moved in a couple days."

"Yeah, the twins freight it to customers all over the

area," Gus piped up. He fell silent when Big Belly reared back to punch him.

Pike saw that Augustus had spoken out of turn and spilled a secret his pa wanted kept close to the chest.

"I don't gossip," he told Big Belly.

"Good. Having a flapping tongue's a sure way to end up out in the potter's field. Now you two, git. I've got work to do." He snatched the jug away as Gus reached for it.

Harvey got to unsteady feet, balanced himself against a chair until he gained some forward motion. He pushed past Pike on his way out the front door.

"Much obliged," Pike said to Big Belly. The man was too busy swilling his own moonshine to answer. Gunning him down would be as easy as pie, but for Pike those days of wanton killing were past. He was now in a position to burrow from within.

He caught up with Harvey Ledbetter halfway down in the street. Pike had hoped to be shown a different warehouse for the moonshine, but Harvey led him to the lot where the burned remnants of Fiddler's wagon stood. All around the square were stores with the windows shot out. This silent testimony to the fierce gunfight that had gone on before the medicine wagon was set ablaze reminded Pike how serious this business was.

Harvey Ledbetter might be a drunken fool, but he was dangerous. How he mooned after Irene Brewster made him a special risk. Big Belly had told his son about finding someone other than Irene in her bed the night before. Pike wondered if Harvey intended to shoot him the instant he turned his back. Something about the way Big Belly had stared at him made him suspect that he had been recognized as someone other than a stranger riding into Kiowa Springs in the rain.

Or, as Irene had said, it might just be that Big Belly

trusted no one who wasn't blood. Even that trust didn't go too far. Pike had seen the looks Big Belly gave his boys. When he called them fools, he wasn't joshing.

"You can throw your gear anywhere," Harvey said. "We got room."

"There'll be even more when you ship all this," Pike said. He rested a hand on a crate filled with jugs.

"The twins take care of that. Your job's to keep it safe 'til then."

"Twins?" Pike tried to sound bored and only idly interested.

"They're my cousins by Aunt Maude and some no account that came through town back in the day. They're not too bright, but Pa trusts them to ship the 'shine to our out-of-town customers. I don't know why. They can't even read or cipher. Either they get cheated or they're cheatin' Pa. I told him but he don't listen."

Pike prowled around the large room. The daylight filtering through cracks in the walls and the broken windows gave him a good look at the small mountain of moonshine stored here. With even a modest price on each jug, Big Belly stood to make hundreds of dollars.

He returned to the spot where Harvey worked off the lid of a crate. Ledbetter fished around and came up with a full jug. He smacked his lips.

"One benefit of workin' guard duty is all the 'shine you can drink." Harvey looked fiercely at Pike. "Not you, just me. Or Gus."

"Might be that the twins sample their cargo, too," Pike said. He had no desire to get soused on the Ledbetter brew. It was hardly nine o'clock in the morning.

"I let Pa know my suspicions. Yeah, they claim high breakage during shipment. Selling some on their own's what they do, mark my words. They're not to be trusted too much, but they're family." Harvey lifted the jug to take a sip.

Pike was already in motion when he yelled, "Get down!"

A shotgun blast blew out what little glass remained in a window facing the vacant lot. The pellets ripped past Harvey Ledbetter's head and tore apart a wooden crate holding jugs of moonshine.

CHAPTER 22

Pike wrapped his arms around Harvey Ledbetter's legs and knocked him hard to the floor. Another shotgun blast tore off part of the window frame.

"Stop kicking!" Pike yelled. "I saved your life."

"The hell you did. You wanted to knock me down and give me a thrashin'." Ledbetter pushed Pike away and sat up.

A new shotgun blast sent a dozen more pellets into the pile of crates. If that failed to get Ledbetter's attention, the rifle slug that followed right behind the shotgun pellets did. Eyes wide in shock, he stared at the hole the rifle bullet made in a crate just inches above his head.

The round had shattered a jug. Moonshine leaked out and puddled on the floor beside him. He stared at it as if he had never seen moonshine before. Harvey scooted away a few feet, then started to stand, oblivious to new torrents of lead and shot tearing apart the wall.

"They're going to put a hole in you if you stand up," Pike warned. He wasn't sure he had done the right thing saving Harvey before, but old instincts die hard. Somehow, in that instant he and Harvey had been partners, and partners never allowed each other to get bushwhacked.

Harvey Ledbetter ignored the warning. With a whoop of

rage, he got to his feet and pulled his gun. He fired through the window. Pike doubted he had a clear target, but venting his wrath was good enough for Ledbetter.

Pike scrambled along the floor and pressed his eye to a knothole in the wall. He moved around until he caught sight of a man with a shotgun. The shooter popped up, fired, and ducked back down. The effort appeared intended not to hit Ledbetter but to lure him out.

And it worked.

Harvey half fell through the window to take a shot. Awkwardly balanced, he was a perfect target for the sniper with the rifle.

Pike fired but not to kill. John Garston's aim was ruined by Pike's slug. He dropped back behind a pile of crates.

"There's two of them!" Harvey Ledbetter sank to the floor and reloaded. "One of 'em's Timmerman."

"The apothecary?"

Pike bit his lip as the question slipped out. As a newcomer to town, he had no reason to know that. For a moment, Harvey ignored the question. Then he turned his head and fixed a hard glare on Pike.

"How'd you know what he does for a living?"

"Keep down or he'll take your head off. Him and the other gunman."

"I can't get a good look at him."

Pike kept his mouth shut this time. To reveal that he recognized Garston would make even a dimwit like Harvey Ledbetter suspicious. If he hadn't needed Big Belly's son to give him information about the Ledbetter family moonshine business, he would have left him to his fate.

"Is there a back way out?" Pike asked. "We can't win a fight with them."

"Are you a yellow belly? Afraid of a shoot-out?"

"I'm almost out of ammo. What about you?"

"I'm good enough a shot to get them both. One bullet each." Ledbetter popped up again and fired at Timmerman.

Pike wouldn't have thought it possible for Ledbetter to fall for the same trick a second time. He did. Timmerman discharged both barrels and hid once more, luring Ledbetter out where Garston had a shot at him. This time Ledbetter screeched and fell back. He sat heavily. His blood mingled with the spilled moonshine.

"Dang it, they got me good. I'm gonna die."

Pike ripped back the man's shirt and pulled down his bib overalls to better examine the wound in Ledbetter's side. He felt nothing but contempt for his unwilling partner.

"It's just a scratch. Looks like you were shot worse than that a couple times." Pike tapped two recent bullet wounds on Ledbetter's torso with his Colt's hot barrel. Ledbetter yelped and pulled away.

"You watch it. If I say I'm sore wounded, then I am."

Pike had inflicted those other wounds. They were even more minor than the one Garston had just inflicted. He vowed to take better aim in the future.

That thought made him rock back and consider how easy it would be to shoot Harvey and then skedaddle. He had the perfect alibi. Unknown gunmen had ambushed him and Harvey. Big Belly might not like it, but the evidence would back up the story.

The only problem was that Pike had moved on from being the type of man capable of shooting another in cold blood.

He found another window and fired a few times to keep Timmerman and Garston pinned down. He had no desire to shoot either of them.

"Pa musta heard the commotion by now," Harvey growled. "Why ain't he comin' to help me?"

"If a couple more of them set an ambush along the street

leading to this lot, they could gun him down if he comes for you." That's what Pike would have done in their shoes. The two men wanted Big Belly Ledbetter dead before he killed them. This was now a full-fledged shooting war over who sold moonshine in Kiowa Springs.

"Pa's too smart to fall for any trap. He's told me countless times how he's escaped gettin' hisself kilt." Harvey rose up and fired a few more times, until his pistol clicked on a spent round. He sank to his knees and leaned against the thin wall.

Pike almost warned him about that. A shotgun carried enough power to blast a big hole in the wall—and Harvey Ledbetter. But giving advice to a man who resented it only wasted his breath. If the other two moonshiners killed Harvey, that would make their own lives easier. All he'd have to do then was remove Big Belly Ledbetter and Gus. From what Harvey said, if the twin cousins heard of the deaths, they'd be in the next county before sundown.

"How many rounds do you have left?" Pike asked. "I've got six, all in the cylinder."

"I dunno. Enough." To show off, Harvey lifted his pistol over the windowsill and fired a few times.

Pike winced when the hammer landed again on a spent cartridge. Eventually their attackers would figure out how little ammo they had and rush them.

He wasn't sure what he'd do if that happened. Irene had worked hard to save John Garston, both nursing him herself and showing Ruth how to bandage him when she was gone. And he had seen what the Ledbetter clan did to Timmerman's store. If he had to pick sides, he'd join the two outside.

However, he had no reason to believe they'd see him as an ally. For all they knew, he was actually working with the Ledbetters. If he tried to surrender, they were as likely to cut him down as they were to accept his word that he bore them no ill. Even if he presented them with Harvey as a prisoner—or corpse—they had no reason to believe he wasn't trying to save his own hide.

"They're gonna rush us," Harvey said. "They want all our moonshine. Well, they ain't gettin' it!"

Pike exclaimed, "What the hell!" when Ledbetter pulled a jug from a nearby crate and popped out the cork.

"What are you doing? Put that down!" Pike stood and almost got his head blown off. Timmerman had opened up again with the shotgun.

Driven back, Pike watched in horror as Harvey ripped off a strip of cloth from his shirt and stuffed it down into the jug like a wick. He fumbled around and found a match.

Even from across the storeroom, Pike smelled the pungent moonshine. The alcohol content was more than enough to get a man drunk with a few sips. It was also volatile enough to set the entire storeroom ablaze.

"Take this, you back shooters!" Harvey lit the cloth fuse, reared back, and prepared to throw the makeshift bomb at Timmerman.

Garston got in the first shot. Harvey yelped more in surprise than pain as the rifle bullet ripped away a chunk of his arm. He dropped his firebomb. The jug shattered and spewed the explosive moonshine everywhere. Then the flame found a mother lode. Bright blue flames leaped upward and engulfed the crate from which Harvey had taken the jug.

Pike acted rather than thought. Again he ran forward. This time his arms circled Ledbetter's rotund body. With a mighty effort, he lifted, twisted, and heaved. Ledbetter crashed through the window and fell outside.

Both Timmerman and Garston charged forward, brandishing the shotgun and rifle. They would have ended

Harvey's life then and there if the blast from exploding moonshine hadn't ripped away the entire wall. Flaming splinters sailed like fire arrows. As Pike dived through the window after Ledbetter, he saw one of the blazing splinters catch Timmerman in the cheek, making him yell and jump. Garston staggered off to the side. Most of the blast's force had missed him, but he was plenty shaken up, anyway.

Pike landed on top of Harvey Ledbetter. It felt like jumping onto a feather mattress, only he bounced up and away as another explosion in the storeroom sent more debris flying.

"Run, John. Run!" Timmerman shouted. "The whole danged place is gonna blow up!"

"Good riddance," Garston called back to Timmerman as he took off, scrambling for safety.

Pike was aware of the two men running hell-bent for leather to get away. The heat from the fire grew at his back. Any second now, more of the jugs would explode into flame. He crawled over to Harvey Ledbetter and shook him hard.

"Get up. I can't carry you. You're too fat. *Get up!*"

Pike's warning caused Ledbetter to stir. He looked around and saw the wall of flames devouring the warehouse. He began scooting away. This gave Pike a chance to grab a double handful of the man's bib overall and heave. Together they got to what remained of Fiddler's burned-out medicine wagon.

The next explosion knocked them flat just as they reached the wagon. Pike wasn't too proud to use Ledbetter as a shield against the raging heat.

"Run for it." He yanked again and got Harvey on his feet and moving. Together they stumbled to the far side of the vacant lot. Behind them flames surged thirty feet into the air as more of the flammable moonshine ignited.

"That's gonna burn the whole town to the ground," Ledbetter gasped.

"I don't want to go up in smoke with it," Pike said. He stopped tugging on Ledbetter. Let him roast if he was so intrigued by watching the fire like an arsonist admiring his own handiwork.

He reached the main street at a dead run. A crack of thunder made him look up at heavy storm clouds rolling in. A big fat cold raindrop hit him smack dab in the eye. He flinched and wiped it away. The rain began to come down in heavy sheets. Pike looked over his shoulder at the fire fed by moonshine. The rain hammered the flames into tiny curlicues of steam. Nature had put out a fire that threatened the entire town.

Dumb luck or divine providence, he would take it either way.

He raised his arms and let the heavy rain wash him clean. By the time he was drenched and free of smoldering embers trying to burn his flesh, Harvey Ledbetter had staggered up, made so unsteady by the violent ordeal that he might as well have been blind drunk.

"Pa's gonna be fierce over this," Ledbetter said. "All our 'shine's gone. Gone! And it's because of . . . them." He squinted at Pike. His eyes vanished into pits of gristle and his chin quivered. Fear and desperation strained his voice as he went on, "Ain't that so? They set fire to the storeroom before we got there. Right?"

"We tried to put out the fire, but it was too late," Pike said. The lie suited him as much as it did Harvey. Trying to save a warehouse filled with moonshine was a good way to win Big Belly's confidence. That his own son was responsible for the destruction wouldn't matter if he decided Pike was at fault. This way he and Harvey alibied each other.

"Glad you see it like I do—like it happened." Harvey Ledbetter pushed past Pike and headed for the Royal Flush.

Pike hoped Timmerman and Garston turned tail and left town. Now that the entire stock of moonshine was destroyed, nowhere in Kiowa Springs would be safe by the time Big Belly Ledbetter began hunting them.

Pike had a temporary ally in Harvey Ledbetter. How could he use the man against his pa and brother?

CHAPTER 23

Big Belly Ledbetter sat like he'd been turned to stone. He was too stunned to feel anything. Anger ought to have filled him. Hatred. The need to kill someone. The perfect target for all that stood in front of him, dripping rainwater all over the Royal Flush's floor.

"All?" Big Belly choked out. "Every last forsaken drop of my moonshine got blown up?"

"Yeah, Pa. That's what happened. They set fire to the place 'fore I got there. There wasn't nary a thing I could do, not me or the owlhoot you sent along with me to protect the place."

"Who? Who torched my moonshine?" Big Belly Ledbetter swallowed hard. The knot in his throat tightened and his mouth turned dryer than the West Texas desert. He grabbed the jug on the table and drained the few drops left.

He lowered the jug and stared at it in dismay. This was going to be the last 'shine passing his lips until he made more. With care he put the jug back onto the table. The small click it made as it touched the table was the only sound inside the casino.

"The fellows what tried to ambush me are responsible," Harvey rattled on. "Timmerman and the grain store owner,

Garston, are in cahoots." When Big Belly failed to say a word, Harvey blurted out what he thought was the ultimate crime. "See? They shot me. One had a shotgun and the other a rifle and they shot me!"

He turned his bare shoulder toward his pa for closer investigation. Big Belly never even glanced at the wound. He fixed his gaze squarely on his son's eyes. Harvey averted his gaze. He might have been butter left in the hot summer sun the way he melted.

"What was the hired gun I sent with you doing when all this was happening?" Big Belly tried to remember the man's name. He wasn't sure he'd ever heard it.

"He saved me, Pa. I was on fire and he saved me. He—"

"Why'd he bother, you worthless pile of cow flop?" The dam inside him burst. He swept the crockery jug from the table and sent it flying across the room to smash into the roulette wheel. Pieces of the gambling device and ceramic crockery flew everywhere. "You worthless, cowardly, skunk! You are a disgrace to the Ledbetter name!" He heaved himself out of the chair. With a wild grab, he reached his son and clamped his huge hands around Harvey's throat.

Harvey gagged and tried to escape. His pa was too strong. When Big Belly leaned forward, he drove his son to the floor. The added leverage made strangling him easier. Harvey turned purple, his eyes bulged, and his tongue poked out.

From across the room someone cleared his throat.

Big Belly looked up. His hired gunman stood just inside the double doors, watching and doing nothing. There wasn't a hint of emotion on his face.

Big Belly's wrath shifted from his son to an outsider. "You let this happen. You're responsible for my moonshine going up in flames."

"I was following Harvey's orders."

Big Belly released Harvey. The boy collapsed to the floor, gasping for air.

"He saved me, Pa. Really. You wouldn't a' wanted me to die, would you?" Harvey rasped out the question.

Big Belly wanted to spit on him to show his contempt, but his mouth was still dry. If it got his moonshine back, he'd murder both his sons and the stranger. But until he had a full wagon loaded with more 'shine, he needed Harvey and Gus. And the stranger.

"Get over here," Big Belly snapped. He sank back into his chair and watched the stranger approach. The way he moved left no doubt that he was a gun-wolf. He almost glided across the floor, each step slow and precise. His hand rested on the slick, hard leather holster slung low on his right hip. Big Belly watched a human spring all coiled up and ready to explode at any instant. There'd be a gun in his hand and leaden death would fill the gambling den at any second.

Big Belly had never hated anyone more in his life.

"Is what he said true?"

The stranger nodded slowly. His cold eyes showed no hint of remorse. There was something more there, though, that made Big Belly hesitate. This was a killer, but he was a killer who knew something. A secret. And he wasn't going to spill it because of money or threats. What was the lever necessary to pry it from him? Irene Brewster?

"Was it Timmerman and Garston?" Big Belly wondered at the flicker of emotion the stranger showed when he named the other two moonshiners in Kiowa Springs.

"If Harvey says that's who they were, then that's them. I wouldn't know their names."

"They're not getting by with this. I want them dead. Go kill them."

"Get somebody else for your dirty work," the man said. "I'm not that kind of hired hand."

Big Belly's lips thinned to a razor slash. He wasn't used to anyone telling him they wouldn't obey his orders. Both his sons jumped when he called "frog." Harvey was trained good enough that he asked "how high?" on the way up.

"You've killed men, using that gun hanging at your hip. I can tell by the way you carry yourself."

Big Belly tried to puzzle out what looked wrong about the gun. He had examined it last night to see if the stranger had fired it. All he'd smelled then was gun oil. If he checked that pistol now, he'd sniff out gunpowder. That made sense if he had shot it out with Timmerman and Garston.

But the gun looked different somehow, as if the man had switched irons.

"I have shot down my share, but you're asking me to murder these two in cold blood. That's not what I do. If I'm going to kill a man, I do it facing him in a fair fight."

Big Belly almost called him a liar. The coldness with which the man spoke warned him to tread carefully.

"What *will* you do, since I'm paying you?"

"Not murder," he said in a measured tone. "But most everything else is on the table."

"Even though Timmerman and Garston tried to fill you full of lead? Why won't you gun them down? They shot Harve. They were shooting at you, too, weren't they?"

"Mostly him. And I *did* take some shots at them. Then the building blew up."

"That's the way it happened, Pa. That's the Gospel truth!" Harvey rubbed his neck and looked like a cornered rat.

"Shut up," Big Belly said to his son. Whatever had gone on, both men were lying to his face. He expected that from Harvey. Nobody else got away with it unless they were blood.

"If you want me to do a job, tell me. Otherwise, I'm moving on."

"Burn down their stills. Both of them. Garston's and Timmerman's. Destroy every last drop they have stored, no matter where it is. I want them hurting. I want them out of the moonshine business." Big Belly waited for the man's response.

"Give me a map showing where to find their equipment. I'll destroy the stills for you as quick as I can ride to them."

"Gus, make the man a map. You know where those bottom feeders built their stills."

"Sure, Pa," Augustus said from the table where he'd been sitting during the confrontation, obviously trying not to draw any attention from the enraged Big Belly. Now, trying to be helpful, he added, "You want me to go along with him to make sure he finds 'em?"

"Shut up and make the map. I've got something else for you and your brother to do."

Out of habit, he reached for the jug on the table, then remembered it wasn't there anymore. His eyes darted across the room to the fragments on the floor. In spite of that display of rage, he hadn't gotten all the hate out of his system.

By the time the stranger returned to Kiowa Springs after putting the other moonshiners out of business, he'd have figured it all out, even if he had to cut off Harvey's ears to discover the truth.

Whatever that was, the stranger wasn't going to ride out of town again. Ever.

CHAPTER 24

"Which way is north?" Pike Shannon turned the map Augustus Ledbetter had given him around and around. He wasn't able to decide where the bottom of the map was, much less directions.

"You're not much of a scout, are you?" Gus Ledbetter smirked. He jerked the scrap of paper from Pike and spun it around. "Like that. The top is north. That way." He pointed out of town along the main road.

"If you knew where the other stills are, why haven't you done something about them yourself? Your old man doesn't talk like the kind of man who'd put up with competition."

"We stole from both Timmerman and Garston. 'Bout half our sales came from their stills this past month. Since moonshining's illegal, they couldn't go to Marshal Nance."

"From what Harvey told me, your pa's got the law all tied up in a nice bow."

"He's scared of us; that's our hold over him. If the marshal ever thought he could get away with tossin' any of us in jail, he'd do it." Gus spat. "The town's likely to hang us if we went to trial. That's not gonna happen as long as they're scared of Pa."

"There's something else about as important," Pike said.

"As long as you supply the moonshine, the good citizens of Kiowa Springs look the other way. At least the ones who didn't vote to go dry."

"Something like that. Now stop flappin' your gums and get to work. Pa's not payin' you to stand around."

Pike looked around town. A dozen people peered out of stores, and some stood around along the main street. All were taking in the sight of Big Belly Ledbetter's new hired gun and drawing conclusions about what he was going to do.

Pike hadn't explained his plan to Irene Brewster or her mother for a reason. They'd soon hear gossip about him throwing in with the iron-fisted tyrant who ran the town. Their reactions wouldn't be feigned. He hoped they were both stunned and outraged. That would help him convince Big Belly that he was loyal.

His best hope of the women knowing that wasn't true came from Dougal. He'd explain about how his grandson came up with harebrained schemes all the time—and acted on them. But that would come after they had shown their outrage to others in town.

Pike considered throwing in with the Ledbetter family as a success so far. He might not be privy to Big Belly's plans, but he had learned plenty about how the man thought. Neither of his sons had the brains to keep their moonshine operation running without Big Belly telling them every little thing to do. Harvey was as much as on his side, whispering good things about him into his pa's ear because they shared a secret. Even being kin wouldn't stop Big Belly from killing Harvey for burning up all the moonshine awaiting delivery by the twins.

More than that, he now had a map to the Ledbetters' competitors. He needed allies. Who better than the town's chemist and the grain store owner since they were already Big Belly's rivals?

"You didn't put distances on the map," Pike said.

"So?"

"So do I ride all day or just a few minutes to find their stills?"

"Figure it out yourself. You think you're so smart." Gus spat. The gob landed between the toes of Pike's boots. Big Belly's younger son smirked some more and pushed past Pike to return to the Royal Flush.

Pike drummed his fingers on the side of his holster. Harvey might be an unwilling ally, but Gus would never be. There was too much of his pa in him. Pike worked it all out and filed it away in his head. Every detail might be useful sooner or later in bringing down the Ledbetter clan.

He went around the casino and mounted his dun. From the scant information on the map, he guessed as to distances. Neither of the other moonshiners would set up their stills too far outside of town. They had businesses to run. Unless they had help, dividing their time between selling prescriptions and seed grain and producing moonshine would keep them busy. Time spent riding back and forth was wasted, both in the legal and illegal businesses.

As he passed the last house in Kiowa Springs going north, Pike looked back over his shoulder and saw somebody on horseback duck behind some trees. He wasn't able to identify whoever trailed him. Either of the Ledbetter boys was his guess. Big Belly wanted to be sure he performed the job he'd assigned.

"Loyalty," Pike whispered. "That's what he wants to know. Am I going to do what he tells me?"

Big Belly Ledbetter trusted no one. There wasn't any reason for him to believe a drifter looking to earn a few dollars would stand fast if shooting started. Saving Harvey was hardly enough to convince him. For all Pike knew, the elder Ledbetter knew his son had been responsible for setting fire to the storeroom with all their moonshine. Harvey simply wasn't a good liar.

Pike worried that he wasn't much better. Big Belly Ledbetter was a cunning man.

He took out the map, oriented himself, and found a landmark. He cut away from the road and rode directly for a stand of trees. As he approached the trees, he found wagon wheel ruts in the ground. The tracks were a week or more old from the look of the weeds already growing along the bottoms of the ruts. The only reason anyone had for driving off the road into the forest was to carry in raw materials and to take out finished moonshine.

When he had a few trees to provide protection from prying eyes, he drew rein and waited. Augustus Ledbetter came up along the main road and stopped, staring after Pike.

He had been right that Big Belly didn't trust him to carry out his orders. Or was there more to it? When Gus turned around and trotted back toward Kiowa Springs, Pike got an inkling of Big Belly's plans. He worked his way deeper into the woods and came out into a clearing less than half a mile from the road.

The still stood cold, abandoned.

Pike circled the lean-to holding the still. The woodpile providing fuel for the cooking fire was depleted. Empty burlap grain sacks strewn about showed signs of weathering. Everything about the still declared this to be an old operation.

He dismounted and poked around under the crude plank roofing. The equipment had been partially dismantled. Kicking at a pile of debris uncovered a large roll of copper tubing. He picked it up and slung it over his shoulder.

He had to laugh at himself. Old habits die hard. He'd salvaged the tubing because it was usable in a bigger still—which he wasn't running any longer.

"Maybe Fiddler will be able to use it," he said. Pike secured it to his saddle and returned to the lean-to. Climbing onto the roof gave him a better view of the area.

He sucked in his breath when he saw the movement of a rider between him and the main road. Pike bided his time, pretending to occupy himself with a loose board at the edge of the roof. His patience paid off. The rider revealed himself.

Gus had trailed him out here, but Harvey spied on him now. Or was it Harvey? The rider's face was hidden in shadow. Other details made him think maybe this really wasn't a Ledbetter. Pike doubted Harvey had changed his clothes just to ride out of town. The man astride a small paint horse wore a different shirt.

Who was spying on him? And should it worry him that Big Belly probably didn't trust Gus and sent a second man out?

He decided the unknown rider presented a danger, but not right now. Let him report what was about to happen to Big Belly.

Pike heaved and tore the plank free. He jumped to the ground and used the board to scrape away some of the dirt under the lean-to. The small firepit was near the open space in front. It took a minute to get a fire started there. The fire was trapped in the dirt depression, but Pike added what remained from the woodpile and then kicked dried debris into the fire. It flared. By keeping it contained, he intensified the heat and caused flames to leap straight up to the lean-to's roof.

He backed out and tossed the board he'd used as a shovel into the fire. The flames danced even higher, and after a minute or so, the roof began to smolder. Pike waited until it was actually burning before turning to his horse. As he mounted, he saw the unknown rider fade back into the woods.

One still down, another to go, but Harvey would be content that his pa's hired gunman was carrying out his orders, if that even was Big Belly's boy lurking in the trees.

Pike had other ideas.

Following the map, he rode deeper into the woods and then cut off down a game trail. Another still popped up unexpectedly. Unlike the other, this one had been hidden with some care. The shed had been camouflaged in brush and a considerable time had been spent to erase wagon tracks. A tiny curl of smoke came from a chimney, but nobody stirred.

Pike felt eyes on him. He had ridden through the forest with one eye on his back trail. There wasn't any way Harvey Ledbetter had gotten around him. That meant only one thing.

"I'm on your side," Pike called, directing the words toward the trees and undergrowth around the still. "Come on out and let's talk." He waited a full minute before bushes rustled in both directions.

The town apothecary, Timmerman, emerged from hiding on the right. He clutched his shotgun with grim determination.

"You were the one who saved Harvey Ledbetter," Timmerman accused. "What are you doing here?"

"Why don't we all talk it over?" Pike looked back to the bushes on his left. "Is that you in there, Garston?"

He wasn't surprised to see the grain and feed store owner show himself. He had his rifle pointed in Pike's general direction. Pike took that to mean both men were willing to discuss matters, at least for a few minutes before getting down to ventilating him. That was the best he could expect.

"We've not got anything to say to you." Timmerman lifted the shotgun to his shoulder.

"The two of you have thrown in together to fight Ledbetter. You're not each other's enemy. That's good. The only way to ever get rid of him, though, is if you get more people on your side."

"You're working for him," Timmerman snapped. "You're lying if you say you want to see him dangling from a noose."

"He beat up a good friend of mine," Pike said, "and he didn't stop there. Dougal Shannon is my grandpa. My name's Pike Shannon."

"That's why Irene Brewster took up with him," Garston said to the other moonshiner. "I wondered why she was consorting with the enemy."

"She patched you up when you needed it. I was there in Ruth's room when she did."

"I don't remember much about that," Garston admitted, "but you were with Harvey Ledbetter when their entire supply of 'shine caught fire." Garston scowled. "What happened? We didn't have anything to do with that. Wish we had, though. It was a real purty sight, all that Ledbetter moonshine going up in bright blue flames."

"*I* didn't want to see it burn," Timmerman said. "There was no reason for you to want it to go up like that, either, John. We wanted to steal back some of what Big Belly took from us."

"You've got a point," Garston said. "It was still a pretty sight, all that flame." He lowered his rifle and asked again, "Why'd the whole shebang catch fire?"

"Harvey got careless."

Pike saw Timmerman relax and point his shotgun away as he chuckled. "He set fire to his own pappy's liquor?"

Garston started laughing so hard he bent double. Then he winced and laid the rifle aside to hold his ribs. “I’m still hurting from getting a bone or two broken,” he said. “But the notion that Harvey set fire to all that moonshine is worth a laugh or two. That’s rich!”

Timmerman advanced. He lifted his shotgun in Pike’s direction again, but the determination to fire faded away. Pike read it in the man’s face.

“What are you doing out here?”

“I joined up with Ledbetter— Hold your horses!” Pike held out his palms to halt Timmerman from shot-gunning him. “I had to find out the best way of running him out of town.”

“On a rail,” said Garston. He came over and motioned to his partner. “You really working against Ledbetter?”

“And his entire family,” Pike said forcefully. “Nobody beats up two old men and gets away with it. Not when one’s a friend and the other’s got Shannon blood pumping in his veins.”

“What are you thinking about doing to get even?”

“Gus trailed me until I cut across country to go to another still.”

“That was mine,” Timmerman said. “I shut it down to come help John when he got beat up.”

“You weren’t turning out that much,” Garston said. He looked past Pike. “You took his spare supply of copper tubing.”

“I’ve got plans for it,” Pike said. “But Gus turned around at the road. Another rider watched me, so I went ahead and burned down the still. At least I’m pretty sure it was someone else.”

“Sorry to see it go,” Timmerman said. “If it gets Big Belly off our backs, though, it’s worth the loss.”

“You say you think someone else other than Harvey was

spying on you?" Garston frowned. "Who might that be? We've been here all day trying to get the still up to capacity."

"I don't know who it was. What do those twins they're always talking about look like?"

Both men shook their heads.

"They're miles off. Big Belly uses them to deliver his booze. Neither of them has sense enough to come in out of the rain. I saw 'em leave Kiowa Springs before we came out to fire up this still." Garston pointed to the thin curl of rising smoke. "Big Belly's got a hideout somewhere east of town. I've heard of rumors about how he has an army there waiting to do his bidding, but it's likely nothing more than lies to keep everyone in town cowed."

Pike knew Ledbetter had plenty of money to hire gunmen. That was how he'd come to ride for the self-styled tyrant of Kiowa Springs.

"You should make tracks. Clear out." Pike wanted them to get out from underfoot. "You'll be the first men Big Belly comes after."

"It's our home!" Garston looked the more indignant of the two. Pike guessed it was because of Ruth. Abandoning her wasn't in the cards.

"Then lay low until I take care of him. It won't be much longer."

"We can hide out here, John," Timmerman said. "We can get another gallon or two of squeezings for our customers."

"That's good. Ruth liked the last batch and—"

"No," Pike said forcefully. "Big Belly knows you've got a still here. Gus drew me a map with this and the other still on it."

"We wouldn't be able to hold off the entire clan if they snuck up on us," Timmerman said. "This is your still, John. What do you want to do? I'll stand with you, whatever you decide."

They argued and finally Garston turned to Pike, shoulders slumped. "We'll run like scalded dogs, if that's what it takes. We'd as soon throw in with everyone else to run that varmint out." He looked sad as he added, "There's not a whole lot of townspeople willing to stand up to him. Not yet."

"You're the kind of man who can whip them into shape," Timmerman said, looking at Pike as if he expected argument.

Pike didn't relish the role of being at the front of a mob roaring for Ledbetter's blood, but if no one else wanted the position, he'd take it. For Fiddler. For Dougal.

"Dismantle your still and hide the kettle, tubing, and anything else that'd be expensive to replace. When all this blows over, you can fire up the still again."

Even as he convinced the two men of the wisdom of taking a small vacation, he knew Irene Brewster wouldn't approve of his advice. She wanted all liquor poured out and every still destroyed. He smiled just a little. She and Sophie had a lot in common when it came to moonshine.

"We'll get to it. What are you fixing to do, Mr. Shannon?" Garston walked to the wood shack and leaned against it. He needed more rest to recuperate from being slammed into the roulette wheel.

Pike started to suggest the two and Ruth make themselves scarce. Then he realized the girl's disappearance, along with Big Belly's two competitors, would stir up the Ledbetters in Kiowa Springs. Better that she kept up her work at the Royal Flush and that Garston didn't alert her. The less she knew, the less she spilled to her employer, either accidentally or through coercion.

"I've got another still to take care of," Pike said.

"But we're the only others still in business," Garston said.

"You're two of three," Pike assured him. He mounted and rode into the woods, taking care to check his back trail.

The mysterious rider at Timmerman's still was nowhere to be seen. Pike doubled around occasionally and then found a stream to slosh along for a half mile or more. Nobody tracked when the trail was drowned in so much running water.

He reached the main road, got his bearings, and cut across a pasture for the patch of trees where Ledbetter's still produced all the moonshine in Kiowa Springs now. Pike approached warily, eyes peeled for any movement. A tiny smoke spiral rose, showing the fire that kept the boiler hot. But with nobody tending the process, the still wasn't producing.

Pike took the better part of a half hour to ride closer, watching for the rider who had spied on him earlier. Nobody appeared. If anything, Pike thought he was being too cautious. It was late afternoon now and another storm was building. At this time of year, they were common in Texas. He listened for thunder. Nothing yet, but the air had a heavy, ominous feel to it.

He rode close to the shed holding Ledbetter's still, climbed up onto the saddle, then jumped to the roof. Pike carried the coil of copper tubing with him. Part of the roof threatened to collapse under his weight. Walking carefully, he avoided the weak spots and went to the stovepipe puffing out smoke.

Working carefully, he unwound the coil of copper tubing until it stretched ten feet straight as an arrow. He pried loose enough flashing to let him look down into the single room below. He fed half the tubing through the hole, then took a single turn around the chimney. The rest of the copper tubing stretched straight up above the roof. A final check assured him it was sturdy enough for what he had in mind.

He dropped to the ground and went into the shed. He took a couple turns of tubing around the still itself. Pike stepped back, fists on his hips, and admired his handiwork.

"Time to get on back to town," he decided. As he mounted he took another careful look around. As far as he saw, he was as alone as a whore's charitable thought. The deep ruts in the grass gave him all the path he needed to find the road to Kiowa Springs.

Pike reached town just before sundown. He had done all he could. The hard part came now. He had to wait. Until then he'd look in on Dougal and Fiddler and see what dinner Mrs. Brewster had whipped up.

Irene Brewster being there, too, only added to the fiesta.

CHAPTER 25

"I just got a telegram from the twins," Augustus Ledbetter said. He held up the flimsy paper and squinted at it.

Big Belly Ledbetter snatched it from his fingers. "You coulda told me what it says," he grumbled. He read what they'd sent, crumpled the sheet, and threw it away. It sailed a few feet and flopped to the floor. It wasn't as satisfactory as throwing a shot glass or a jug against the wall, but it would have to do.

"A jug," Big Belly said, his anger mounting. He felt his face burning red. "A jug! They don't want a single jug. They want an entire shipment. We got obligations. You hear that?"

Gus's head bobbed up and down like it was on a spring.

"You know what they want? They want two wagonloads of moonshine. Two! How many do we have?"

"We don't have any, Pa. It all got burned up."

"That's the first thing you've said that's true. We don't have nary a drop left because it all got sent up in flames."

Gus looked confused. "How're we gonna send that much? We need a case or two for the Royal Flush. The weekend's comin' up. The cowboys work up a powerful thirst during the week."

"We don't have any, you fool. Not any!" Big Belly raged.

He stormed around the gambling den, kicking chairs and overturning tables. When he got to the roulette table, he put his fingers under the edge and started to heave. He would have sent it flying into the back wall.

However, looking at the battered gambling device caused him to cool down a mite. He'd paid plenty for the roulette wheel from a New Orleans company, and it was already damaged from his prior temper tantrum.

"What are we gonna do?"

"I swear your ma switched my legitimate son for a dimwit at birth. What do you think I should do?" Big Belly sank into a chair and stared off into space. His mind sorted through all sorts of schemes without hitting on any that he thought might work.

"We could steal more from Timmerman and Garston," Gus suggested.

"I just sent that new fellow out to burn their stills to the ground." Big Belly hoped that the hired gun had doubled-crossed him and those stills were intact. Rather than getting rid of the competition, he needed their moonshine now.

"I saw him headin' for Timmerman's," Gus said. "He's real good at followin' a map."

"Too good," Big Belly said. "By now he's on his way back to town. Unlike you and that dunderhead brother of yours, he can follow orders." Big Belly drummed his fingers on the table. "He's just a mite too good at doing what he's told."

He wondered if the man shared Irene Brewster's hatred for 'shine. If so, it wouldn't be long before he got rid of the last still anywhere around Kiowa Springs just when Big Belly needed one running at full capacity.

"We can work all night at our still," Gus said. "It'll take a spell to get two wagonloads, plus what we need here for the Royal Flush, but we won't never have none unless we get started."

For once, the boy had said something that made sense. "Harve took a load of grain out a day or two back," Big Belly said. "Is everything else ready to fire up the still?"

"I reckon it is, Pa. I can ask Harvey, but I don't know where he is."

"Find him. Me and him'll get a new batch going as quick as we can get there. You stay here and see that everything runs smoothly in the Royal Flush."

"I can do that, Pa. You can count on me." Gus beamed at the trust placed in him. Big Belly wanted to smash him in the mouth to let him know how much trust he actually had in his youngest.

"The first couple gallons will come here," Big Belly went on. "Then I'll do what I can to get enough to keep the twins' customers from finding other moonshiners."

"They can't do that," Gus said. "We can convince them to buy our 'shine, like we did before."

"We had a crate or two to sell them right away. There's a powerful lot of countryside north of here. Every ranch, every town, everywhere there are more than a handful of people, there's somebody who thinks he can distill moonshine. We'll lose most of our customers because of this, but we'll get them back when our supply is flowing again."

"Sure thing, Pa. Let me go fetch Harvey." Gus Ledbetter hurried from the casino, leaving his pa to fume over the lack of booze.

"I've got to do it myself. There's no way to trust those two sons of mine." Big Belly heaved up out of the chair and started toward the entrance, but he stopped just inside the doors when a short man with a huge handlebar mustache pushed aside the batwings and bustled into the gambling den.

The newcomer wore a battered tin star on his vest. His rheumy eyes darted around, and he nervously ran his hand up and down his holster.

"Did you see him, Marshal?" Big Belly demanded.

"Of course I did, Mr. Ledbetter. You told me what to do, and I did it. I watched him burn that still to the ground. I don't know what he did inside the lean-to, not exactly, but he dug a pit, maybe, then lit a fire in it. The whole shebang went up in smoke a couple minutes later."

"Arrest him for destruction of private property when he gets back to town."

Marshal Nance looked frightened.

"He's got the look of an expert gun handler, Mr. Ledbetter. Tangling with him could be dangerous."

"That's why you're paid so well, Nance," snapped Big Belly. "I want him locked up or run out of town. Don't make it look like I had anything to do with it. Your choice on how to do it."

"What if he resists?"

"Gun him down. Do I have to tell you everything? It's too much of a coincidence that he rode into town when he did."

"After you whupped up on the pair o' snake oil salesmen?"

"I tried to get Dobbs to tell me if either of them sent a telegram. He refused. I'm thinking it might be time to find a new telegrapher who's not so intent on following Western Union rules."

"He was probably just too drunk to remember," Nance said. "I've had more than one complaint about Dobbs being too drunk to send a telegram, but that's no concern of mine. It's up to the telegraph company to take care of any soused employee. It doesn't seem like they're much interested in firing him, if I can say so."

"Might be he thinks he's got a secure job," Big Belly said. "I applied some persuasion, and he still wasn't telling me. But the stranger showed up less than a week after the two in the medicine wagon rolled into my town. That's about how long it'd take someone from down south to get here."

"Your town?" Marshal Nance sucked in his breath, puffed out his chest to better show off the badge, then deflated under Big Belly's withering glare.

"Get rid of him." Big Belly bumped the marshal out of the way with his protruding gut and went outside.

A small smile came to his lips as Harvey drove up in their buggy just then. Gus had found him and passed along their pa's orders, and finally, one of Big Belly's boys thought ahead. Harvey knew better than to expect his father to ride a saddle horse out to their still.

Besides the indignity of actually sitting astride a horse, the heavy clouds building up threatened yet another rainstorm. The canvas top over the buggy seat would keep him from getting too wet if the sky decided to open up.

He climbed in, almost toppling the buggy over. Harvey shifted his own considerable weight to compensate. The springs just about flattened out from the weight.

"Don't just sit here. Let's get to work." Big Belly peered out from under the canopy. "It's not going to rain for an hour or two."

"That's about how long it'll take to get to the shack. Its roof leaks, Pa. You all right with that?"

"Of course I'm not. But I have to be out in weather like this because neither you nor Gus can fix the mash and get the process started."

"We've done all right on our own," Harvey said.

"Don't make me tell you what your last batch tasted like. Now let's go."

Big Belly rocked back as Harvey snapped the reins and got the horse pulling its heavy load. As they drove along the road out of town, Big Belly kept a sharp eye out for any trouble brewing. He didn't have much confidence in Nance being able to deal with the hired gun. He might have to take care of the stranger himself when he got back. More than once he had shown how quick with a six-shooter he was. If he left Harvey at the still, once he got things going, it could run all night long.

Numbers and dollars rolled through Big Belly's head as he calculated how long it would take to get a supply laid in for the Royal Flush and then send a few gallons north for the twins to sell. Losing hard-won customers wasn't in the cards.

Not for Big Belly Ledbetter.

"Hang on, Pa. We're in for some rough terrain."

Even with the warning, he was almost thrown out of the buggy when they left the road and started across a grassy patch. The previous rains had caused the ground to turn soft. The wheels sunk deeper and deeper under all the weight the buggy carried.

"Get out," Big Belly ordered. "I'll drive the rest of the way to the still."

"But, Pa, it's more than a mile off. I don't want to walk that far!"

"I'll have everything set up by the time you get there."

Reluctantly, Harvey climbed out of the buggy. Big Belly snapped the reins and urged the horse to a faster gait. The buggy wheels still sank but not as deeply. Removing Harvey's weight sped up the trip. When he reached a double rutted trail, he steered higher on one shoulder where the earth was firmer.

Pleased with himself, Big Belly maneuvered the turns through the forest until the still appeared in its clearing.

He looked up at the sky. The clouds gathered faster now, but rain was more than an hour off, he estimated. Maybe longer. He'd have the fire at the right temperature and all the ingredients mixed together just right in the kettle. He intended to have a gallon made before midnight.

Big Belly brought the buggy to a creaking halt by the woodpile. He went into the shack and began working. He preferred to make money gambling, but he felt a certain satisfaction with running his still. Here he produced something plenty of folks paid good money for.

"Everyone but those damn temperance females," he grumbled. He had backed them in the vote to go dry to get rid of legal competition. But the ones like Ada Brewster and her daughter carried the crusade against John Barleycorn a step beyond what Big Belly had expected.

She and Irene and too many other women in town tried to stamp out the illegal supply of liquor. He had expected them to go off feeling all proud of winning the vote and never bother with him supplying the Royal Flush and towns all around Kiowa Springs. Their vote had closed down competing saloons. Why couldn't they have been content with that and gone back to their baking and housekeeping?

"What's that, Pa?"

Big Belly scowled as Harvey pushed into the shack. There was hardly room for the equipment and both of them.

"What's what?"

"You were mutterin' about something when I came in."

"Never mind about that," Big Belly said. "Get more wood. The fire's not hot enough."

"Let me rest for a minute. I'm all tuckered out from hikin' all the way from where you tossed me out of the buggy."

"Wood. Now."

His tone brooked no argument. Moaning, Harvey went to fetch the wood. Big Belly stoked the fire, then checked the fittings to be sure not a single drop would be lost. He stepped back and frowned.

"What's this? Why'd you wrap that tube around the top of the still?"

"I didn't do anything to the still, Pa. I know how upset you get when anybody else messes with it." Harvey dropped an armload of wood and bent closer to look at the copper tubing. "Nope, nothing I've done. Maybe Gus thought it looked good. It don't seem to do anything to help the process."

Big Belly stepped out of the shed and looked up. A heavy raindrop hit him in the face. He cursed and stepped back another few feet for a better look at the shack's roof. Harvey followed him.

"What's that pokin' up?" Harvey pointed. "It's hard to see since it's gettin' so dark."

As if calling him a liar, a lightning bolt crossed the sky.

"I can't make it out. You get up there and take it down. It's not supposed to be there," Big Belly said.

"Aw, Pa, it's hard for me to climb up there."

Another dazzling lightning bolt crossed the leaden sky.

"You get up there right now and—"

Big Belly never finished his order. A lightning fork stabbed downward and caressed the copper tubing. The tube exploded as the power from the sky followed it downward into the still. The shack and its contents erupted like a volcano. The force of the blast lifted Big Belly and cast him aside as if he were nothing more than a rag doll.

Chapter 26

Big Belly Ledbetter screeched, "I'm on fire! I'm on fire!"

Flames licked at his clothes. He swatted at cinders on his face and felt blisters on his cheeks as he brushed the fiery debris away. He began rolling over and over, sloshing through a mud puddle, and kept rolling until he came to a grassy patch. Face down, he began venting his anger into the ground.

Big Belly bellowed curses and hammered his fists against soft dirt, then lashed out when hands grabbed at him.

"Pa, stop fightin' me. I'm tryin' to put out the fire. Your clothes are burnin' up!"

He turned over onto his side. His son loomed over him. For a split second, Harvey looked like the devil. A lightning flash lit his face and cast shadows in all the wrong places. Soot smeared under his eyes made him into an even more diabolical figure.

Then Big Belly's vision blurred as raindrops flowed into his eyes. He flopped onto his back and swatted Harvey's hands away.

"Stop fussing like that. Tell me what happened. I stepped

out to—" Big Belly sat up and swung around to look as he realized what had happened.

The metal tube fixed to the stovepipe had acted as a lightning rod. The powerful bolt had raced down into the still and blown up the equipment. Anything the least bit explosive had ignited.

Big Belly went cold inside. If he had been inside the shack when the lightning struck, he'd be dead. Without realizing he was doing it, he began wiping off his clothing. Burnt holes under his fingers showed how extensive the blast had been.

"I'm hurting all over," he complained. He started to brush off Harvey's renewed attempt to help him onto his feet. When he found his legs weren't acting right, he let Harvey support him enough to stand. He stumbled back and almost fell when a wave of heat from the burning still smacked him in the face.

Big Belly stared at the ruined still. Something inside suddenly added to the blaze and created a new explosion. Then everything collapsed into a fiery pile. As he watched, the increasingly heavy rain sizzled and popped in a futile attempt to drown out the fire. The flames were too strong for that to occur right away.

"It'll get put out in a minute or two, Pa."

"Get your hands off me. I can stand on my own two feet now." Big Belly pushed away his son's hands. On shaky legs, he began circling the fire. "It's a complete loss. The metal pot's even melted."

"I saw what happened to Tanner's barn when it got struck by lightnin' a couple years back. Even the nails got melted down," Harvey said. "Lightning's nothin' to fool with."

"How'd that tubing get strung up like a lightning rod?"

"I didn't do it, Pa. Honest. Maybe Gus—"

"Shut up. Let me think." Big Belly spat dirt and wiped

his lips. His boys weren't likely to string up copper like that. Dumb enough to, but also too lazy to climb onto the roof. And what would they gain? "There's only one man who'd do this."

"That stranger, Pa? You think Timmerman or Garston bought him off?"

"It wasn't Garston. He's still in a bad way from you busting him up. For once you did good."

"Thanks, Pa."

"Shut up." Big Belly screwed up his face and thought hard until the solution came to him. "It's got to be the stranger I hired. But he did as I told him. He destroyed Timmerman's still."

"Maybe he read the map wrong and thought our still belonged to Garston."

Big Belly ignored Harvey's speculation. That made no sense. And even Gus wasn't stupid enough to mark the location of the Ledbetter still on the map.

"If he heard I'd set the marshal on him, he might have done this. But why not just burn it down and then hightail it out of town?" Big Belly thought more on the matter. "He's staying in Kiowa Springs for a reason. He wanted to have an alibi when the lightning took out my still."

"Why'd he want to stay in town, Pa? Because he's sweet on Irene Brewster? I want her for mine, Pa. He can't go cuttin' into my action with her!"

"You leave that filly alone, boy. She's bad news." A pointed finger and a hard look from Big Belly silenced Harvey. "She's one of the temperance crusaders, her and her ma, but the two snake oil salesmen make better sense. He's in cahoots with them."

"He wants to get even for you beatin' up the two old geezers?"

If even Harvey came to that conclusion, it had to be right.

Why hadn't Marshal Nance arrested the stranger the instant he rode into town? He paid the marshal enough to keep order, meaning taking care of anyone upsetting the Ledbetter rule over Kiowa Springs. And beyond taking a bit of graft, the marshal was scared of what Ledbetter would do if he crossed him. Marshal Nance was not a brave man, much less much of a lawman.

"The rain's 'bout put out the fire, Pa. You want me to poke through the ruins and see what I can salvage?"

Big Belly almost told his son to do that while he drove back to town. Let Harvey walk the whole way. Then he snarled, "Get the buggy. We're heading back to the Royal Flush. I need to talk to the marshal."

"Sure thing, Pa. Me and Gus can come out here later and fix things up just like they was."

Big Belly doubted anything could be salvaged. Fire was bad. Lightning was worse.

All the way as they returned to town in the rain, he glowered and thought of how to get even for not only losing his still but almost being killed. If he hadn't been curious enough to step away and look at the lightning rod, he'd be dead. Through some quirk of fate, his son had been fetching more wood. Both of them had been in the shack only a minute earlier.

By the time the buggy came to a halt in front of the casino, Big Belly had made his decision about what to do.

The next morning at the Royal Flush, Big Belly told Harvey, "Tell Nance to get over here right now. He's layin' down on the job."

Even dimwitted Harvey knew what his pa had in mind for the marshal to do.

Big Belly flopped into a chair. His clothes had been

ruined in the fire, he had burns all over his body, his ears rang from the explosion, and worst of all, there wasn't a drop of 'shine in all of Kiowa Springs to drink. He slammed his fist on the table so hard that one leg broke.

"What's got you so riled, Mr. Ledbetter?" Marshal Nance had come in and stood just far enough away that Big Belly couldn't land a punch in the middle of his ugly face.

"The stranger," he said. "You got rid of him?"

"Well, not exactly," Nance said, shuffling his feet like a schoolchild caught cheating.

"You'd better mean you locked him up. Get over to the jail and shoot him. Cut him down. I want him dead!"

"You see, Mr. Ledbetter, it's like this." The lawman took a deep breath and plowed ahead. "I hunted high and low and coudn't find him. Nobody will fess up to having seen him, either. I reckon he's left town for good. He knew you wanted him, and he just rode on out, never looking back."

"You're more of a fool than either of my two dimwitted sons," Big Belly roared. "He's not the kind to scare off easy." He settled down and fumed. If anything, the man would stay in town to find out if his trap out at the still worked. If lightning didn't destroy the still—and its owner—he'd try something else.

"Why'd you hire him on, Mr. Ledbetter?"

"I wanted to keep him close to find out what he was up to."

"That didn't work out too well for you," Nance said, then gulped as he realized that had been an unwise thought to express.

Big Belly boiled up out of his chair and took a powerful swing at the marshal. If it had landed, bones would have broken. Nance dodged the blow and backpedaled fast before Big Belly regained his balance.

"I'll track him down for you, Mr. Ledbetter. You wait and see." The marshal ran from the Royal Flush.

Big Belly went to the bar and leaned against it. He felt a vein in his forehead throbbing, and his hands shook. Everyone worked against him, either through incompetence or utter stupidity.

"If you want a job done right, do it yourself."

He reached over the bar and found a double-barreled, sawed-off shotgun. A quick check showed shells loaded and waiting in the chambers. All his trouble had started when the snake oil salesmen came to town.

"It's those two old peddlers," he muttered aloud. "Somehow, they caused all this."

His trouble would go away when he took care of them once and for all.

The floorboards sagged as he stormed out of the casino. It was drizzling outside. This only added to Big Belly's fury as he stomped along, splashing through mud puddles, on his way to the Brewster house and the end of his problems.

CHAPTER 27

Irene Brewster cringed down when Big Belly Ledbetter's meaty hand came groping over the bar. She closed her eyes and held her breath. If she wished hard enough, he would go away and not find her, she told herself.

In spite of hoping that he'd leave if she didn't open her eyes, a metallic scraping sound made her look. He had snared a shotgun on a shelf just inches above her head. Sneaking into the Royal Flush to spy on the Ledbetters seemed more and more foolish as Big Belly cursed and stomped around on the other side of the bar.

She had overheard everything said between the moonshiner and the marshal. It hadn't been much of a secret that Ledbetter owned the marshal, lock, stock, and barrel. What she heard erased any lingering doubt she had. The lawman was crooked and beholden to a criminal.

After a full minute she didn't hear any more ranting and rampaging from Big Belly. Like a timid rabbit poking its nose from its burrow, she peered around the edge of the bar. A destroyed table testified to Big Belly's wrath. Scooting along a little more, she surveyed the empty room. It wouldn't be long before gamblers started coming in.

Or would they bother? Everything she'd overheard told

her someone had blown up the only remaining source of moonshine in Kiowa Springs. Pike? It had to be. She felt a glow of pride that she had been right about him and his honesty. Then the sensation was replaced by a cold lump.

He had almost killed Big Belly and in doing so turned the huge man's ire toward Fiddler and Dougal. Irene stood, knowing she had to get home and warn everyone there that trouble was on the way, in the form of the enraged Big Belly Ledbetter.

Before she could take a step, Gus pushed through the double doors leading out to the main street. He spotted her immediately.

"What are you doing here, Miss Brewster? If you're lookin' for Harvey, you missed him. He went to the stable to look after our horse and buggy. It looks like he drove it through a forest fire. Pa's not gonna be pleased with that, no ma'am."

Having overheard the conversation between Big Belly and the marshal, Irene knew why the buggy looked like that, even if Gus didn't.

"I . . . I wanted to ask your father something." The lie sounded incredibly weak, but Gus swallowed it whole.

"Ask me. I know everything he does. And I'm a sight better looking than Harvey."

His leer chilled her. He came across the room toward her. She read nothing but evil intent in his eyes.

Irene moved fast. She feinted right, went left, and brushed off his hand as he tried to grab her arm. The expression of pure hatred on her face kept him from pursuing her. Tangling with a wildcat would have had a better outcome for him, and he realized it.

"You forget about my brother if you want a real man," he called after her. "I'm available. You hear?"

Irene ran out into the rain and looked around frantically.

Big Belly was nowhere to be seen. She'd never be able to reach the house to warn Dougal and Fiddler of Big Belly and his fury before he got there.

"Pike. He'll be able to stop Big Belly." Even under these desperate circumstances, she smiled for a second, thinking of him destroying the Ledbetter still. He had done what no one else in Kiowa Springs had been able to do in months and months since they'd voted in a temperance law.

In rain that had turned more into a mist, she tried to figure out where Pike would be. The only place that came to mind was the vacant lot where the Ledbetter brothers had burned Fiddler's wagon down to the axles. Hoping she did the right thing, she turned away from her ma's boarding-house and ran down the street in the opposite direction.

Irene found the alley leading back to the storehouses. Even in the dampness, the heavy burnt odor made her nose wrinkle. With skirts flying, she burst into the lot and looked around frantically.

"Pike! Pike, please! We've got trouble."

Irene jumped a foot when a hand touched her shoulder. She spun and faced him. She put her hand to her throat and sagged in relief.

"You frightened me. How'd you sneak up on me so quietlike?"

"What's the problem?" Pike asked, ignoring her question.

"Big Belly," she panted out. "He's got blood in his eye."

"So you heard about what happened to his still?" Pike laughed. "News travels fast in this town. Did it burn down with him in it?"

"Almost."

He grabbed her by the arms so she had to look him squarely in the eye. "He's not dead?"

"I didn't understand it all, but he barely escaped getting

fried when the whole place went up in an explosion. Him and Harvey barely escaped. And now Big Belly is on his way to the house with a sawed-off shotgun to take care of Dougal and Fiddler. He's sure they're responsible for him almost getting killed."

"He must have figured out Dougal and I are related."

"No, no, but he thinks there's some connection. He doesn't know you're Dougal's grandson."

"It doesn't matter the reason if he intends to do them harm. He's going to the boardinghouse, you say?"

"He's got too much of a head start, Pike. You'll have to ride like the wind."

"My horse is at the stables," he said. "It'll take too long to fetch it. There's got to be some other way."

"Gus said Harvey was at the stable. If Big Belly tries to do anything, you can catch Harvey and use him as a bargaining chip."

Pike snorted. "As if he cared about his sons."

"Blood's thicker than water. He might insult them in public and do terrible things to them, but they're his kin." She clutched his arms and moved closer. Looking up into his eyes she said, "You can't let them get hurt more. Fiddler and Dougal are barely on the road to recovery from the first beating he gave them. This time he's got a shotgun." She shivered, remembering how she'd thought he had discovered her hiding behind the bar.

"Taking Harvey hostage is all I can do right now." Pike turned away from her to head for the livery stables.

"Wait, Pike. There's something else." She caught his arm and held it. "The marshal is hunting for you. Big Belly ordered him to gun you down."

"I won't tangle with a lawman, not like that. If Big Belly's gone, the marshal will fall right into line. That'll take care of that problem."

Irene looked up into his eyes and saw the steel there. And something more. She saw Pike's devotion to Fiddler and his love for his grandfather. If Big Belly harmed either of those men, Pike Shannon would never rest until he had avenged them.

"What are you going to do?"

"Harvey is the weak link," Pike said. "You stay here where it's safe. I went through these storage buildings hunting for any more moonshine and didn't find any. You might take a look around and see if I missed anything."

She knew he was giving her a fruitless task to keep her out of the fight. Irene impulsively stood on tiptoe and kissed him. She wasn't sure who was more surprised.

"Be careful," she said in a small voice.

Pike nodded once and hurried off in the direction of the stables. She watched him go, then looked around. Staying here would drive her crazy with worry. Retracing her route to the main street, she heaved a deep sigh, hiked her skirts to keep the hem from getting too wet and muddy, and ran for the boardinghouse.

What she could do to stop Big Belly from harming the two men so near and dear to Pike wasn't obvious. If nothing else, she might slow Big Belly down enough for Pike to get there.

She'd have to see.

CHAPTER 28

Pike glanced over his shoulder as he made his way from the vacant lot. He almost stopped and went back. He had a hunch that Irene wouldn't do as he asked. He imagined her rushing to her house, only to tangle with Big Belly Ledbetter.

He broke into a run to get to the stables. The plan of taking Harvey prisoner and using Big Belly's boy as a bargaining lever became even more important. If Big Belly wanted to shoot Fiddler and Dougal, there was no telling what he'd do to Irene.

Pike slowed when he rounded a corner and saw someone lying under a buggy parked in front of the stable, fixing a spring that had popped free. From the rotund gut poking up, Pike knew he had found Harvey.

Walking steadily, he slid his Colt from its holster. He cleared his throat and called, "Don't do anything stupid, Ledbetter. Keep your hands raised."

"Raised? What is this?" Harvey scooted clear of the buggy and looked up to see that Pike had the drop on him. He scowled and said, "Pa's gonna blow your fool head off. You can't come traipsin' into his town and—"

"Shut up." Pike almost laughed when he realized how

much he sounded like Harvey's pa. It was easy to fall into such behavior when dealing with a couple of dolts like Harvey and Augustus Ledbetter.

The way Harvey reacted was completely unexpected. With a bull-throated roar, Harvey reared up, lifted the buggy off its wheels, and heaved it toward Pike. The buggy half turned in the air, then righted and rolled into him. Pike triggered a round that tore up a dry spot on the ground a few feet in front of him. He jerked aside to avoid getting tangled up more in the buggy and fell to his knees.

By then Harvey was on his feet and had his iron out.

"Pa wants you dead. He's told Marshal Nance to take care of you, but I'll do it since I'm as good as he is."

Harvey opened fire.

The buggy that had upended Pike now saved him. Harvey's bullets tore through the buggy and missed hitting Pike by a foot or more. Pike kicked with his right foot and sent the buggy rolling back toward Harvey. This caused a wild flurry of rounds until Pike heard the other man's hammer fall on a spent round.

"I won't kill you if you surrender."

Harvey cursed a blue streak and dived for the stable's open door. Pike got off a shot but missed.

"Yeah, right, you won't try to kill me," Harvey yelled back at him. "You'll fill me full of lead!"

"The extra weight'd never be noticed when they bury you," Pike said. He rushed to the door. He had to catch Harvey before he had a chance to reload.

As he twisted from side to side with his gun leveled, searching for Harvey, he almost died. There were other weapons besides pistols, and Pike was almost skewered by a pitchfork.

Harvey shrieked like a banshee as he yanked the three-pronged pitchfork from the wall where a tine had caught in the wood. Pike fired again, but Harvey was quicker for his size than he looked. He drew back with the pitchfork and thrust hard.

Pike winced. The tine that had torn through the wall now ripped the flesh on his right leg. He fanned off the rounds remaining to him, forcing Harvey to retreat. Then his Colt came up empty.

Pike started to rush forward in spite of the leg wound, but Harvey had disappeared into the rear of the stable. Pike took the opportunity to reload. The horses in the stalls were all spooked by the gunfire and the sharp tang of powder smoke. One started kicking at the wall of its stall. It wasn't any consolation that the horse doing the most damage was Pike's own dun.

Pike advanced slowly. At first his step was sure. Then pain radiated from the hole in his leg and turned his thigh numb. Worse, the blood trickled down into his boot. Every step now squished as if he waded through a gory mud puddle.

"You hurtin' bad, mister? Did I pink you, just a little?"

Pike homed in on Harvey's taunting voice. He was hidden in the third stall. Flushing him out wasn't going to be easy with horses in the adjoining stalls.

"You're the one who's going to be hurting," Pike called. He made his way to a ladder leading to a hayloft. Getting up the rungs presented a problem. If Harvey had reloaded, he'd be an easy target. Worse, his wounded leg began to twitch. He'd be in a real pickle if he got halfway up and it gave out on him. Hopping up a ladder on one leg wasn't something to do if he wanted to go on living.

Pike braced himself, then lunged forward. A final jump took him halfway up the ladder. Using his hands and good leg, he pulled himself up to the loft. Barely had he flopped belly down on the fragrant hay than Harvey opened fire.

Bullets exploded all around him, punching through the planks of the loft's floor.

He counted four rounds. His jaw tightened in frustration when the final two rounds weren't fired. Harvey was smarter than Pike expected. Or cagier. Hold back a couple rounds and wait for his adversary to make a mistake.

"I've got the high ground, Ledbetter. You can't get out of that stall without me plugging you. Give up."

"Pa didn't raise no fools," Harvey answered.

Pike wasn't in a position to argue. All he hoped for was to prove Harvey too confident in his own abilities. Rolling brought him to the edge of the hayloft. Looking down, he had a good shot at the side door leading out, as well as one at the rear. He had six rounds ready to fire, but by now so did Harvey.

Pike waited for what seemed an eternity. He began to grow antsy, thinking that Big Belly had reached Ada Brewster's place by now. Unless Dougal was alert, Big Belly had the pair from Warbonnet County in his sights. Pike swallowed hard when a lump formed in his throat. By now Big Belly might have done more than get the drop on Fiddler and Dougal.

Harvey's life would be forfeit if any of the Shannons were harmed. And Gus would pay for his pa's crimes, too. And the twins, wherever they were. Anyone beholden to Big Belly would end up as buzzard bait. The marshal and—

Pike almost paid for his inattention with his life. Harvey stepped out and looked up. When he saw movement, he fired. Accurately. Pike yelped in pain as a bullet tore through his right biceps. His entire arm went numb. He rocked to the side, putting him out of sight from below, and shifted his pistol to his left hand.

"Gotcha!" Harvey gloated. He stepped farther out into the stable.

Pike bit back a moan. He moved a little and let blood from his new wound drip between the boards and down into the stall below. This caused Harvey to dance a jig.

"Pa's gonna tell me I'm his favorite son now, for certain sure. I did what Nance couldn't. I put a hole in the skunk who blew up our still. You were the one, weren't you?"

Pike squeezed more blood from his arm. A sporadic drip became a steady stream now. Harvey saw it and grew careless, stepping farther out to get a look into the loft.

Colt gripped in his left hand, Pike waited. More than once he'd had to shoot it out left-handed. His patience paid off. When Harvey tried to shift position to get a better look into the loft, Pike acted. His gun blared once, twice, a third time.

Every round found a target in Harvey Ledbetter.

Pike came up to his knees and braced his pistol against the edge of the loft. Harvey sat on the floor, clutching his belly.

The bulky man looked up, face drawn. "You shot me. You shot me!"

"Not the first time," Pike said. He had grazed Ledbetter at least three times in their previous gunfights. This time he had done it right.

Or so he thought. He moved to the edge of the loft. Harvey pressed his hand into his belly—but Pike hadn't counted on all that fat protecting the man's life. He had hit Harvey three times, but all three rounds had gone through the bulge overhanging his waistband. Not a single round had drilled through a vital organ.

He stood to remedy that. As Pike cocked his gun for the killing shot, a loud screeching of nails pulling out of wood filled the stable. The loft wobbled under him, then collapsed entirely. Pike plunged down to the floor. Unprepared for the drop, he hit hard. His injured leg gave under him as he tried to stand.

Flat on his belly, using both hands to steady his Colt, he lifted it to finish what he had started. He pointed his gun at . . . empty space.

Harvey had hightailed it.

The only place he could have run was out the side door. Pike drew himself up on his good leg and hopped to the wall to support himself. Rushing out would be a mistake, probably his last. He reloaded instead.

"You're out there, Harvey. I can hear you gasping for breath. Give up and I won't kill you."

"Liar. That's all you've tried to do."

"You can't run, can you? All my slugs hit you in the gut. Moving's sending pain through your entire body. I can tell how bad you're hurt. You need medical attention."

"Not gettin' it in Kiowa Springs. The doc left months back."

"The vet can patch you up. I never trusted a doctor. I always trust a vet."

Pike didn't add that a vet was perfect for dealing with Harvey's wounds. Any animal doctor dealt with pigs on a regular basis.

"You're gonna die, mister. I'll see to that." Harvey fell silent, then asked, "What's your name, anyway? Pa never said."

"Pike Shannon. That was my grandpappy your pa beat up."

As he spoke, Pike moved out of the stable. Harvey had positioned himself exactly where Pike expected. The man sat on the side of the buggy, half bent over and holding his belly.

"So you're with them snake oil salesmen? That means you know all about moonshine, since that's what they was sellin'."

"Drop your iron, Harvey." Pike moved painfully to get a clean shot.

"I'm faster'n you. I can take you. You look like some kind of gunslinger, but you're all shot up. You're shot up because *I* put a couple rounds through you."

Harvey heaved himself upright. He wobbled, but he had his pistol in his hand.

"You want a showdown? Face-to-face?"

"You and me, Mr. Pike Shannon." Harvey dropped his six-gun into his holster and widened his stance.

Pike took in the man's wounds. His shirt was completely soaked with blood from the three slugs he'd taken in the belly. His face was ashen, and his lower lip trembled.

"It doesn't have to end this way," Pike said.

"Yeah, right, you won't shoot me if I give up. I'm a Ledbetter. This is my town and I'll never give up."

Pike thrust his Colt into his waistband. He squared off against Harvey. In all his wild days, he'd never thrown down left-handed. But he wasn't one to walk away from a fight, and this was as even a fight as either of them could expect.

Harvey went for his gun first. Pike was slower, clumsier—and more accurate when he dragged his hogleg out. The Colt bucked in his grip. There wasn't any need to fire again.

Harvey had cleared leather but was slow raising the muzzle. When Pike's bullet tore through his heart, his finger tightened. His bullet blew the toe off his own boot. Then he fell forward and lay still.

Deathly still.

Pike watched Harvey closely for a moment, then sighed and slid the Colt back into leather. The sting of gun smoke was in his nose, and a bitter taste lurked in his mouth.

He had just lost his only bargaining chip with Big Belly Ledbetter.

CHAPTER 29

Some of Big Belly's anger had faded by the time he stomped up to the Brewster house. Some, but not all. The men inside deserved whatever punishment he dished out to them. He gripped the sawed-off shotgun's stock and steeled himself. He'd blow the two snake oil salesmen to hell and gone. Then he'd laugh.

He kicked open the gate and broke a hinge. A second kick tore it entirely free. He stormed to the door. Big Belly never tried the knob to see if the door was unlocked. He reared back and kicked hard. The entire door frame, door and all, exploded inward.

"Get out here, you mangy excuses for humanity. Now!" His roar caused the windows to rattle.

Big Belly went to the table by the door and yanked open the drawer. Ada Brewster's puny little four-shot pistol lay inside. He tucked it into his waistband. There was no way Ada Brewster or anyone else could use it against him now. It might be fun shooting both of the medicine peddlers with it and watching them die real slow.

"Everyone in this house, get out here right now!" He swung the shotgun's short barrels around and smashed a vase to a thousand pieces. Even this wanton destruction failed to bring anyone running.

He stomped down the hall and shouldered open the first door. A lump on the bed in the dimly lit room was the first recipient of his ire. He triggered one barrel. The weapon bucked hard and sent a load of buckshot ripping into the comforter. Feathers from the pillow fluttered into the air and drifted around.

This made him even madder. What he had thought was Fiddler sleeping in the bed was only a rolled-up blanket. He swung around and threw open the next door. This bedroom was empty, too. Across the hall he kicked open the door to Ada Brewster's bedroom.

Empty!

He discharged his second barrel into the bed and sent more feathers sailing in the air. Big Belly reloaded and prowled the house for any trace of its occupants. The back door stood ajar. He barreled out and saw Dougal trying to harness a horse to the Brewster buckboard. With a guttural roar that started deep in his gut and rose like a tornado, he discharged both barrels. He was rewarded when Dougal jerked around and sat heavily, looking stunned.

"I'll kill you and—" That was as far as Big Belly got. The roar from the Greener made his sawed-off shotgun sound puny. Pellets tore into the ground at his feet. Tiny plumes of dirt and mud rose and caused him to retreat a step.

"You missed the varmint, Fiddler. Shoot him again. Don't miss this time!" Dougal scrambled to pull himself to his feet using the buckboard as a support.

In Big Belly's rush to shoot Dougal, he had overlooked Fiddler standing on the far side of the shed. He braced a long-barreled shotgun against the structure. The bore wobbled but was close enough to centering on Big Belly that he retreated farther and ducked into the house.

"Dang it, Fiddler, you let him get away. What's wrong with you?"

"I can barely stand. Firing this goose gun's a chore when I'm feeling up to snuff. And right now I'm as far from that as I can be without being ready for the grave."

Big Belly saw his chance. He slid two more shells into his shotgun and rushed forward. His tactics became clear. Fiddler was farther away. He made a beeline for Dougal. When Dougal saw this, he tried to run. Big Belly fired low and hit him in the leg. It looked as if Dougal stood on a rug that was abruptly jerked from under him. His feet shot into the air, and he fell straight down. Only a patch of mud softened his fall.

"You throw down that shotgun or this one's getting my second barrel in the head!" Big Belly stood over Dougal.

"Do as he says, Fiddler. He means it. I see it in his eyes. He's a killer!"

"You got that right, you no-account snake oil peddler." Big Belly circled the supine man so he faced Fiddler. "Get out here. Now! Get out here now or he's a goner!"

"Don't shoot. There's no call to get all murderous on us." Fiddler dropped the shotgun and hobbled out.

"Get those hands in the air where I can see them!"

"Can't. You tore up the muscle in my shoulder when you beat the hell out of me. This is the best I can do." Fiddler grumbled and forced his right arm higher when Big Belly shoved the shotgun barrel down into Dougal's chest. "Don't get an itchy trigger finger now."

"I'll do anything I please. This is my town and your friend blew up my still."

"Do tell," Fiddler said. "That's a real pity."

"I was almost blown up with it. Me and my boy."

"A double pity. Or should I say that's a triple pity?" Fiddler reached the buckboard and collapsed forward into the bed.

Big Belly thought he was faking injury, then saw Fiddler's face. It was pale and drawn. He had lost a dozen pounds since he'd come to town. More than walking on shaky legs, his hands trembled like he had the ague. He might be a performer selling his witch's brew from the back of his wagon, but this was no act. Big Belly felt almost proud of the job he'd done to show Fiddler how wrong he'd been coming to Kiowa Springs.

"Get up," he said, poking Dougal again.

"I need help." Dougal flopped around like a turtle rolled over on its back. "I'm all shot up."

"I can help you. Three, two . . ." Big Belly stepped away and pointed his shotgun straight at Dougal's face. This gave the incentive for the old-timer to do as he was told. With a groan, Dougal climbed to his feet and hung on to the buckboard.

"You're going to pay for this," Fiddler said. "Pike will make you pay plenty."

"Pike? Is that the tall stranger's name?"

"Pike Shannon," Dougal said. He and Fiddler helped support each other. The buckboard did most of the work. "He's my grandson."

"I'll see that his name's put on his gravestone."

"You don't know Pike. He—" Fiddler bit off his words when he saw Big Belly smirking. "You've killed him?"

"As good as done," Big Belly said. "If the marshal didn't do it, my son's been told to lay him low."

"You don't know Pike. He's not dead," Dougal said. "He can't be."

"His death's on your heads. You should never have come to town. My town!" Big Belly motioned with the shotgun.

"You two get up on the driver's box. We're going for a little ride."

"Where?" Fiddler and Dougal exchanged concerned looks.

Big Belly got a laugh out of that. He enjoyed it when men realized their fate—and that he, Big Belly Ledbetter, was the one dishing it out.

"You do as you're told and you might live to see another sunrise. Otherwise . . ." Big Belly held up his shotgun. Its aim drifted from one man to the other. "Now get up there and drive!"

Big Belly expected them to resist, but they were in no shape to do so. Helping each other, moaning in pain, they clambered onto the driver's seat. Big Belly got into the back of the buckboard, holding the shotgun on them the whole time.

He braced himself when Fiddler snapped the reins and tried to make the horse bolt. Such a leapfrog start might have thrown him from the back of the buckboard. As it was, he gloated some more that he continued to outsmart them. They obviously thought of themselves as being better than everyone else. They peddled snake oil and promised miracles, after all.

"To the main street and then out of town. Head east."

"We don't want trouble," Dougal said, "but you're in for more than you can handle if you don't let us go."

"From the stranger who rode in and tried to kill me?"

"Pike did that?" Dougal's eyes narrowed. "What do you know about him?"

"He did things that got him killed, that's what I know. There hasn't been time to bury him yet, but I'm in no hurry to feed him to the worms. No way he's not dead."

"You're lying!" Fiddler swung around in the driver's

seat. Big Belly expected it. He reared back and laid the short shotgun barrel alongside the snake oil salesman's head.

Fiddler recoiled and dropped into the foot well. The buckboard rocked to a halt with Fiddler no longer handling the reins.

"You can't do that!" Dougal struggled to stand up and turn around. Then he sank back down on the seat when he saw Big Belly's expression.

Big Belly thought about how good it would feel to blow these two old pelicans apart. Real good. He thought on all the ways he'd celebrate after piling up another corpse or two. Showing the dead men off ought to cement his control over everyone else in Kiowa Springs.

"Get to driving," Big Belly ordered. "Straight out of town." He thrust out the shotgun to emphasize how serious he was about Dougal obeying. His finger caressed the triggers, but he wanted to have a little fun with the two before he ended their miserable lives.

Dougal reached for the reins Fiddler had dropped when Big Belly clouted him.

"Wait, don't go. Stop!" The cry from behind came high and shrill.

Big Belly knew he should keep his shotgun trained on Dougal, but the old man looked up and the expression on his face mixed hope and fear. Big Belly had to see what Dougal was looking at. He pivoted in the buckboard's bed. Running hard to catch up came Irene Brewster.

Big Belly knew he had made a mistake when he heard Dougal's gusty cry. The old galoot dived from the driver's box. His arms wrapped around Big Belly's giant frame, at least part of the way. For a wounded old man, Dougal showed surprising strength as he tackled Big Belly.

"Let them go! You can't take them." Irene gasped and stumbled along, waving her arms like a windmill.

For two cents Big Belly would have fired both barrels into her, but he was occupied with fighting off Dougal. With a deep-throated growl, Big Belly rose to his feet. Dougal clung to him for an instant before his grip loosened. He went flying through the air as Big Belly gave him a hard shove off the buckboard.

"Dougal, Dougal, are you all right?" Irene ran to where he lay in the mud alongside the road. She knelt to see if he was hurt.

"Get in the wagon. Both of you." Big Belly pointed his shotgun at them.

"I can't move. You done paralyzed me." Dougal weakly flopped around.

"I'll blow her head off if you're not in the wagon by the time I count to three."

Big Belly was pleased that his threat worked so fast. Dougal got to his feet, more agile than he had any right to be at his age and in his condition.

"Don't hurt her." Dougal stepped between the shotgun bore and the girl. "Go on, Miss Brewster. Go back and—"

"Both of you," Big Belly interrupted. "Into the wagon. I've got me three hostages now. Move!"

"Why'd you come?" Dougal asked as he helped Irene up into the driver's box. "That was a danged foolish thing to do."

She ignored Dougal and said to Big Belly, "Pike has your boy Harvey. If you don't let us go, there's no telling what he'll do."

"Who's got him? Are you saying that Pike Shannon's taken my boy prisoner?" Big Belly cursed under his breath. This meant Marshal Nance and Harvey had both failed to gun down the stranger, the man responsible for blowing up his still and almost causing him to burn to death. Nobody was able to do what they were told these days.

"He sent me to tell you he'll trade Harvey for them." Irene swallowed hard and nodded toward Dougal and Fiddler. "And I reckon me, too, now."

"That's a poor trade, if I agree to it. Three for one."

"It's an even-steven trade on a pound for pound basis," Dougal said.

Big Belly never tried to control his anger. He lashed out with the shotgun barrel and laid Dougal out next to Fiddler.

"Harvey's not got the brains God gave a gnat, but he's my flesh and blood. We'll see about a swap later. You, Miss Brewster, you drive the rig since the other two are in no condition. Keep on along this road until I tell you different."

"You're lying," she said in a small, choked voice. "I can read your face. You intend to kill us all."

"You might survive. Not them. Would Pike Shannon swap you for Harvey?"

"No, he wants his grandpa and friend."

Big Belly laughed and pointed ahead. "Drive. And don't you go looking back at me."

"That won't be hard. Who'd want to stare at your ugly old face?" Irene settled down in the seat and took the reins. She wasn't too experienced at driving, but the chore wasn't too demanding.

From the rear of the buckboard, Big Belly stared at the back of her head. The snake oil salesmen could be buried anywhere the ground was soft enough to dig, but Irene Brewster? He'd save her for Harvey. The boy didn't deserve such a gift, but it was about the best way he could think of to get even with her.

With her and Pike Shannon.

CHAPTER 30

Pike hid Harvey Ledbetter's body in a burned-out storeroom. His wounded arm and leg made the grim chore both painful and difficult. He covered the corpse with a pile of debris and topped off the makeshift grave with a few crates that hadn't been too badly damaged in the fire.

"Seems fitting," Pike said as he stared at his handiwork. "You burned down your own building and destroyed your pa's moonshine."

Now he had his grandpappy and Fiddler to rescue from Big Belly. If Harvey hadn't put up such a fight, there wouldn't have been such a delay getting to the Brewster house.

"Brewster," he said softly. If Irene had run straight for her home to warn Fiddler and Dougal, chances were good Big Belly Ledbetter found himself with three captives. Pike closed his eyes for a moment. "There'd better be three captives."

Pike mounted and galloped to the boardinghouse. A quick check of the house and then the shed out back where Ada Brewster let her guests stable their horses confirmed his suspicion. The buckboard was gone and the depth of the tracks where it had rolled away showed it was heavily laden.

With Fiddler, Dougal, and a man the size of both of them combined.

There was no sign of Irene or Ada, no indication of whether either or both of the women were Big Belly's prisoners, as well, but it was a distinct possibility, Pike knew.

In ground softened by the frequent rains, the tracks leading out of town were distinct enough for a blind man to follow. Then Pike saw even more. He spotted tiny footprints in the mud, going in the same direction. The prints were just about Irene's size. The girl had tried to warn Dougal and Fiddler that Big Belly was coming for them, and failing that, had chased after the wagon.

Pike dismounted when he came to a spot in the road where Irene's footprints ended. It took no imagination at all for him to imagine Big Belly ordering her into the wagon when she caught up to them. From there, the twin ruts continued east.

Pike mounted and galloped off. He had three people to save now.

He rode for better than half an hour and never spotted the buckboard or its occupants.

"Missed them. How could I have not seen where a heavily loaded buckboard pulled off the road?" He rode back toward Kiowa Springs, eyes scanning both sides of the road for a spot where the buckboard had cut across country.

He was almost back at the Brewster house when he was forced to admit he had lost them. How that happened was a mystery since he thought of himself as a good tracker, but he had. Big Belly had three hostages and Pike's only bargaining chip was dead and hidden under a pile of debris.

In front of the Brewster house, he stopped when he

heard a loud voice rolling down the main street from the center of town.

"Come on over, step right up, take part in a great medical experiment. You, yes, you, can sample the most marvelous creation since asafetida." The voice lowered to where Pike no longer heard it, then came the bellow, "Our medicine is better than the food of the gods. And it's only one dollar a bottle!"

Pike tapped the flanks of his dun and trotted forward. He turned down the street leading to the vacant lot where the Ledbetters had burned out Fiddler's wagon. Parked next to the pile of rubble was a new medicine wagon. Standing atop the vehicle was a figure he knew well.

The handwritten banner hanging on the side of the wagon read: *Professor Horace T. Hathaway, Purveyor of Powerful Potions.*

The man haranguing the large crowd gathered around three sides of the wagon was Pike's brother, Torrance, wearing a frock coat and a top hat. He had finally arrived in response to the telegram Pike had sent.

As he swung down from the saddle, Pike listened to Torrance give his spiel and approved. He hadn't thought his younger brother had the ability to lie with such a straight face. Pike almost believed some of the claims made for the wonder juice Torrance had bottled up. But one thing made Pike uneasy.

Not twenty feet away in a burned-out building lay the hidden body of Harvey Ledbetter. With so many people crowded around, one of them might take it into his head to poke around in the vacant storefronts.

Torrance was winding up his pitch and getting ready to take money. Pike saw the problem right away, one that Torrance hadn't thought through. Standing atop the wagon and haranguing as "Professor Hathaway" made it impossible to sell the product to members of the crowd down on the ground.

Pike wondered how Torrance was going to manage that, when the wagon's back door swung open.

Nessa stepped out, wearing a bright green dress snug enough to show off her lithe figure and draw the attention of the men in the crowd. As they pressed forward to get a better look at her, she took a small brown bottle from the wicker basket she held in her left arm and held it up.

"Here you are, gentlemen, the elixir that will cure all your ills, for only one dollar a bottle," she said in a loud, clear voice.

Pike was furious. What the hell had Torrance been thinking, bringing their sister along on a dangerous mission like this?

Torrance spotted Pike coming and lifted his voice again. "There's no need to rush forward to purchase a bottle. I know you want to be healed by my potent elixir, but my lovely assistant will satisfy you all, each and every one."

"Wait just a blasted second," Pike called, pushing through the crowd lining up to hand their money to Nessa.

"Wait your turn, mister," Nessa said. She smiled sweetly, then ignored him to swap a crumpled greenback for a bottle of the purplish fluid. Pike had no idea what Torrance had mixed into the moonshine to give it such a color. He hoped the alcohol killed off both the foul taste and any poison used to create the vile concoction.

Fuming, Pike stood to one side and let his brother and sister work the crowd. It took almost fifteen minutes for the last of the eager buyers to be relieved of their money in exchange for the bogus medicine.

"It's your turn now, mister," Nessa said. She gestured toward the door into the enclosed back of the wagon.

"Would you like to step inside and see how our miraculous fluid of vitality is made?"

Pike climbed into the back of the wagon. Torrance had already dropped onto the driver's box and twisted around to join his brother and sister through the door at that end of the bed.

"You took your time showing up," Torrance said when the three siblings were in the wagon and the doors were closed. "What's the all-fired hurry? We got here and then you were nowhere around—"

Pike interrupted him, saying, "What in blue blazes were you thinking, bringing Nessa along?"

"You think I could stop her, once she figured out something was going on and was bound and determined to find out what it was? When she heard that Dougal and Fiddler had been hurt—"

"You should have told her she couldn't come—"

"Both of you, stop it," Nessa said, sharply enough that her brothers fell silent and looked at her in surprise. She stared hard at Pike and his grim expression. "Never mind about me. Bring us up to date on what's happening here, Pike."

She made sense, as usual. She was here and there was nothing Pike could do about it, so he quickly explained everything that had happened in the days since he'd ridden into Kiowa Springs, concluding with the fact that Dougal, Fiddler, and Irene Brewster were Big Belly's prisoners—or worse.

"So trade him his son for them," Torrance said. "That's the simplest solution."

"I left out part of the story," Pike admitted. "Harvey is deader than a doornail." He patted the Colt resting in his holster. "It was him or me. There's one other son, Augustus, but I don't know where he is."

"You'd better find him," Nessa said. "If you lost track of this Big Belly person, there's no telling where Grandpappy and Fiddler are." She eyed him shrewdly. "And your Miss Brewster, too."

"She's not 'my Miss Brewster,'" he said sourly. "She got involved when her mother took Dougal and Fiddler in and nursed them."

"So we owe it to her ma to get her back, as well as Dougal and Fiddler," Torrance said. "What're you planning?"

Pike shook his head sadly. He didn't have a plan. Not really.

Torrance read his silence and said, "Then we need to get cracking."

"Torrance is right. Time matters with a man like this Big Belly fellow," Nessa said. "He doesn't think things through. He reacts. He's probably sorry for what he's done later, but it's too late by then."

"You're wrong there," Pike said. "No matter what he's done, he's not ashamed of having done any of it. The man is without a conscience."

"We need a local to help us organize," Nessa said. "Mrs. Brewster fits the bill."

"I don't know where she is. Her house was deserted when I rode back into town and heard Torrance's sales pitch."

"They voted the town dry," Torrance said, rubbing his chin as he thought. "That's the bunch we need to form a posse. From everything you said, the marshal's not going to help." Torrance pulled back his cutaway coat and showed a small Colt sheathed in a shoulder rig. "We can deal with the law, but we need everyone in town on our side."

"We can whip up a crowd," Nessa said. "Look at how many people came to listen, and it's only midafternoon. About sundown folks will have closed up their stores. If we catch them before dinner, we can get a sizable number to help bring down Big Belly and his clan."

"How many will risk their necks?" Pike was always skeptical when recruiting folks like that was necessary. A posse formed in the heat of the moment burned out quickly. If shooting started, they'd evaporate as fast as a raindrop falling into a smithy's forge.

"We only need enough to buck the marshal and run Big Belly and his son out of town," Nessa said.

"There are also twins out there somewhere," Pike said. "If they're like Harvey, they won't bother coming back if they hear their uncle's in trouble."

"Give the people a shield against Ledbetter's threats and, well, that's all we need," Torrance said.

"Did you read that in one of your books?" Pike doubted it would be that easy.

"You should spend more time reading and less getting into trouble," Torrance said, his dander up.

"Arguing isn't getting us anywhere," Nessa said, acting as the peacemaker as she often did. "We can get a crowd together and sell them the idea of freedom rather than that horrid blend. I swear, Torrance just threw in whatever was at hand." She smiled a bit. "And some moonshine, of course."

"Where did you get it?" Pike asked. He had hidden Fiddler's still well.

"It's not hard," Nessa said. "I helped whip up a batch and it's pretty good, if I say so myself."

This surprised Pike. He looked at her askance.

"You didn't think I knew how to turn out a batch of Shannon's best? Ha!" Nessa grinned as she said, "It was getting boring around the ranch. This whole thing, except for Fiddler and Dougal being beaten up, breaks the monotony." She laid her hand on Pike's arm. "Oh, I'm sorry, Pike.

I forgot to mention your new girlfriend. What's her name again?"

"Irene," Torrance said. "That's a pretty name."

"Don't you think Irene Shannon is, too? Very Irish."

Pike ignored the pair of them poking and prodding him like that. He had tangled with Big Belly and knew how dangerous the man was. To his brother and sister, he was still a distant threat.

"We need someone everyone can believe will stand up to this Big Belly owlhoot," Nessa said. Both she and Torrance turned toward Pike.

They were right. Pike sighed and nodded.

"Get the crowd, I'll tell them what has to be done."

"We need to whip up another batch of Doc Hathaway's prescriptive medicine," Nessa said. "That'll pass the time. Torrance is right that a couple of hours from now will be the best time."

"Pull the wagon out to a spot directly in front of the Royal Flush. That's Big Belly's casino. This will let everyone know how serious we are about getting rid of Ledbetter."

They both nodded in agreement. Nobody was arguing. The Shannons were united in their determination to end Big Belly Ledbetter's reign of terror.

All Pike had to do was come up with something to say that would sway enough people. Otherwise, he would have to tangle with Big Belly Ledbetter alone.

Alone . . . except for his Colt.

CHAPTER 31

"Take that bag off. Take it off me right now!" Irene Brewster struggled but Big Belly Ledbetter had tied her wrists securely, then pulled a burlap bag over her head. She bounced from side to side in the rear of the buckboard, completely disoriented. All she heard was Big Belly sniggering and him occasionally warning Fiddler to drive faster.

Irene had no idea where they were or how long they'd traveled. Less than a mile outside town, Big Belly had insisted she stay in the back while Fiddler drove, since the old-timer now had his wits back about him.

She wasn't too familiar with the countryside, hardly ever straying from town, but he must worry that she'd recognize landmarks. All she really knew was that they were heading east. Or maybe it was south because the sun warmed the side of her face through the coarse cloth. Or maybe she had no idea at all where they were.

"What are you going to do? You can't kidnap us. There are laws!"

"Hush up, missy. You wouldn't like it one little bit if I bashed your teeth out with this shotgun."

She cringed when cold metal touched her arm.

"Pike will get you for this. He will!"

"Did you talk to Pike before you came after us?" Fiddler asked. "What's he going to do to free us?"

"Yeah, let's hear it," Big Belly said. "I intend to swap the two snake oil salesmen for my boy."

"What about me?" Irene's words caught in her throat. The implication was frightening.

"I reckon you're a prize for Harvey. He's been through a lot, even if most of it is his own danged fault. You say Pike Shannon's got him all trussed up?"

"Like the pig that he is," she spat out. She instantly regretted it. Big Belly whacked her on the side of the head with his shotgun. Not too hard, but enough to make her fall over onto her side and get bounced around even more. By the time she sat up and pressed her back against the side of the buckboard, she was so lost she wondered if she'd ever get home again.

And if she did, would it be as Harvey Ledbetter's prisoner?

"Then again, I might just cut down those two because you're mouthing off," Big Belly said. There wasn't a hint of joking in his tone.

"Pike will do for your boy if you kill us," Dougal said. "I don't think he's the kind who'll kill in cold blood."

"You don't know him," Fiddler said. "He was one of the most dangerous gunmen in all the West. He hired out for jobs nobody else wanted."

"And he's alive. They're not," Dougal finished.

"He did try to kill me and Harvey," Big Belly said thoughtfully. "But that part could have been an accident. He wanted to blow up my still. It was my bad luck I happened to be there when lightning struck."

"Talk about lightning, he's chain lightning with a six-gun, fat man," Fiddler said. "You don't want to cross him."

Big Belly laughed heartily. "Stop it, you're making me

hurt myself listening to your lies. And no matter what you think, I'm fast with a six-shooter."

"He doesn't lie," Dougal said. "Not about this."

Dougal groaned. Irene imagined Big Belly hitting him alongside the head with his shotgun to silence him. If they kept up their constant goading, Big Belly would blow them to kingdom come with the buckshot loaded into those twin sawed-off barrels.

"Where are we going?" Fiddler asked. "I can't see anything for all the trees." The buckboard came to a halt. Irene rolled around in the bed and fetched up hard against Dougal.

"I'm climbing up onto the driver's seat with you. Try anything and you'll have parts scattered all around to feed the coyotes."

The buckboard sagged and tilted as Big Belly settled onto the seat.

"You ready to run for it?" Dougal whispered. "Me and Fiddler'll distract him while you get on back to town. Tell Pike everything."

"I can't," Irene whispered back. "I'm tied up."

"Just your hands. That won't stop you from runnin'. Get out now!"

Irene barely stifled her cry of surprise as Dougal hoisted her up and over the drop gate. She hit the ground hard but stayed on her feet. Even though her fingers felt like sausages from the tight bonds around her wrists, she was able to jerk the bag from her head and look around. The wagon lurched and hit one rock after another as it drove deeper into the woods.

Whether by accident or design, Fiddler and Dougal had worked together well. Dougal had dumped Irene out of the wagon just as Fiddler caused the buckboard to lurch forward over a particularly rough bit of ground. Big Belly never heard or felt a thing as she escaped.

Irene scrambled for a hiding place until the buckboard was out of sight. She sank down behind a thorn bush and listened as the vehicle rattled on through the forest. Big Belly didn't yell or fire his shotgun, which meant he hadn't looked around and realized he was missing a prisoner. She had escaped successfully.

But where was she? Moving carefully, she backtracked the buckboard, then began running. Following the deep ruts was easy enough. She was out of breath when she reached the road.

Then she had another problem. Which way?

"We drove east out of town. The sun's in that direction." With the sun in her face, she started walking as fast as she could. As she walked, she worked at the twine around her wrists and eventually got it loose. Big Belly hadn't been as careful about tying her up as he would have been if she were a man, she figured.

Within an hour she recognized the terrain. Irene cut across country and got back to Kiowa Springs much faster than if she'd stayed on the road.

Footsore and aching, she went to her house. As she started inside, a loud voice echoed across town, the familiar hawking spiel of some sort of pitchman.

"Another medicine show?" After the ordeal she had undergone, Irene wanted nothing but to rest, but the voice sounded familiar. Something about the timbre, the way the words rolled out, all reminded her of someone. Drawn by her curiosity, her steps continued on past her house.

She soon found herself at the edge of a crowd outside the Royal Flush. The medicine wagon was parked directly in front, and the top-hatted snake oil salesman stood on the roof, hawking his goods.

"You good people deserve to be cured of what ails you.

Normally, you would pay for my fine nostrum, but today my lovely assistant will pass out bottles for free."

A murmur went through the crowd. Irene straightened and cried, "You look like Pike Shannon. You even sound like him!"

A hand touched her elbow. She turned to see a lovely redhead standing there with an urgent expression on her face. Irene's mouth opened in surprise, because she saw a family resemblance in this young woman, too.

"You must be Irene Brewster," the redhead said quietly. "I'm Nessa. Vanessa Shannon."

"Pike's sister!" She turned back to the man standing on the wagon. "Is that his brother?"

"Our brother, Torrance," Nessa said. "Come on. Pike will be happy to see you."

"He will?" For a moment Irene wasn't able to get everything right in her head. Then she brightened and said, "He will! And I need to tell him about Fiddler and Dougal."

"That's why we're here. Come on. Climb into the wagon through the front. Pike's inside. I've got joy juice to pass out."

Nessa lifted the wicker basket she held with its supply of small, dark brown bottles.

"Joy juice?" Irene frowned. "You're giving them moonshine?"

"I do declare," Nessa said, "you look just like Sophie Truesdale does when anybody mentions liquor."

"Who?"

"Never mind. In you go," Nessa urged.

Irene let Nessa help her up onto the driver's box. Her feet and legs were rubbery from the long hike back to town. She pushed aside a curtain and cried, "Pike!" She stumbled forward and threw her arms around him. Irene wasn't the type to let emotions get the better of her, but she began sobbing as she clung to him.

"Settle down. Here." Pike handed her a bottle of his brother's medicine.

She took it and downed a swallow before she realized what she was doing. The fiery liquid choked her, but enough spiraled down into her stomach to puddle there warmly. Somehow, it calmed her nerves.

"Good, isn't it?" Nessa said.

"It's still burning." She eyed the bottle in her hand and shuddered. One slug of that white lightning was more than enough for her. "But I'd drink it all if it got rid of the Ledbetters."

"Torrance is getting a good crowd," Pike said. "It's time for me to convince them they're not alone in this fight."

He stepped out of the wagon through the curtained front entrance.

"Big Belly might harm Fiddler and Dougal," Irene said. "What are you going to do to rescue them?"

"We need to discuss that," Nessa said, putting her arm around Irene's shoulders. "Pike can track a snowflake in a blizzard, but he lost the tracks. What can you tell me to help us find where Ledbetter took you?"

"He had a bag over my head, so that must mean I'd recognize where he's got Dougal and Fiddler."

"You found your way back to Kiowa Springs using the sun. That will help Pike figure out where to go. Now . . ." Nessa and Irene began piecing together small clues.

At one point Irene jumped. Heavy footfalls on the roof went the length of the wagon. She caught her breath, imagining Big Belly coming for her. Then she heard Pike begin talking to the crowd.

"You don't know me yet, folks, but you will," Pike began in a loud voice that penetrated clearly into the wagon. "I spent ten years on the trail, working for men who hired my fast gun."

Irene opened the back door a crack and peered out at the crowd. They had all taken a step back as they looked up, apparently in awe. Then Pike explained the reaction.

"I'm fast, really fast, as you can see from that draw I just demonstrated. And I don't miss. But my gun can only back you up, all of you. If you want to get out from under Big Belly Ledbetter's boot heel, *you* have to do it for yourselves. Only by standing together can you get rid of him and his family."

Questions shouted from the audience all carried skepticism that Pike would leave them at Ledbetter's mercy if things got rough. Irene was impressed by how confident Pike sounded as he denied that would ever happen. His sincerity made her believe.

"He means it, too," Nessa whispered in her ear. "Pike never goes back on his word. Ever."

"He won't leave as soon as he gets Fiddler and Dougal away from Big Belly?"

"Not until Kiowa Springs is able to run its own affairs," Nessa said. "You might consider what to do for a new marshal. I'm not sure Nance will want to stay in a town where he's not given bucketfuls of graft to do what a boss wants."

Irene smiled as she considered this. Once Ledbetter was gone and Marshal Nance had resigned, she knew the perfect man to be the next marshal. She glanced up at the wagon roof, then went back to trying to figure out where Dougal and Fiddler were being held prisoner.

Chapter 32

"Let's just kill 'em, Pa." Augustus Ledbetter glared at the tree where his father had lashed Fiddler and Dougal Shannon.

Big Belly Ledbetter reared back and cuffed his younger son. "I got plans for them. Don't you want to see your brother again?"

"What'd you do that for?" Gus held his ear and cringed away when Big Belly started to hit him again.

"He's your brother. If we get rid of these two, they might do something to him." Big Belly fell quiet and thought, *Pike Shannon might kill Harvey.*

"Harve can take care of himself. And we'd have three of 'em if you hadn't let that Brewster girl get away."

Gus faced his father squarely and thrust out his belly. The expression called out his pa, and Big Belly almost met the challenge. Taking backtalk from any of his family was never allowed. Ever. To allow it meant the family was falling apart.

"They're scheming against us," Gus went on. "I heard a new snake oil salesman calling on the entire town to come after us. I slipped away before anybody noticed me and come straight here to warn you."

Big Belly snorted in contempt. "It'll take more than that to give them all spines. I got the whole town cowed."

"They had their medicine wagon parked right in front of the Royal Flush, Pa. And the huckster claimed that Pike Shannon was some kind of notorious gunman."

"So they expect a hired gun to back them up when they make their play." Big Belly fumed at this. If he wasn't able to buy off opposition, he simply made it go away. There were a dozen graves scattered around outside Kiowa Springs where nobody would ever find them. At one time there had been a dozen other moonshiners. He had whittled that number to two.

And Pike Shannon had destroyed Timmerman's still. For all Big Belly knew, he had also destroyed Garston's. He rubbed his palms on his shirt. Tiny burnt spots flaked off. Pike Shannon had also demolished his still and almost killed him and Harvey.

"Shannon intends to move in and take over the moonshine supply," he said. That made perfect sense to him. "Gus, how many were in that crowd listening to Shannon and the new snake oil salesman?"

"A lot, Pa. Forty? Fifty?"

"Why should we swap two of them for Harvey? Shannon would trade for one of them just as soon as he would both." Big Belly walked to where Fiddler struggled to breathe. The ropes tying him to the tree had been cinched tight around his chest. "Which of them's likely more valuable? Is it you, old-timer?" Big Belly kicked Fiddler. Then he spun on Dougal. "Or is it you? Now that I look real close, you and Shannon got the same facial features."

"I'm proud to be his grandpappy!" Dougal blurted.

"So you're bragging on being family? And this one's not? No, not kith and kin." Big Belly stepped back and leveled his shotgun. "Gus, get this one into the buckboard. We're going to use him to get Shannon's attention."

Fiddler fought weakly as Gus cut the ropes, then used the shorter pieces to tie his hands behind his back. A couple of quick turns around Fiddler's ankles hogtied him. Gus stepped back and brushed off his hands in satisfaction.

Big Belly whacked him on the head again.

"Pa, stop that! What'd I do?"

"How's he supposed to climb into the wagon when you got him all trussed up like a holiday pig?" Big Belly pointed using his shotgun. He was glad that Gus got the idea right away.

Grunting, Gus pulled Fiddler to his feet. As he tipped over, Gus got his shoulder under his middle and heaved. Fiddler cried out in pain, then fell silent when Gus dumped him into the buckboard.

"Get on up there and drive," Big Belly said. "I'll keep an eye on the varmint."

"Which one?" Gus asked. "You fixing on leaving that one tied up and all by his lonesome?"

"He's not going anywhere." Big Belly towered over Dougal. "If that grandson of yours don't cooperate, this is where you're gonna die. Truth is, you might die before anyone finds you. There are wild hogs all through this forest." He laughed harshly. "That's real fitting, you being fed to the pigs."

"You ought to know pigs," Dougal cried. He gasped when Big Belly kicked him in the ribs.

"Keep a civil tongue in your head, or I'll cut it out." He swung around and climbed into the rear of the buckboard. It took a few seconds for him to settle down on a stack of burlap bags. "Get rolling," he called to his son. "Take the back way into town and come up behind the Royal Flush. I want to get onto the roof."

Big Belly settled back and endured the bouncing around until they reached the road. It was smoother but did nothing to soothe him. Pike Shannon occupied his thoughts like a swamp leech. The man had been the source of too much trouble, and all over a whiskey peddler. He kicked Fiddler out of spite. He thought it should make him feel better, but it didn't.

The only way he'd feel better was when he controlled Kiowa Springs again. There'd be a passel of fresh graves before that happened, and he stared at one of them flopping around next to him. Fiddler was going to rue the day he drove into town.

"Pull up real close to the back wall of the casino," he told Gus. "Then get on up to the roof. There's a rope in the back room. Take it up with you and drop one end over. Put a loop on it."

Fiddler sat up, eyes wide when he heard that. Big Belly enjoyed his panic.

"We'll need it to hoist him to the roof."

"What are you up to?" Fiddler demanded as Gus hustled into the gambling hall. "You can't kidnap a citizen like this. That's against the law."

"As if Marshal Nance cares. He's probably not even in town. He makes most of his money serving process. That's fine by me since it keeps him out of town and out of my hair."

Gus emerged from the building carrying a coiled rope. He climbed the ladder to the roof, tossed the rope over the edge, and then hoisted himself onto the roof, with a lot of grunting and huffing for breath accompanying the effort. A minute or so later, one end of the rope, with a loop form in it as Big Belly had commanded, sailed down from the roof.

"Here you go, Pa."

The rope banged against the side of the Royal Flush. Big Belly adjusted the honda and dropped the lasso around Fiddler's shoulders, then pulled it tight under the old-timer's arms. The man struggled but was too weak to put up much of a fight.

"Haul him up, Gus."

Big Belly stepped to the edge of the buckboard and watched Fiddler being drawn up. Their captive kicked feebly and then gave up. Gus finally pulled him over the edge.

Big Belly went to the ladder that was leaning against the building a few feet away and climbed up it to the roof. One rung after another creaked under his weight. He ignored the way the wood sagged with each step. If the ladder had supported Gus, it would hold him.

Puffing hard, he stepped onto the roof. He motioned for Gus to bring Fiddler and pointed to a flagstaff poking out above the street from the roof over the front door.

"Tie the rope around that."

Gus hurried to obey his pa.

"You . . . you're not gonna string me up! You can't do that." Fiddler tried again to get free, writhing around. Big Belly held the rope a few feet from the loop.

"Stop fighting or I'll tighten the rope around your neck."

"It's cutting off circulation to my arms. They've gone numb."

"Ready, Pa," Gus called.

"You better hope the rope doesn't slip."

With that Big Belly hooked a foot under Fiddler's shoulder and rolled him right off the roof. Fiddler fell a few feet. The rope snapped him tight around until he spun, cutting into his body even more cruelly.

"That new snake oil peddler's got quite a crowd around him, Pa. What do we do now?"

He ignored his son. Big Belly took a deep breath and let out a bull-throated cry.

"Listen up, all you snivelers," he called. Shocked faces lifted to stare up at him. "You got it good with me running this town. Don't go buying a stranger's lies. What he's telling you is no more medicine than what's in them fancy bottles. You might feel good for a minute or two swilling that witch's brew—or believing what he has to say—but it's all worthless. Forget him. I live in Kiowa Springs. I'm the one to look after you."

Big Belly stared down into the street, which was now gloomy with approaching night. Light from inside the Royal Flush spilled out and illuminated a few dozen townspeople crowded around the wagon.

"I got one of them lying varmints dangling from a rope right here. He's helpless. So are the rest of them. You follow them and you won't end up like this one. You'll end up with the rope around your dirty necks!"

The crowd muttered. A few men called out taunts.

"You want to see him dancing at the end of the rope? I'll do it to show you what happens if you cross me. Gus, pull him up and put the noose around his neck." Big Belly stood at the very edge of the roof. "Then you can watch him dance around. Maybe not for very long since he's got such a scrawny neck."

Some in the crowd called out for him to let his prisoner go. Others begged for mercy as Gus hauled Fiddler up and adjusted the rope, pulling the loop tight around the old-timer's neck. Fiddler was in too bad a shape to even struggle now.

To Big Belly, the desperate cries were music to his ears. The townspeople wanted him to do them a favor by letting the old geezer live. His mind turned over the possibilities.

If he let Fiddler go, was he caving in to the crowd by giving them what they wanted, or was he being merciful?

"Get ready to shove him over the side. Make sure the rope's not too long."

"Just long enough to hang him, Pa?"

Big Belly nodded. Fiddler sputtered and choked when Gus yanked the rope tighter around his neck. Sheer terror gave him strength and made him try to get away, but Gus was too big and strong.

Then something went wrong. Gus yelled in alarm and flailed his arms around in a frantic attempt to keep his balance, but he failed and toppled from the roof to land with a meaty thud below. Big Belly swung around. Someone had joined them on the roof, coming up quietly from behind as the racket from the crowd covered any sounds he made.

"Who're you?" Big Belly demanded.

"Don't fall, Fiddler," the man said. A knife flashed in the light reflected from below. The blade severed the rope. The cut end dangled down across Fiddler's chest.

"I can breathe again. Thanks, Torrance."

Torrance Shannon stepped away and lowered the wicked knife.

"I don't take kindly to anyone threatening my friends." He advanced on Big Belly.

"Torrance, he's still got Dougal. Don't kill him 'til he tells where he's got your grandpappy all trussed up."

"He just saved your miserable life." Torrance moved closer, then laughed harshly. "I see why they call you Big Belly. That's quite a load you're carrying around your midsection."

"Makes it easier to brace my shotgun." Big Belly lifted the sawed-off weapon from behind his leg and pulled one trigger. The left barrel spat two feet of orange fire.

Torrance was spun around and fell to his knees, but

Fiddler toppled backward, toward the empty air. Making a wild grab, Torrance caught Fiddler's shoulder. His fingers cut into flesh. Fiddler's shirt began to stretch, then ripped.

"Fiddler!" Torrance made a final grab but missed. The bound man crashed to the street.

"You're another of Dougal's meddling grandsons? That makes Pike your brother."

Torrance rolled over and brandished his knife. On his back, half falling off the roof, he saw how futile fighting was. Big Belly pointed the shotgun squarely at him.

"You'll make an even better hostage than that mouthy old geezer. Thanks for helping me make the trade." He gestured for Torrance to stand.

As he did, Big Belly swung the shotgun barrel down hard. Metal hit bone. Torrance cried out in pain as he dropped the knife.

"You broke my wrist." Torrance looked daggers at Big Belly.

It was good to be hated by the likes of another Shannon offspring. It proved he controlled the entire family, grandfather and two grandsons. He was only sorry he had to kill them all. Tormenting them was such fun.

"Down the back. We're going to do some horse trading. You for my boy." Big Belly chanced a quick look down into the street. Gus was nowhere to be seen. Good. The boy had been able to skedaddle, and sense enough to do so. The fall must not have hurt him too badly.

Big Belly didn't see Fiddler from where he was. The old-timer must have landed too close to the building.

Torrance told him what he thought about being swapped for Gus.

"If you're not up to making the trade, what good are you?" Big Belly lifted the shotgun and aimed it squarely at Torrance. Killing him would feel real good.

CHAPTER 33

Moments before, Pike had ducked into the medicine wagon as soon as he saw Big Belly on the roof of the Royal Flush. He wasn't hiding, but he wanted to take the Ledbetters by surprise. He didn't think Big Belly had spotted him in that brief moment, especially with twilight settling over Kiowa Springs.

He heard Big Belly ranting but didn't really pay much attention to what the man was saying as he slipped out the front of the wagon and moved quickly into the shadows of the alley next to the gambling hall. He had just started toward the back of the building when a heavy step sounded behind him.

Pike twisted, his hand going to his Colt, but he held off as he recognized his brother.

"They've got Fiddler up there," Torrance said.

"What?"

"Ledbetter . . . I guess it's the one called Big Belly, from the looks of him . . . has Fiddler and is threatening to hang him. I'm going up there to stop them."

"That's where I was headed."

Torrance shook his head. "No, Pike, you need to stay

down here, in case I fail. If they push Fiddler off the roof, you'll have to save him."

"How in blazes can I do that from down here?"

"Shoot the rope," Torrance said.

Pike drew in a sharp breath. "That would be one hell of a trick," he said.

"If anybody in Texas can do it, it's you, brother."

Under normal circumstances, Pike would have been proud to hear Torrance express such confidence in his hand and eyes and shooting ability. Now there wasn't time to think about such things. But Torrance was right, and Pike nodded as he drew his Colt.

"Go," he told Torrance. "Those lard-buckets got up there, so there must be a ladder."

Torrance hurried on down the alley.

Pike called after him, "Where are Nessa and Irene?"

"Still in the wagon when I left there," Torrance flung over his shoulder.

Pike moved back to the street. Big Belly was still threatening to hang Fiddler. Pike stood tensely at the corner of the building, wondering if he could jump out, turn around, and drill Big Belly and Gus before they could make good on their threat to drop Fiddler over the edge.

Then he heard a sudden scuffle, followed almost instantly by Augustus Ledbetter falling off the building and crashing into the street. Pike hoped he had broken his neck, or at least an arm or a leg, but Gus rolled over, climbed to his feet, and staggered off into the gathering gloom. None of the townspeople tried to stop him. They were still too afraid of the Ledbetters.

Then a shotgun boomed on the roof. Shouts rose into the dusk. Pike couldn't wait any longer. He bounded out into the street and looked up, raising his gun . . .

Fiddler plummeted toward him.

Pike proved in that moment that he wasn't just fast at drawing his gun. He could holster it mighty darned fast, too. He pouched the iron, set himself, and caught Fiddler as the old-timer dropped toward the ground.

Fiddler was a small man, but even so, that much dead weight striking Pike drove him off his feet. When he hit the ground with Fiddler on top of him, the impact made the wounds he had suffered in the past few days hurt like blazes. But he had broken Fiddler's fall, and although both of them were shaken up, neither seemed to be badly hurt. Pike rolled Fiddler off of him and then leaned over the old-timer.

"Fiddler," he said. "Fiddler!"

"No need to shout," Fiddler said in a weak voice. "It isn't my ears that are all banged up. My hearing is still fine."

Pike helped him sit up. As he did so he poked and prodded, hunting for broken bones. The beating Big Belly had given him had busted a couple of ribs before. Thanks to Pike, Fiddler had come through this fall from the roof without dying.

"Thunderation, but my head hurts something fierce. I may have to have a sip of Torrance's medicine."

"You don't need any moonshine," Pike said. "Where's Torrance?"

"He saved me, the gallant lad, but I believe he may have been wounded. And now Ledbetter has him."

"Pike!" That was Nessa, pushing through the crowd with Irene Brewster beside her. "Pike, is Fiddler—"

"He's alive," Pike said as he came to his feet. "See to him. I don't think he's hurt too bad, but—"

"But he wasn't healed from before," Irene finished. "I know what his earlier injuries were. I can see if he has any more."

Pike exchanged a look with Nessa. "He said Torrance saved him, but that now Torrance is Ledbetter's prisoner."

Nessa gripped his arm. “You have to find them, Pike.”

“I intend to,” Pike said grimly.

He checked around the back of the building. A ladder leaning against the wall led to the roof. There was no sign of Big Belly’s wagon. Pike fished a lucifer from his pocket and snapped it to life with his thumbnail. He found wagon tracks easily enough in the flickering glare, but he had followed those tracks before and been stymied.

He returned to the street.

“It was Big Belly Ledbetter and his son, Gus,” one excited townie told him. “Gus took a tumble off the roof, too, but he lit a shuck.”

Pike had seen that with his own eyes, but he didn’t waste time pointing that out. “Which way did he go?”

The man shook his head. Too much had happened for him to be a reliable witness.

“Pike, Pike!” Nessa waved to him from the back of the wagon. He went over.

“Fiddler’s going to be all right. Irene is looking after him. Are you going after Big Belly?”

“He took Torrance hostage,” Pike said. “That’s better than him having Fiddler, I suppose, but if Torrance mouths off, he’s likely to get himself shot. Big Belly isn’t the type to take lip from anyone, especially with the mood he’s in now.” Pike frowned in thought. “With Big Belly gone in the buckboard, Gus will need a horse. Maybe I can stop him.”

“He’ll have his horse stabled behind the Royal Flush,” Irene called from inside the wagon. “I’ve been thinking and—”

Pike wasted no time running through the Royal Flush. To his surprise, a dozen men scattered around the interior were settling down to poker games. Almost seeing Fiddler hanged and Gus Ledbetter falling off the roof meant nothing to them. He reached the back room and burst out the door. Fifty feet away a small shed he'd never noticed before had to be the Ledbetter stables. He ran to it.

He heard a skittish horse inside—and a man cursing. With a powerful kick, he battered down the flimsy door. Making a smooth, quick move, he drew his gun.

"Give up, Gus. You're not going anywhere."

"Says you!" Gus Ledbetter was half hidden in shadow. He must have had his gun already drawn and cocked. Muzzle flame spurted in the shadows. A slug ripped past Pike's head.

Gus could still be valuable to him. Instead of triggering a return shot, Pike whirled around and crouched just outside the shed.

"There's no need to die," he shouted. "Your pa's got my brother and grandpappy. I need you to make a swap. Blood for blood."

"You've already got Harvey. What do you need me for?" Gus's voice sank. He cursed. "You don't have him, do you? What happened? Harvey didn't get away. You killed him!"

Pike waited. If Gus acted without thinking in his anger, Pike had him.

Unfortunately, Gus reacted differently from what Pike expected. Silence. No flurry of lead.

"Gus? Give up. You don't have to die!" Pike showed part of his arm to draw fire. When it didn't come, he dived parallel to the ground and skidded along, his iron ready to fire.

He pointed his gun at . . . nothing. Pike scrambled to his feet and made a quick search. A horse stood nervously in its stall, but Gus was gone. At the rear of the stall a board had been pried loose. A strip of Gus's shirt had ripped off as he squeezed out into the night.

Pike left the shed and circled, wary of a trap. He found the broken board and scuff marks in the dirt where Gus had run off. In the distance he heard a galloping horse. But was it Gus or someone else? He had no way of knowing. Disgusted, Pike jammed his pistol back into his holster and returned to the medicine wagon.

"I didn't hear any shots," Nessa said. She looked at Pike and saw his expression. "You didn't get him, did you?"

"He got clean away. And he figured out that his brother's dead. When he tells his pa, both Dougal and Torrance are likely to come to a sudden end."

"Do you have any idea where they went?" Nessa asked.

"Tracking at night is always hard, and I failed when the sun was high up in the sky."

"I think I know where they might be."

Pike looked past his sister. Irene stood in the back door of the wagon.

"The Ledbetters have a house somewhere out east of here," she went on.

"That's where Big Belly took you? Or where he was taking you when you escaped?"

"I don't know the exact location, but I heard Harvey bragging on how it was a fortress. I've never seen anything like that, and I don't have any notion where it might be."

"Has Fiddler?" Pike climbed into the wagon. Fiddler was stretched out. He held an open bottle of Torrance's snake oil. He looked up at Pike.

"Don't go worrying yourself, Pike. All I'm doing is partaking of the delicious aroma from this potion. I'm not going to take a sip, as much as I want to." He heaved a deep sigh. "Your mother's been good to me. Starting to drink again would be a betrayal of her trust."

"What can you tell me of where Ledbetter took you and Dougal? I've got to get them free before Gus can tell his pa that I killed Harvey."

"That would be bad," Fiddler said. "Fetch me a rifle. I'll go out with you to find them."

He tried to sit up but only fell back flat onto the makeshift bed.

"You're not going anywhere, but you can still help save them. Did you see a big house? A fort? Tell me everything you can think of."

"I was driving most of the way. Get me paper and a pencil. I can draw a map, but I never saw anything like a house. He tied me and Dougal to trees."

Pike found the paper and Fiddler carefully drew a map. For a man so beat up and in a sorry way, his hand was steady and the map precise. This was the sort of thing he was good at—along with playing the fiddle, of course. Every landmark he thought could be useful was added with a detailed note describing it. The longer he worked, the more anxious Pike became.

"Time's against us, Fiddler," he finally said. He took the map.

"There's more. I need to remember all the details."

"This'll do. If I save Dougal and Torrance, this'll be the reason." Pike held up the map.

"You mean *when* you pull their fat from the fire."

"Rest up. We'll all be back as quick as we can."

Pike jumped from the wagon and collided with Irene Brewster. She clung to him for an instant, then pushed back, looking flustered.

"Sorry, Mr. Shannon—Pike. That was clumsy of me."

"I ran into you. Have you remembered any more about Ledbetter's fort?"

"Not really." She looked at the paper in his hand. "Is that Fiddler's map? May I see it?"

Pike was champing at the bit but knew any additional

details Irene supplied might cut down on the time it took to find Ledbetter's hideout.

"This bend in the road is tricky. I've heard stagecoach drivers say it's blind all around. They all worry about outlaws holding them up there. If they get past it, it's a quick and safe trip into town. I suspect this is where Big Belly leaves the road to go to his fort. There's a deep ravine that hides everything around it, or so I've heard."

"This will help," he said. "Will you see to Fiddler? Talk him out of it if he gets a yen to sample any of Torrance's potion."

"You mean your brother's moonshine."

"He hasn't touched a drop in months and wants to stay sober."

"Good for him," she said. She laid her palm on Pike's chest and looked up at him. "Be careful, Pike. Don't go getting yourself shot up. Big Belly likely has a lot of his gang there. Not all of them are his family, but enough are. They'll fight to the death to protect him." She looked up into his eyes. Irene hesitated, then kissed him quickly before jumping into the wagon.

Pike had no time to work out what he felt about that quick kiss—or what it meant to Irene. He hurried to the livery stable and saddled his dun. A quick check showed his rifle was fully loaded, and he had several boxes of cartridges for both his Winchester and his Colt in his saddlebags. All he needed now was luck and for Fiddler's map to be accurate enough that he rode straight to Ledbetter's stronghold.

He led the dun from the stable and started to mount. Another rider blocked his way. His hand drifted to the pistol at his hip before he recognized the other horsebacker. Nessa wore boots, trousers, and a man's shirt under a gray duster, and her long red hair was tucked up under a brown hat, but he knew instantly who she was.

"You're not leaving me behind, Pike Shannon."

"Blast it, this is no place for you, Nessa. It's going to be bloody."

"I've been practicing," she said, patting the rifle in her saddle scabbard. "And I can't match your speedy draw, but I'll bet you a dollar I can shoot better than plenty of men with a six-gun."

She had strapped on a gun belt. The bone handle on the Colt gleamed in the starlight.

"You know it's hard to shoot a man."

"I won't hesitate to do whatever I need to if it saves Dougal and Torrance." She laughed. "I've got to save Torrance. I'll be able to josh him about it for years and years."

Pike knew that arguing with Nessa would waste time, and, in the end, she would get her way. All his arguments with her ended that way, for some reason. He won his share of debates with Torrance, but never their sister.

He settled in the saddle, then put his heels to the dun and rocketed off. Nessa kept pace as they raced into the night.

CHAPTER 34

"It took long enough to find this trail," Pike said. He stood and studied the terrain off the main road. Brush had been used to wipe out hoofprints and any tracks left by wagons. A rocky patch helped hide the trail that led into a deep ravine.

"You'd have found it without Fiddler's map," Nessa said.

Pike doubted that, or at least that he'd have discovered the road in time to save Dougal and Torrance. As it was, he fretted that they were too late.

Gus Ledbetter had ridden here directly with the news that Harvey was dead. How long would it take Big Belly to react? From everything Pike had seen, the Ledbetter family patriarch had a fierce, sudden temper.

"What are we waiting for? Let's go." Nessa urged her horse forward.

Pike grabbed the reins and pulled hard, stopping her.

"You're the one who said time was running out," she told him. "Standing here isn't going to save Dougal or Torrance."

"Neither is getting ourselves killed. Look up on the rims of the ravine. What do you see?"

"Nothing," she said. "Are you worried about sentries?"

"Ledbetter isn't the kind to leave an open path into his stronghold. Why aren't there guards?"

"Something in the ravine takes care of intruders," Nessa guessed. "It'll take us hours to circle around and come at him from a different direction if we don't want to be seen."

Pike stewed. She was right, but if they advanced without knowing what lay in wait for them, they might well be doomed.

"Pike, somebody's coming from the east. Riding fast."

He swung into the saddle. She followed his lead.

"What do we do now?" Nessa asked. "Find some place to hide?"

"No traveler gallops like that. It'd wear out their horse in a couple miles. Somebody's in a powerful hurry to get somewhere." He looked down the narrow, rugged canyon. To him it looked like a grave with the ends knocked out. "Let's see how this plays out. Follow my lead. And keep your head down. In that getup, they might not be able to tell right away that you're a girl."

Two riders rounded a bend in the road and bore down on them. Pike shifted in the saddle to be sure his gun rode easy in the holster. He slipped the leather thong off the hammer just as the pair spotted them. They slowed and walked their exhausted horses forward. The two kept looking from Pike and Nessa to the hidden trail into the ravine.

These were the men Pike needed right now.

"Howdy," one rider called. The other hung back, hand on his gun butt. "You two need some help?"

"No, but Big Belly does," Pike replied. "You heading up to the house, too?"

"House?" The man laughed harshly. "That's one name for it."

"Who are you?" Pike demanded. He rested his hand on his gun. Beside him his sister did likewise.

"Paul and Troop."

"Cousins," Pike ventured, making his voice sound confident. He hadn't seen these two around Kiowa Springs, so it stood to reason they were new to the area.

"From up in Fort Worth," one of them answered. "We got the call and rode here straightaway."

"They're all right," Pike said loudly. He took his hand off his pistol and nodded to Nessa to do the same.

"Who're you?" the one who had spoken asked. Pike suspected this was Paul.

"Big Belly told us to join him, too," Pike responded without really answering the question. "He's preparing for a big attack. Come on."

Pike wheeled his horse around and jumped over the brush camouflage on the trail leading into the canyon. The hair on the back of his neck prickled, as if he expected a bullet at any instant.

Nessa rode alongside and whispered, "They're talking it over. The one who hung back is reluctant."

"They'll be along in a second. Just wait." Pike looked up at the steep walls. At one time a powerful stream had cut through the hills to make this canyon, but the water was long gone.

As he predicted, the two men followed. Pike gauged their progress by the crunch of their horses' hooves against the gravel. While he didn't like having enemies behind him, he felt more confident with them along. If Big Belly had guards posted, at least two of the party would be identified as family.

Suddenly, Nessa pulled back on the reins and jumped to the ground to check her horse's right front hoof. Looking up at Pike, she winked to let him know she was running some sort of bluff.

"Horse pull up lame?" asked the one Pike had decided was Troop.

"Just a stone under the shoe, looks like," Pike said. He didn't want Nessa answering and revealing that she was female. "I can pick it out."

He dismounted, too, and drew his knife from its sheath with his left hand. At the same time, he waved the other two on with his right hand.

Pike heard Paul and Troop discussing the matter. The way they spoke in hurried whispers put him on guard. He glanced at Nessa and saw the way her eyes abruptly widened. That was all the warning he needed to turn and reach for his gun.

He was barely in time. Both men were already drawing. Pike got off the first shot and hit Paul in the head. The man snapped backward in the saddle and tumbled off his horse. The animal bucked and kicked, its hooves catching its former rider in midair. Even if Pike hadn't ended Paul's life with his accurate shot, the horse had finished off its own rider.

Nessa had her gun out. She fired at Troop but missed. The shot came close enough to spook the man's horse and ruined his shot. A bullet tore past Pike, missing by a foot or more. He fanned off three fast shots. All of them missed Troop, whose horse had reared and lashed out with its front hooves.

The Ledbetter cousin tried to race past. He should have made a stand where he was. Nessa tracked him with her gun. As he rode past her, she fired. Troop slumped in the saddle but kept going.

Nessa stared at the pistol in her hand. In a low voice she said, "I shot him, Pike. I shot him."

"You'd better hope you killed him. If he reaches Big Belly, they'll know we're coming."

He reloaded and mounted. His sister swung up into her saddle but then sat there staring after Troop. Pike reached over and put his hand on her shoulder.

"You saved us, sister. They had figured out we weren't part of their family, not even distant relatives."

"I'd never fired at anyone before, much less . . . much less—"

"Fired in self-defense," he finished for her. "It's not going to get any easier. You want to ride back to town? If you do, now's the time to leave."

"No!" Nessa's vehement reply settled Pike's nerves a little. Killing a man was a burden that had to be carried around forever. She had to be completely committed to the fight or they'd both end up dead. "Dougal and Torrance need us."

He nodded, then led the way through the winding ravine. Alert for an ambush, his keen eyes spotted a branching route hardly wide enough for a horse and rider. He touched his Colt, then moved his hand away before Nessa saw.

Troop had tried to escape down this narrow passage. He hadn't gone ten yards before he died. The riderless horse had gone on, but Troop's body lay sprawled on the ravine's rocky floor. Pike's sister had been deadly accurate.

"The ravine opens up, Pike," she said. He was glad she was focused ahead and hadn't noticed Troop's body. "I smell smoke, too."

He inhaled deeply. "A cooking fire. They're fixing a meal," he said. "Venison, from the aroma."

"It's making me hungry," she said. "Maybe they'll invite us in for a bite."

Big Belly wasn't likely to invite them in for anything other than to hang them like he'd tried to do with Fiddler. As they came to the end of the trail, he halted beside Nessa and studied the broad, shallow bowl where Big Belly had built his camp that opened up before them.

"It is a fortress," Nessa said. "That's not an understatement at all."

A sturdy ten-foot-tall palisade circled a compound with three buildings inside. The gate was secured and at least two guards patrolled catwalks around the wall.

"There's no quick way to get in," Pike said. "We'll have to wait for complete dark before I sneak in."

"I'm going, too. Torrance and Dougal are kin. Both of us stand a better chance of getting them free."

Pike wondered if Big Belly had murdered them already. Gus must have arrived and told his father that Harvey was dead by Pike's hand.

"They're still alive," he said suddenly. "Even if he knows one boy is dead, he won't kill Dougal or Torrance. That'd get some revenge, but he'll want me to die, too."

"Pike, no! You're not going to swap yourself for them. He'd never honor a trade. Then he'd have all three of you. Mama could never accept that all the Shannon men were dead. It was hard enough on her when Tyree and Papa died."

"I can get in. You have to hang back to take word to Fiddler about what's happened. He'll be our last chance at stopping the Ledbetters."

"I'm sorry *I* didn't kill *both* of those cousins. I won't rest until they're all dead. Big Belly and the rest are just plain evil."

"No argument on that, but they're also smart. Somebody who knew how to lay out a fort built that place. Approaching it will be hard the way the ground is scrubbed clean of all vegetation. I'll have to get in quick before the moon rises."

"That's a while from now, Pike. There's no telling what Big Belly will do before then."

"He built this as a hideout. He kept his still close to town so shipping the moonshine was easier. But here?" Pike shook his head. The more he studied the fort, the more he realized the difficulty getting in. Big Belly had fire pits scattered around the bare ground. If those were ignited, the entire area outside the walls would be lit up like day.

From this hideout he could hold off an entire cavalry company.

They couldn't stay here, out in the open, Pike realized. If somebody down there had field glasses, they might be spotted. He motioned for Nessa to follow him and led the way to the left, to a thick grove of post oaks about a quarter of a mile from where the trail opened up.

"Look, there!" Nessa pointed off into the distance almost as soon as they had gotten into the cover. "Someone else is coming."

"There must be other ways to reach the fort. We came in from the west, but that road's going east."

"And another comes in from the north. Where do you think it leads?"

Pike wasn't much for speculating. What was real and faced him was always more important than "what if?"

"Four more coming to join him. He must have sent out the call across all of north Texas. The two we took care of back in the ravine said they rode down from Fort Worth."

"The only reason to gather such a force is to crush any revolt in Kiowa Springs," Nessa said.

Pike watched the riders approach the gate. The sentries on the wall spotted them right away. When the four came to a halt in front of the gate, a conversation went on for several minutes. Finally, the gate opened and they disappeared inside. Pike tried to make out details beyond the gate, but he was too far away. He let out his pent-up breath when the gate slammed shut.

Big Belly had added to his army in an already impenetrable fortress.

"It's now or never, Pike. If Big Belly leads his men out, he might leave Dougal and Torrance behind and—"

Pike held up his hand, silencing her. From the west, following the same route they had taken, came a wagon—but not just any wagon.

"That's Torrance's medicine wagon!" Nessa blurted. "What's Fiddler doing driving it out here? And how'd he find the trail?"

"He's the one who drew the map that put us on the right track, remember? Never underestimate Fiddler. He's smart and stubborn." Pike studied the wagon rolling toward the Ledbetter stronghold, then exclaimed, "That's not Fiddler driving. It's Ada Brewster."

"Irene's mother? What's she doing out here?"

"I have no idea."

Ada Brewster never slowed as she neared the fort. The men on the wall leveled their rifles at her but didn't open fire. She pulled up outside the gate and yelled out, "I want to see Big Belly."

"What's your business?" came the retort. "And how come you're driving that wagon? Gus said that belongs to the Shannons."

"The ones you're holding prisoner. Torrance and Dougal Shannon. I want to talk to Big Belly about them."

A heated argument went on between those on the wall, leaving Ada Brewster sitting in the wagon. Pike halfway expected to see Fiddler pop up beside her with a shotgun in his hands. She had been smitten by Dougal, and Fiddler had a way about him of convincing people to go along with his schemes. The only thing Pike could figure was that they intended to make a daring rescue attempt.

And from what he had seen of the fort it would be a futile attempt. At best they'd end up prisoners, too. At worst? Pike clamped his teeth together hard thinking about that. Big Belly wasn't the kind to care if he killed a woman in cold blood.

"Fiddler wasn't in any shape to ride out with her," Nessa said, voicing his own concern. "She must be alone. What's she up to?"

"It's now or never," Pike said. "Do what you can to distract them if I get into trouble."

"Pike, wait!"

He started running on foot, taking advantage of what scant cover there was. On horseback he would have had no chance of escaping detection. A few gullies and knobs gave a little protection—but darned little. Bent low, he ran for the space directly behind the wagon.

Just when he thought he might make it without being spotted, a cry from the sentries went up. Pike braced himself for the bullet that would take his life.

Chapter 35

"Up there, at the end of the ravine!"

Pike heard other guards join in the frantic alarm. They *hadn't* seen him, after all. Instead, Nessa was waving frantically to draw their attention, he saw when he glanced over his shoulder. When the guards opened fire on her, she faded back into the ravine, out of sight.

"You danged fools," Ada Brewster shouted. "Let me in. You're under attack! I don't want to be stranded on this side of the wall."

Pike skidded along on his belly and came to a halt under the wagon. Flipping over on his back, he reached up with both hands and grabbed the front bolster on the wagon's undercarriage. Just as he wrapped his hands around that grip, the wagon lurched forward and dragged him with it as Ada drove into the compound.

He exerted all his strength to pull himself up off the ground. He kicked his right foot up and got the toe of his boot hooked over one of the braces on the wagon's frame. The rough ground slid beneath him, only inches under his back.

The gate slammed shut, and he heard more commotion all around as the wagon jolted to a halt. Pike stayed where he was, straining to hold himself up so he was less likely to be noticed.

"What're you dimwits shooting at?" Big Belly waddled out of the main building and passed a few feet from where Pike hung underneath the medicine wagon.

"There was a rider comin' toward the west wall from the passage through the ravine. You want us to go find who it was?"

"Troop and Paul are supposed to get here sometime today. Was it them?" Big Belly asked. "You didn't shoot your own cousins, did you?"

"There was only a single rider," the guard who was doing the talking replied. "And I know Troop and Paul. This was somebody else. Smaller."

"Don't leave the compound. That might be Pike Shannon thinking to lure us out so he can kill us off one by one."

Murmured agreement told Pike none of Big Belly's gang wanted to risk their necks by riding out to see if they could discover who the stranger was. It would have pleased him that they were so afraid of him if he hadn't been hanging precariously under Torrance's wagon at the moment, gritting his teeth from the effort of doing so.

Big Belly went to the driver's box.

"What're you doing out here, Ada?"

"You know why I came, Big Belly Ledbetter," she said sternly. "Help me climb down from this contraption. Somebody took my buckboard while I was at a meeting with the church ladies, and I don't ride a horse like I used to."

Well, that explained why Ada hadn't been in the house when he went back there earlier, Pike thought. It was pure luck that both he and Big Belly had missed her and *she* hadn't been taken hostage, too.

"Climb down your own self," Big Belly said. "You figured

out where the road was to get here. You can keep on getting yourself mixed up in things that don't affect you."

"Not affect me? I ought to thrash you good and proper. You kidnapped my girl. I heard all about it when she got back to town."

"She was playing with fire," Big Belly said sullenly. "She's lucky she didn't get herself killed."

"You would pay dearly for that if she had," Ada said.

"Don't go threatening me," Big Belly said, his tone cold.

"Don't *you* go threatening me, you old goose. You couldn't keep a secret in Kiowa Springs if you glued everyone's mouth shut."

"More likely, I'd slit their throats. That way works a whole lot better."

Ada Brewster's feet appeared just inches from Pike's face as she dropped to the ground.

"You're certainly no gentleman, not helping me."

"You're no lady. I don't know why I let you in."

"Because you're still sweet on me, that's why. And don't give me that guff about you being a married man. Nobody's seen your missus in years. For all anybody knows, you killed her and buried her under this fancy fort of yours."

The gunshot startled Pike so much he let go of the wagon and hit the ground. Not falling far, he made little noise. But within arm's reach, Ada Brewster sprawled on the ground. A red bloom on her breast told the tale. Big Belly had gunned her down in cold blood.

"Why'd you do that, Pa?" Gus Ledbetter knelt beside Ada. If he looked away from the woman, he'd be sure to spot Pike, who lay absolutely still.

"I don't let anyone get by with saying things like she did. She disrespected your ma."

"She's not dead. I feel a pulse in her throat," Gus said. "But she's in a bad way."

"Don't let her die for a minute or two. I know why she came out here," Big Belly said. He walked away and disappeared into the main building.

Pike looked for a better hiding spot. The wagon was ringed with Big Belly's men. He heard one open the vehicle's back door and footsteps tromp the length. Glass broke and a general ruckus came from inside as he searched drawers and boxes. Liquids dripped between the floorboards onto Pike, and there wasn't anything he could do about it.

Big Belly returned, half dragging someone else with him. Pike went cold inside when he realized it was Dougal.

"See what I did to her? That's going to happen to you, old man. You want to be put in a grave alongside hers? Or maybe I'll just bury the two of you together in the same hole. You and her was sparking, weren't you?"

"You shot her!" Dougal cried in outrage. Pike was furious at Big Belly's brutal act, too, but trapped under the wagon like this, he wasn't able to act. Not yet.

Dougal dropped to his knees beside Ada and cradled her head in his lap.

"Where do you want to be buried?" Big Belly asked with a sneer in his tone.

Pike wasn't able to see Torrance, but he recognized his brother's voice coming from a ways off as he snapped, "I want to be buried after you. Years later. You are the epitome of evil."

"I don't rightly know what that is, but I like the sound of it. Your brother gunned down my boy. Killing the lot of you's just getting even. Barely. I ought to think of ways to string it out and make sure you all suffer."

"Pa," Gus said with a sudden warning sound in his voice.

"Shut up," Big Belly snapped.

"Pa! There's somebody under the wagon."

Gus dropped to his hands and knees and stared straight at Pike.

Hanging under the wagon had been a dangerous, spur-of-the-moment plan. Pike hadn't had time to figure out what he wanted to do, other than get inside the compound.

Well, he had gotten in, all right, but now any further chance of surprise was gone.

He drew his pistol and fired point blank into Gus's face. The man made a squeaking sound and keeled over. Pike fired at Big Belly's feet and hit the right ankle. Big Belly stumbled and fell to the ground.

"You!" he shrieked. "Get him! Kill him! It's Pike Shannon. A thousand dollars to the man who kills him!"

Pike fired at Big Belly again but missed. The horse pulling the wagon tried to bolt and a wheel rolling in front of him spoiled his aim. By the time he wiggled from under the wagon, Big Belly had made it back to his feet and was hobbling away. His men were confused and milled around, but they couldn't have provided better protection for him if they'd been trying. Pike couldn't get a clear shot.

But he had plenty of targets anyway. As two men finally realized he was a threat and tried to swing their rifles in his direction, Pike shot them both, his bullets spilling them off their feet.

That emptied his pistol, but he didn't take the time to reload. Instead he dashed to Torrance's side and dropped to a knee. His brother had been bowled over when Big Belly ran for the building behind him.

"You must have had a rough ride," Torrance said as Pike used his knife to cut through the rope around Torrance's wrists. "It's smoother riding inside the wagon."

"Stop the palaver. Grab a gun." Pike reloaded, his hands working automatically as he thumbed fresh cartridges into the Colt. The wagon gave them some cover, since most of

Big Belly's men happened to be on the far side of it, but that slight respite wouldn't last long, Pike knew.

He glanced down at Dougal. His grandpappy still cradled Ada's head. Tears ran down his cheeks.

"He gunned her down," Dougal wailed. "Without so much as a fare-thee-well, he shot her."

"Get her into the wagon," Pike ordered. He used his knife to sever the ropes on Dougal's wrists.

"Help mé. She's too much for me to get inside alone." Dougal stroked Ada's hair.

"Torrance and I have our hands full," Pike said. He leaned around the back of the wagon and dropped another of Big Belly's clan with a swift, accurate shot. Moving quickly, he returned the Colt to his holster and grabbed a rifle that one of the first men he'd shot had dropped. This worked better to pick off the guards on the walls. They were only now beginning to realize the extent of the massacre going on behind them.

Torrance had the other guard's rifle. Following Pike's lead, he emptied the Winchester, spraying lead along the parapet inside the stockade fence, then tossed it aside and rolled over a body to pluck the dead man's pistol from his belt.

"You took your sweet time getting here," he told Pike.

"Nessa slowed me down," Pike said.

"You let her come along? Ma is going to have a fit when she hears that."

"I'm sure you'll want to be the one telling her. You take such pleasure in making me look bad," Pike said. He took another guard off the parapet. The man dropped his rifle, clapped both hands to his belly where Pike's bullet had drilled him, and toppled forward, turning over completely in the air before crashing to the ground.

Pike and Torrance stood back to back now, taking potshots

at any of Big Belly's gang foolish enough to poke out their heads. The first barrage had been their most successful. Now that the gang was alerted, neither Pike nor Torrance had clean shots.

Worse, they were being fired on by men able to take cover. It was only a matter of time before they caught some lead.

"Grandpappy's got her loaded into the wagon," Torrance said. "It's time for us to take our leave."

"I hate letting any of them get away," Pike said. He especially wanted to end Big Belly Ledbetter's moonshining career once and for all.

Torrance read his mind. "He's all barricaded inside the main house. There's no way we'll pry him loose, not with a half dozen of his gunmen trying to ventilate us."

Pike threw down the pistol he had taken from the dead man and said, "Get into the wagon. Mix up something explosive."

"What's that likely to be?" Torrance edged toward the wagon, holding his fire.

"You're the one with book learning. Just mix up a lot of it."

"You always want me to do the impossible," Torrance complained. "For once, you ought to be the one coming up with all the miracles."

Pike glanced at Gus Ledbetter's still body. He had taken out both of Big Belly's sons. That hardly seemed enough payment for all the Kiowa Springs tyrant had done.

"I'll skin you alive, Pike Shannon!" came the furious cry from the house. "You've ruined me. You've killed my sons. You'll pay for all that and burning down my still and—"

Pike emptied his pistol at the loophole through which Big Belly was shouting. Big Belly stopped his ranting, but

Pike knew the chances he'd actually hit the man and killed him were slim. He bent over and grabbed Gus Ledbetter's pistol. Shooting Big Belly with his son's gun would be ironic justice.

But he had no chance to squeeze off even a single round. A rifle barrel poked out of the loophole. Flame leaped from the muzzle. Slug after slug tore past Pike and forced him to take cover under the wagon.

"I got it, Pike. I got a couple bottles all whipped up," Torrance shouted from inside the vehicle.

"Throw it at the building," Pike ordered. He fumbled in his pocket for a tin holding a few lucifers he used to start campfires.

Torrance climbed onto the driver's box through the curtained entrance at the front of the wagon. He held a corked bottle by the neck in each hand. One after the other he flung them, and they spun through the air to crash into the wall and spew a noxious fluid everywhere.

"What now?" Torrance asked.

"The gate!" Pike yelled as he surged out from under the wagon. "Drive to the gate!"

With all of Big Belly's men shooting at them, nobody had thought to close the gate.

As Pike ran toward the house, he threw lead from the Colt in his right hand at the half dozen outlaws still shooting at him. With his left hand, he struck the lucifer he had dug out. The flare momentarily revealed his position in the shadows. Three gunmen opened fire on him from the house. He winced as he felt a sting on the side of his neck.

Then he tossed the match into the puddle that had collected at the base of the wall.

For an instant, nothing happened, then flames exploded upward, licking hungrily at the wall.

"Roast in hell," Pike said, hoping Big Belly Ledbetter heard him. Then he ran after the medicine wagon, which Torrance had wheeled around. He was whipping up the team, urging them into a run.

The wagon's back door flapped open. As soon as Pike was close enough, he leaped, landed in the doorway, and grabbed hold of the frame with his left hand. Though Pike knew his right hand still wasn't perfect, he used it to empty the remaining rounds in his Colt. Two more men pitched off the parapet as the wagon raced through the gate and out of the compound.

Behind them, the big house in the center of the stronghold exploded in a huge blast that sent a towering column of flame shooting high in the night sky. Pike looked back in astonishment. He'd planned on burning the place down, not blowing it to smithereens. He didn't know what Big Belly had stored in there. A lot of ammunition and blasting powder, judging by the size of the explosion.

What caused it wasn't important. What mattered was that there was no way Big Belly Ledbetter had escaped. Justice had finally caught up to him.

Pike was about to let out a victorious whoop when he remembered the price paid for this triumph. Big Belly had gunned down Ada Brewster. He didn't know if she was still alive or not, but if she was, they needed to get to Kiowa Springs as quickly as possible. Irene might be able to do something to help her mother.

Dougal sat on the floor with Ada cradled in his arms. As Pike pulled the door closed, shutting out the sight of the huge fire behind them, he said, "Is she . . . ?"

"She's still breathin'," Dougal said, "but I don't know for how much longer."

Pike nodded. He moved to the front of the wagon, climbed out onto the box, and pointed out the way to Torrance.

"Head for that ravine. Nessa's waiting for us there."

Torrance nodded and urged the team on, and that was when they saw muzzle flashes split the darkness at the mouth of the ravine.

CHAPTER 36

"I'm gonna have some fun with you, you little hellcat," Big Belly Ledbetter said as he closed his hands cruelly around Nessa's arms and dragged her against him. "Your brothers are dead. I killed them for what they did to me. They killed my boys."

"You're lying," Nessa cried. "You've done no such thing. Pike and Torrance are alive. So is Dougal! You're lying!"

Big Belly laughed. It echoed long, loud, and harsh.

"I watched Torrance crawl. I shot him a dozen times after I blew the head off your grandpa. He begged me not to shoot him, but I enjoyed watching him grovel."

"No!"

"And Pike. Pike Shannon was the most cowardly of them all. He sobbed. He cried like a baby. He was on his knees praying for me not to shoot him, but I did."

Big Belly was hurting from the places where bullets had creased him during the battle, but it made him feel better to torment Pike's sister like this. He hurt, as well, from the knowledge that Harvey and Augustus were both dead and his empire was gone along with his stronghold, destroyed by the fiery holocaust burning half a mile away.

He wasn't quite sure what had happened, other than that cache of powder and ammunition he had in the house had blown up for some reason, after he'd slipped out the back, grabbed a horse, and gotten away from there. He hoped Pike had been killed in the blast, but even if that wasn't the case, Big Belly was still going to win. He was going to hang on to Nessa until he was sure he was safe—and then he would kill her, too.

He was about to brag more about how Pike had groveled before dying, when from somewhere nearby a voice declared, "You've got quite an imagination, Big Belly."

Jerking around but still holding Nessa in his brutal grip, Big Belly said, "Shannon!"

"That's right. Dougal and Torrance and I are still alive. You never came close to killing any of us. All you did was gun down Ada Brewster. She wasn't armed, Big Belly. You shot a helpless old woman."

The taunting voice enraged Big Belly. He let go of Nessa with his right hand and used it to draw his pistol.

"I've got her, Pike," he called. "I've got a gun pointed at your sister's head."

"I'm sorry, Pike," Nessa said. "I never thought he could sneak up on me, but he did. I . . . I guess I'm not as ready for something like this as I thought I was."

"Don't worry about it," Pike called reassuringly. "He won't get away."

"The hell I won't!" Big Belly blustered. "Should I blow her brains out or maybe put a few rounds into her belly so she'll die of lead poisoning? There wouldn't be a thing you could do but watch her die a slow, painful death. Yeah, Shannon, I like that. I'm going to kill her that way."

Nessa clapped her hands over her face and sobbed,

"It's my fault, it's all my fault!" She bent over, apparently wracked by misery and guilt. Big Belly didn't try to stop her.

Then he saw her reach into the top of her boot, twist around almost faster than the eye could follow, and lash out at him. Pain lanced into him, and he looked down in amazement to see the handle of a knife sticking out, right where the top of his enormous belly started sloping out from his chest.

Nessa tore free, dived to the side, and yelled, "Get him, Pike!"

Pike had been working his way closer through the shadows. He drew and fanned off a single round as Big Belly tried to jerk his gun into line. Pike wasn't sure at first where his bullet struck, but Big Belly reached up with his left hand and pressed it where his heart should have been—if he had a heart.

Big Belly swayed and let out a growl like an enraged bear. Then he toppled forward. He hit the ground so hard it seemed to shake.

Pike stared at the fallen giant. Then with a quick spin, he twirled the gun around and dropped it into his holster. Only then did he go to the body to be certain Big Belly was dead.

He had drilled Big Belly Ledbetter squarely through the heart.

"Pike, Pike, did you get him?" That was Nessa. He hurried to her side and helped her up.

"He won't be a problem any longer. Between my bullet and that knife you planted in him, he's done for." Pike glanced toward the still-burning stronghold. "He won't be escaping certain death this time."

"Good," Nessa said, leaning forward and hugging him. "If anybody ever had it coming, it was Big Belly Ledbetter."

Pike couldn't argue with that. Instead he cupped a hand to his mouth and shouted for Torrance to come ahead with the wagon.

They still needed to get back to Kiowa Springs.

Chapter 37

"It just doesn't seem fair," Fiddler groused. "Dougal and I did all the work whipping up enthusiasm in a crowd for our magical elixir, and yet it's Torrance that's reaping the profits."

Pike had to laugh. His brother was selling the bottles of his remaining snake oil so he wouldn't have to carry them back to Warbonnet.

"He'd better be careful what he's peddling," Pike said. "Those might be the same chemicals he mixed up to set fire to Ledbetter's compound."

"From the sound of it, they made the whole place go up like a midwinter bonfire." Fiddler heaved a sigh. "I wish I'd seen it." He looked at Pike. "I wish I'd been there when you gave Big Belly his final comeuppance, too. Never did anyone deserve getting a bullet in the heart more."

"That, gentlemen, is that," Torrance said, dusting off his hands. His coat pocket bulged with greenbacks and not a few silver dollars from the sales. "I'm ready to head home. You have everything packed, Fiddler?"

"Most of what Dougal and I brought with us was

destroyed when the Ledbetter boys set fire to my wagon. So I'm raring to go, as they say."

"Was this exciting enough for you?" Nessa asked, coming from inside the Brewster house. "I admit it was more than I expected. It'll make a better story to tell than it was to live through."

Pike felt the same way. Even his family never understood why he spoke so little of his years on the trail. There was only so much to say, and once it was told, everyone wanted a new tale. Most of what happened to him wasn't fit for retelling. He vented a deep sigh. Most of it he wished he could forget. He looked past Torrance's wagon toward Kiowa Springs. Much of what had happened here was like that.

"It did break the boredom," he admitted.

"All aboard," called Torrance. "Has Dougal decided what he's going to do?"

"He wants to nurse Ada back to health," Nessa said. "He claims it's only fair since she nursed him and Fiddler after they got beat up. Those buckshot wounds in his leg aren't bothering him too much now, so he can get around fairly well."

Dougal's decision wasn't much of a surprise to Pike. He had seen how his grandpappy and Ada Brewster got on so well. And she had risked her life going to the Ledbetter compound to demand Big Belly release him. Pike doubted Ada would complain much about having Dougal fussing over her.

"You riding up here with me or in the back with Fiddler?" Torrance asked Nessa.

"I'll keep him company. We need to get our stories straight for when we tell Mama where we've been and what we've done." Nessa helped Fiddler into the back of the wagon, then hopped in after him.

"I don't envy him coming up with a story. Ma always sees through a lie," Pike said as he moved up alongside the driver's box and rested a hand on the seat.

"Your lies, maybe," Torrance said. "You never put any thought into what you say."

"Unlike you, I tell the truth and let the chips fall where they may."

"Are you calling me a liar?"

"Born and bred. You inherited Pa's thinking that you can get by skirting the truth."

Torrance leaned over and thrust out his hand. "It might be dull around the spread, but we need you." He glanced over his shoulder at the medicine wagon. "Fiddler and Nessa, too. Ma needs the lot of us."

Pike shook his brother's hand. He stepped away as Torrance flicked the reins, got the team moving, and started the long trip back home.

Pike watched the wagon disappear in a cloud of dust. The storms had died down. His brother, sister, and friend likely would have a pleasant trip back to Warbonnet County.

Warbonnet County. Home. The Shannon horse ranch. Men worked all their lives for half that success. In spite of everything waiting for him, he wasn't sure if he was in any hurry to return.

He and Sophie Truesdale were finished, except as friends, Pike hoped, and that might not be possible. And Belle Ramsey? The only way to explain her behavior toward him was to think she had found another beau. She was worth fighting over, but absence didn't make the heart grow fonder. Not that Pike had ever found.

He heaved a sigh thinking about what had started all

this. Fiddler had been bored. Dougal had joined him in running the still and going out to sell their snake oil because he was bored, too. Torrance would never come out and say so, but he had to feel a bit fenced in, too, and so did Nessa.

Pike wasn't sure anything had changed back in Warbonnet.

"Pike?"

He turned to see Irene Brewster. She had come from the house, wiping flour from her hands. She had been preparing the noonday meal.

"How's your ma getting on?" he inquired.

"Dougal won't let her do a thing for herself. He's quite the caretaker, isn't he?" She moved a step closer. The aroma of freshly baked biscuits clung to her. "But that's a trait that runs through all the Shannons, isn't it?"

"Everything's settling down in town now that the Ledbetters are gone," he said. "Torrance and Nessa are on their way back home. I don't envy them too much."

"Why's that?" Irene stepped closer yet.

"They have to put up with Fiddler. You and your ma fixed him up so good that nothing shuts him up now."

"I heard him going on about how dull it was back in Warbonnet. That's why he and Dougal started their medicine show. Fiddler got his excitement, and Dougal might be settling in here."

Pike nodded.

"Have you decided where you're headed?"

"I'm not sure I want to go back to the ranch. I'll hit the trail and make a decision as I ride."

"Don't go," she said. She came close enough to brush up against him. "Stay. Stay for lunch. You can make a decision like this over a good meal better than you can from a saddle."

"Are you asking me to stay?"

Irene's face showed the answer.

Pike Shannon had some big decisions to make. After the noon meal.

And maybe after supper, too.

Chapter 1

West of the Arizona Territory's Tinajas Altas Mountains, west of Vopoki Ridge, west of anywhere, Fort Benjamin Grierson, better known to its sweating, suffering garrison as Fort Misery, sprawled like a suppurating sore on the arid edge of the Yuma Desert, a barren, scorching wilderness of sandy plains and dunes relieved here and there by outcroppings of creosote bush, bur oak, and sage . . . and white skeletons of the dead, both animal and human.

The dawning sun came up like a flaming Catherine wheel, adding its heat to the furnace of the morning and to the airless prison cell that masqueraded as Captain Peter Joseph Kellerman's office. Already half drunk, he glanced at the clock on the wall. Twenty minutes until seven.

Twenty minutes before he'd mount the scaffold and hang a man.

A rap-rap-rap on the door.

"Come in," Kellerman said.

Sergeant Major Saul Olinger slammed to attention and snapped off the palm forward salute of the old Union cavalry. "The prisoner is ready, Captain."

Kellerman nodded and said, "Stand easy, Saul, for

God's sake. There's nobody here but us, and you know where it is."

Olinger, a burly man with muttonchop whiskers and the florid, broken-veined cheeks of a heavy drinker, opened the top drawer of the captain's desk and fished out a bottle of whiskey and two glasses. He poured generous shots for himself and his commanding officer.

"How is he taking it?" Kellerman said.

"Not well. He knows he's dying."

Kellerman, tall, wide-shouldered, handsome in a rugged way, his features enhanced by a large dragoon mustache, nodded and said, "Dying. I guess he started to die the moment we found him guilty three days ago."

Olinger downed his drink, poured another. He looked around as though making sure there was no one within earshot and said, "Joe, you don't have to do this. I can see it done."

"I'm his commanding officer. It's my duty to be there."

The sergeant major's gaze moved to the window, and he briefly looked through dusty panes into the sunbaked parade ground. His eyes returned to Kellerman. "Private Patrick McCarthy did the crime and now he's paying for it. That's how it goes."

The captain drank his whiskey. "He's eighteen years old, for God's sake. Just a boy."

"When we were with the First Maryland, how many eighteen-year-old boys did we kill at Brandy Station and Gettysburg, Joe? At least they died honorably."

"Hanging is a dishonorable death."

"Rape and murder is a dishonorable crime. The Lipan girl was only sixteen."

Kellerman sighed. "How are the men?"

"Angry. Most of them say murdering an Apache girl is not a hanging offense."

"That doesn't surprise me. How many rapists and murderers do we have?"

Olinger's smile was bitter. "Maybe half the troop."

"And the rest are deserters, thieves, malingerers, and mutineers, commanded by a drunk." Kellerman shook his head. "Why don't you ask for a transfer out of this hellhole, Saul? You have the Medal of Honor. Hell, man, you can choose your posting."

"Joe, we've been together since Bull Run. I'm not quitting you now." The sergeant major glanced at the clock and slammed to attention. "Almost time, sir."

"Go ahead. I'll be right there."

Olinger saluted and left.

Captain Kellerman donned his campaign hat, buckled on his saber, a weapon useless against Apache but effective enough in a close fight with Comancheros, and returned the whiskey bottle to his desk. His old, forgotten rosary caught his eye. He picked up the beads and stared at them for a long moment and then tossed them back in the drawer. God had stopped listening to his prayers long ago . . . and right now he had a soldier to hang.

CHAPTER 2

No other frontier army post had gallows, but in Fort Misery they were a permanent fixture, lovingly cared for by Tobias Zimmermann, the civilian carpenter, a severe man of high intelligence who also acted as hangman. So far, in the fort's year of existence, he'd pulled the lever on two soldiers and at night he slept like a baby.

Zimmermann, Sergeant Major Olinger, and a Slavic Catholic priest with a name nobody could pronounce, stood on the platform along with the condemned man, a thin young towhead with vicious green eyes. Fort Misery's only other officer, Lieutenant James Hall, was thirty years old and some questionable bookkeeping of regimental funds had earned him a one-way ticket from Fort Grant to the wastelands. A beautiful officer with shoulder-length black hair and a full beard that hung halfway down his chest, Hall stood, saber drawn, in front of the dismounted troop: thirty-seven hard-bitten, shabby men standing more or less to attention. The troop had no designation, was not part of a regiment, and did not appear in army rolls. Wages and supplies were the responsibility of a corporal and a civilian clerk in Yuma, and deliveries of both were hit or miss. As one old soldier told a reporter in 1923, "The army sent us to hell for our sins, and our only chance of redemption was to lay low and die under the guidon like heroes."

A murmur buzzed like a crazed bee through the troop as Captain Kellerman mounted the steps to the gallows platform. Private McCarthy's arms and legs were bound with rope and Sergeant Major Olinger had to lift him onto the trapdoor. Zimmermann slipped a black hood over the young man's head, then the hemp noose. He then returned to the lever that would drop the door and plunge the young soldier into eternity.

The army considered their castoffs less than human, and McCarthy lived up to that opinion. He died like a dog, howling for mercy, his cries muffled by the hood. Despite the efforts of Lieutenant Hall, the flat of his saber wielded with force, the solders broke ranks and crowded around the scaffold. Horrified upturned faces revealed the strain of the execution, soldiers pushed to the limit of their endurance.

"Let him go!" a man yelled, and the rest took it up as a chant . . . .

Let him go! Let him go!

A few soldiers tried to climb onto the gallows, but Sergeant Major Olinger drew his revolver and stepped forward. "I'll kill any man who sets foot on these gallows!" he roared. "Get back you damned scum, or you'll join McCarthy in the grave."

That morning Saul Olinger was a fearsome figure, and there wasn't a man present who doubted he'd shoot to kill. One by one they stepped away, muttering as the condemned man's spiking shrieks shattered their already shredded nerves.

The priest's prayer for the dead rose above the din. Sent by his superiors to convert the heathen Comanche, he'd attended six firing squads, but this was his first hanging, and it showed on him, his face the color of wood ash.

Captain Joe Kellerman—he used his middle name because Peter had been the handle of his abusive father—said, loud enough that all could hear, "This man had a fair court-martial, was found guilty of rape and murder, and sentenced to hang. There's nothing more to be said."

He turned his head. "Mr. Zimmermann, carry out the sentence."

The carpenter nodded and yanked on the lever. The trap opened, and Private Patrick McCarthy plunged to his death. His neck broke clean, and his screeches stopped abruptly, like water when a faucet is shut off.

But the ensuing silence was clamorous, as though a thousand phantom alarm bells rang in the still, thick air.

And then Private Dewey Bullard took things a step further.

As Lieutenant Hall ushered the men toward the mess for breakfast, Bullard, thirty years old and a known thief and mutineer, turned and yelled, "Kellerman, you're a damned murderer!"

"Lieutenant Hall, arrest that man," the captain said, pointing. "I'll deal with him later."

Sergeant Major Olinger stepped closer to Kellerman and said, "His name is Bullard. A troublemaker."

"I know who he is. He won't trouble us for much longer."

"Insubordination, plain and simple," Olinger said.

"Yes, it was, and I won't allow him to infect the rest of the men with it," Captain Kellerman said, his mouth set in a grim line.

CHAPTER 3

After breakfast, the troop was assembled on the western edge of the post that looked out over the harsh wasteland of the Yuma Desert. A few blanket Apache, mostly Lipan, camped nearby, close to a boarded-up sutler's store that had never opened and a few storage shacks. The parade ground, headquarters building, enlisted men's barracks, latrines, and stables lay behind Captain Joe Kellerman as he walked in front of his ranked men. Dewey Bullard, under guard, stood a distance away, facing a stark sea of sand and distant dunes ranked among the most brutal deserts on earth.

"You men know why we're here," the captain said. "Under any circumstances I will not have insubordination at Fort Benjamin Grierson. I will not tolerate it. Deserters, thieves, malingerers, murderers, and rapists some of you; you're the soldiers no one wants. Damn your eyes, you're all condemned men, but the army is stretched thin on the frontier, and you were given a choice: death by firing squad or hanging, or the joys of Fort Misery. Well, you chose this hell on earth and now you're stuck with it."

Kellerman needed a drink, the effect of his morning bourbons wearing thin.

"Look around you," he said. "There were eighty of you when this post opened and now there's thirty-six, since Private Bullard will not be rejoining us. Forty-four dead. Nine of them were deserters whose bones are no doubt out there bleaching in the desert. I executed three of you by firing squad and two by hanging, as you just witnessed. The other twenty-nine were killed by bronco Comanche and Comancheros. I know because I saw most of them die. And why did they die? I'll tell you why. It's because they were poor soldiers, coming to us half-trained and barely able to ride a horse. As a result the Comanche gunned them down like ducks in a shooting gallery. That will now change. By God, I'll make fighting men of you or kill you all in the process. In the meantime, I will not have an insubordinate piece of dirt like Dewey Bullard undermining my authority, especially now, when this post is under siege." Kellerman paused for effect and then said, "In an alliance from hell, the Comanche and the Mexican slaver Santiago Lozado and his Comancheros vow to wipe us off the map by executing every man in the garrison. Well I say, let them try!"

To the captain's surprise, that last drew a ragged cheer, and Lieutenant Hall whispered, "There's hope for them yet, Captain."

"Yes, be hopeful, Lieutenant, Just don't bet the farm on it," Kellerman said. Then, "Canteen!"

Sergeant Major Olinger formally presented a filled canteen to Kellerman, who hung it around Bullard's neck and then said, "Youngest soldier, step forward!"

A fresh-faced seventeen-year-old with a penchant for desertion took a step from the ranks, saluted, and said, "Private Reid reporting for duty, sir."

"You know what you have to do?"

"Yes sir."

"Don't stint. Private Reid."

"No sir."

"Then stand by." Kellerman directed his attention to Bullard. "Private Dewey Bullard, for the offense of rank insubordination to the detriment of military discipline and other past transgressions, I banish you from this post in perpetuity. If you make any attempt to return, you will be shot on sight. Do you understand?" Bullard said nothing and the captain repeated, "Do you understand?"

Bullard's black eyes blazed dark fire. "You're sending me to my death."

"You have water, make good use of it," Kellerman said. "Now begone from here and let us never see your face again. Youngest soldier Reid, get ready." Then to the pair of troopers holding Bullard: "Bend him over. No, right over." Bullard cursed and struggled but the captain had chosen the two strongest men in the troop to hold him. His arms elevated in vice-like grips, chest parallel to the ground, he ceased to battle his captors, and Kellerman said, "Youngest soldier Reid, carry out your order."

Private Reid grinned, relishing the task at hand. In the past he'd been bulled by Bullard, and now it was payback time. Reid took a few steps running and slammed the toe of his riding boot into the man's butt. The kick was so furious, so powerful, that the two soldiers holding Bullard lost their grip, and the man tumbled headfirst into hot sand.

"About . . . face!" Lieutenant Hall immediately ordered, and the troop turned its back on the stunned and hurting Bullard, as did Captain Kellerman and Sergeant Major Olinger.

"Forward march!"

The soldiers stepped away, and not an eye turned in Bullard's direction. The man was banished and was now invisible . . . as though he never existed.

CHAPTER 4

"Rider came in under a white flag, Captain," Sergeant Major Olinger said. "Comanchero by the look of him."

"You figure he's here to negotiate a truce?"

"I have my doubts about that, sir. He looks arrogant; like a man with an ultimatum."

Joe Kellerman rose from his desk and swayed slightly, his morning bourbon taking effect. "I'll talk to him," he said. "By the way, my breakfast bacon had green spots, the beans tasted stale, and the coffee was weak."

"Supplies are low, sir."

"Send a patrol to Devil's Rock, see if Yuma got up off its ass long enough to send us a supply wagon."

"Yes sir."

"Have the Navajo ride scout for the patrol."

"Do you trust him?"

"No, but he's all we've got. I reckon Ahiga doesn't like eating rotten bacon any more I do."

"I'll send out Corporal Hawes and six men right away."

The captain shook his head. "Hawes! Damn it, I know Hawes. When he was at Fort Griffin everybody knew he murdered and robbed that whiskey drummer for the ten dollars and five cents in his pocket."

"And that's the truth, but Dave Hawes is a good soldier, and we don't have many of them," Olinger said.

Kellerman buckled on his recently issued .45 Colt Single Action Army revolver and grabbed his hat from the rack. "Right now I'd forgive a hundred mortal sins for a hundred good soldiers. Now let's talk with the Comanchero. This should be interesting."

The Comanchero was a smallish man who wore the white shirt and pants of the Mexican peon, his chest crossed by bandoliers, a wide sombrero tipped back on his head, robe sandals on his feet revealing calloused, gnarled toes. He sat a paint pony, probably of Comanche origin, and had a Colt in an open holster buckled around his waist. He carried a white sheet tied to a 10thCavalry guidon, a deliberate insult.

When the man saw the shoulder straps on Captain Kellerman's shirt, he saluted and said, "Buenos días, mi Capitan."

"Buenos días. What can I do for you?"

"For me, nothing," the Comanchero said. He had quick, black eyes, and the mouth under his mustache was a straight, tough line that now relaxed in a smile. "But I bring you greetings and a wish for good health from the hidalgo, don Santiago Miguel Lozado."

"So, the raggedy-assed bandido is calling himself a hidalgo now. He's come up in the world."

The Mexican's smile slipped. "Oh, señor, I cannot tell mi general that. He would be very hurt. He is a man of a sensitive nature who longs for peace, not war."

"And what does he want from me? War or peace?"

"Don Santiago wants very little."

"And that's what he'll get . . . very little."

The Comanchero smiled, his hand waving. "It is but a small request."

"Name it."

"The general and hidalgo desires that you and your soldiers immediately pack up, leave this stinking fort, and never return." The man smiled. "Don Santiago is being generous. He wants only what is best for you and your soldados."

"And if I don't leave?"

The Comanchero chewed on the corner of his mustache, then said, "Then it will be very bad for you, I think."

"I have a message for Lozado," Kellerman said.

"Ah, then you've come to your senses at last."

"Tell Lozado he must immediately put a halt to his bandit activities, including running guns to the Apache and slaves to the Comanche. If he complies, I will allow him and his rabble to return peaceably to Sonora. Tell him I can't offer the same generous terms to the Comanche."

"And if he refuses?" The Comanchero's voice was tight, hardened by anger.

"Then I will kill Santiago Lozado and all with him."

"You already killed his son. Isn't that enough for you?"

"I killed Comancheros. I didn't know his son was among them."

The Mexican fell silent. He pulled down the brim of his sombrero like a monk's cowl, his shaded eyes glittering. The heat had bleached the sky into faded blue and the morning was heavy and oppressive, lying mercilessly on the suffering land like a smallpox blanket. A few idling soldiers crowded close, listening to every word, their faces carved from stone.

Finally, the Comanchero spoke. "Capitán, though grieving

for his son, the hidalgo don Santiago Miguel Lozado extended the hand of friendship and you knocked it away. The result will be the death of every man on this post, and for you, a terrible fate. My general has made it clear that if you refuse his offer, he will nail you to the wall of a building and skin you alive. I beg you to reconsider and pack your bags and leave. Leave now, before it's too late. This will not be the first time that mi general has extended mercy to the undeserving."

"You heard my terms. I will not change them," Kellerman said.

The Mexican leaned from his horse and spat into the dirt. "Pah! Your terms are worthless, the bluff of a frightened man. Do as the general says and save your lives." Then, talking to the soldiers, "Time is running out for all of you. You're all dead men. Surrender now while you still can."

Concern and some fear showed on the faces of the surrounding soldiers as Kellerman said, "I made a mistake. Perhaps I didn't put my refusal in strong enough terms."

He unbuttoned his holster flap, drew his Colt, and fired. His bullet hit the middle of the X made by the Comanchero's bandoliers, crashed through leather, bone, and flesh, and tore into the man's heart. The Comanchero shrieked, tumbled off his horse, and was as dead as hell in a parson's parlor when he thudded to the ground.

"Perhaps that answer was strong enough," Kellerman said as smoke trickled from the muzzle of his revolver. "One of you men, bring me Mr. Zimmermann. I have a job for him."

It was a measure of Sergeant Major Olinger's shocked surprise that he momentarily forgot his military discipline and addressed his commanding officer by name. "Joe, what the hell?"

"Lozado wanted an answer to his ultimatum. Well, I gave him one," Kellerman said.

"But . . . but he was under a flag of truce."

Captain Kellerman holstered his revolver. "A flag of truce means nothing to Santiago Lozado and his kind. All they understand is force."

"He'll come at us," Olinger said.

"No doubt he will. We burned him the last time."

"And it cost us three dead and a couple close to it, Captain. That was a month ago, and the Navajo says Lozado's numbers have grown since then. He says twelve more Comancheros came up from Sonora with the latest slave train and six cases of Henry rifles, and there are at least fifty Comanche in camp."

"If the Navajo isn't lying, we figure Lozado now has about a hundred fighting men," Kellerman said.

"And maybe more."

"Yeah, and maybe more." Kellerman smiled. "And that's why we're here at Fort Misery, Sergeant Major."

"'You are requested and required, with all expedition, to abolish slave and gun running from Mexico into the Arizona Territory and bring the perpetrators to swift justice.' I recollect that part of General Sherman's letter."

"So do I. Easy for him to say from his cozy berth in Washington." Kellerman thought for a moment and then said, "I don't want us to meet him in the open field again, so we'll let Lozado come to us. As before, station the pickets and we'll fortify the headquarters building and the infirmary. My compliments to Lieutenant Hall and ask him to report to my office in an hour."

"Yes sir, and I'll give Corporal Hawes his orders."

"Yes, tell him to take the wagon and woe betide him if he doesn't come back with supplies."

Sergeant Major Olinger saluted and left, just as Tobias

Zimmermann elbowed his way through a crowd of gawking soldiers and said, "You wanted to see me, Cap'n." He glanced at the body. "I heard the shot. A coffin?"

"No, I have other plans for this man. I think very soon we'll come under attack from Comancheros, so tell your wife not to leave headquarters. If she needs water, tell her to ask a soldier to take a bucket to the seep."

Mary Zimmermann was a tall, thin woman, strait-laced, much given to prayer, good works, lectures on the evils of demon drink and fornication and the power of prune juice to keep a person regular. She was the camp washerwoman and cook and the soldiers referred to her as the Virgin Mary.

Tobias Zimmermann listened to Captain Kellerman's instructions for the Comanchero's corpse and said, "Cap'n, I've never done the like before."

"There's a first time for everything, Mr. Zimmermann, so get it done."

"He brought a guidon."

"Yes, and he's taking it back. Nail the pole to his hand if you have to, but I want him carrying the guidon when he leaves here."

"It's a strange order, Cap'n Kellerman."

"And one you'll carry out. Just get it done. Tell me when you're finished."

The carpenter shook his head. "Fought in the war, didn't you?"

"Yes."

"It hardened you."

"How very perceptive you are, Mr. Zimmermann. Life hardened me. And now just surviving in this hellhole is finishing the job."

Zimmermann nodded. "Your dead man will be all ready to go in an hour."